Christopher Crown
& the
Immortal Signal

Tricia Price

TSL Publications

Author's Note

H.M.S. *NONESUCH* never rode out a gale, never fired a shot in anger, never lost a man in action. She is a shadow of the past, remembering some of the men and some of the ships who sailed with Nelson. Some of the sayings and some of the doings aboard her have been adapted from things said and done aboard the vessels which took part in the autumn campaign of 1805. The rest, like the White Knight's little box, is my own invention.

The Voyage of
H.M.S. Nonesuch
from Plymouth
to Cadiz
September 1805

Plymouth

Isles of Scilly

Ushant Cruising ground

Boulogne   Here Napoleon waited

Cruising Squadron   Brest
Lorient

Rochefort
(Missiessy escaped from here in January)
Allemand slipped out from here too.

Cape Finistere

Ferrol
Here Villeneuve sheltered after the battle in July

Toulon
Villeneuve left with N. Italies in March

Gulf of Lyons

Barcelona

Corsica

Sardinia

Lisbon
Here the fleet transports took shelter

Cape St Vincent

Gulf of Cadiz   Cadiz — Here the Combined Fleet anchored

Cape Trafalgar

Straits of Gibraltar
Gibraltar

Tetuan

1

The thinking place, where Christopher always went when he most particularly wanted to be alone, was beside the beach path just where it started to curve down to the shore. There was a thorn-bush of splendid proportions, and behind that was a grassy space almost hidden from the passers-by. But the view over the little cove was uninterrupted. Christopher could stay there for hours at a time listening to the gulls and watching the ships passing to and fro on the horizon. There was nearly always something to be seen. Sometimes a slender white yacht made her way up channel with billowing sails: or a small coasting vessel caught in rough sea would seem to stand almost on her head and then reverse slowly until her stern dipped under and you felt seasick as you watched. Once, a school of porpoises had bounded across the mouth of the cove, gleaming black backs visible for an instant and then disappearing again under the rippling waves, while the gulls rode unconcernedly about them. It was a good place for swimming, too, with its gently shelving shore, though the water was always cold – too cold for bathing today, in September, although the lovely Indian summer weather was just perfect for lying in the thinking place with nothing in particular to do.

For some time now Christopher had had the cove to himself. It was getting late in the year for summer visitors, and sea traffic was scarce this afternoon. There was nothing to be heard but the screaming of the seabirds, nothing to be seen but the heaving grey-blue water, right out to the skyline. It was still heaving beyond that, Christopher knew, until it broke against the shore of France: and he wondered idly at just what point the water would start to break in the opposite direction, and if perhaps some boy in Brittany were lying by the shore and seeing the same sea wash home. Perhaps it was where the Channel opened out to the Atlantic and the huge rollers come surging in? A ship sailing beyond that again could go for thousands of miles down the coasts of Portugal and Africa until it came to the Cape of Good Hope, and there that surging Atlantic would merge with the Indian and Antarctic Oceans . Christopher thought how funny it might be if a ship were sailing right over the place where they met, and half the crew would be sunbathing perhaps on the deck and the rest at the other end might be wrapped in heavy dufflecoats and seaboots because of the ice floating all about. But he knew it couldn't be like that really. And then, if you went on sailing far enough, you'd be past the South Pole, and you'd start coming up again on the other side of the world; and would you, he wondered, seem to climb upwards or would you, as seemed most probably, simply go on sailing as if you hadn't been anywhere near the tip of the world at all? Then you'd go right on through the hot Pacific, on and on till the winds and waves turned cold again up Alaska way, and so right up to the North Pole: and then you'd turn and come downhill once more, as it were, past the shores of Greenland and Iceland and Scotland until you were home again, here in the cove with the thinking place: and you'd have gone all round the world one way and never come to the end of the sea at all.

Somewhere beyond the point a gun boomed, shocking the stillness, and a flight of startled seagulls rose squalling over the cliff. Christopher sat up straight, wondering what on earth was happening. As the sound died throbbing away, others came to his ears: a scrabbling of shoes on the shale, and the gasping of breath. Someone was running up the cliff path from the town, running desperately. Christopher peeped out through the bushes just as a boy came panting round the bend. His cravat was under one ear, and his buckled shoes skidded as he ran. He stared straight at Christopher without seeing him, then dived through the hedge on the other side of the path and vanished. Moments passed. Then a rough looking man in a striped jersey came lumbering round the bend and went on past, cursing under his breath. Some yards further on he stopped, stared all round, turned, and came back. For an awful moment Christopher thought he'd been spotted, but the man took no notice of him and went back round the bend, calling "Not here, mateys!

He must be somewhere in town!" and the sound of his footsteps faded away.

When Christopher felt certain the man was gone, he crept out from his hiding-place and peeped through the hedge. There was no one to be seen. He called softly, "Hi!" There was no reply, and the only sound was the scraping of a grasshopper. He called more loudly, "It's all right! It's only me!" but nobody answered. The boy must have made good his escape. Christopher drew back, and looked up and down the narrow lane. He went to the bend where the path sloped down towards the harbour. It was quite empty. The man, whoever he was, was out of sight, probably searching through the twisting streets of the old town. Christopher wondered why the boy had looked so desperate, and why the man was chasing him so angrily. Perhaps he'd stolen something, but he didn't look like a thief. It was the man who looked rough and ready for anything. Perhaps he was a pirate, and wanted to kidnap the boy and hold him to ransom. Some people said Drake had been a pirate, sailing round the world looking for plunder. That must have been exciting, thought Christopher, wandering slowly down the sandy path towards the beach; for some reason he felt the man wouldn't come down there, though he didn't know why. Drake really had sailed round the world, but he'd gone the other way. His way, the usual way, you'd turn right across the Atlantic and so on into the Pacific Ocean, on and on among the South Sea Islands, on and on past New Zealand and Australia, past the tip of India until you sighted land again, and up through the Red Sea between Egypt and Arabia. Then you'd bear left across the Mediterranean, past Gibraltar, turn right for the north and so home. Christopher sat down on the shingle and wrapped his arms round his knees, staring out to sea. "Wait a minute!" he thought. Drake couldn't have done that. There was no Panama Canal then, no Suez either; he'd had to go the long way, all round South America, round the Cape of Good Hope too. It wasn't much fun down Cape Horn way, so Christopher had heard, even in a modern ship with powerful engines and computers and all sorts of electronic gadgets. What on earth had it been like in a little wooden tub with only its canvas sails to keep it going? Not so much as a wireless set to keep Drake in touch with the world he was sailing around. No one would know where he was or what was happening to him. That went for a lot of others, too, who came after him. Possibly they had bigger ships, but it must have been very uncomfortable and they must have been a brave and hardy lot, one way and another. Of course, later on they would have had charts and maps and things. He lay on his back and stared up at the sky. But there were other dangers too, he thought; pirates like the man he'd just seen. What was he doing? And what had the boy done? Oh well, it was none of his business! Pirates and storms and shipwrecks. But they'd kept on going hadn't they? All those little ships, across all those thousands of miles of water coming from the middle of the deep, deep oceans, rushing to the shore, drawing back and surging out again where it came from – never still, never the same. It was bursting with creatures, too; and the men had come last of all to travel on it, live on it, work on it and fight on it too, in all sorts of places, even here in the Channel when the Spanish Armada had come. Christopher propped himself on his elbows, gazing out towards the mouth of the Channel, where the enemy had appeared and where the grey seas ran big. There it was: mile upon mile of it, no end to it, and this shifting surge of water had gone tirelessly on for thousands – no, millions of years. Thousands and thousands of miles, and it went down a goodish way, too...

BOOM! The gun thundered again, and again the seagulls rose screeching over the beach. Christopher shot up, as startled as the birds were, and as the echoes died away a small boat appeared round the corner of the cove. It came towards the shore, and rowing it was a boy of Christopher's own age, or maybe just a little older, fair-haired and broad-shouldered. He beached the boat, climbed out and waved. Christopher jumped to his feet and raced across the sandy foreshore, slipping between the rock pools until he came to the curling edge of the sea. It seemed to him afterwards, when he stopped to think about it, that the fair boy in the boat seemed to have been expecting him; as if he knew that he would find him just in that spot, just at that time. But right now Christopher didn't stop to think. He liked the look of the newcomer, whose grey eyes were crinkled at the corners, oddly lined for his years; there was a merry twinkle in them, as if he found life a huge joke. He had funny clothes on but really, they were most practical for an afternoon's sea-rowing. He wore long white duck trousers and short round jacket of some dark stuff, and plain black slip-ons on his feet.

"That's a grand boat," said Christopher as he reached it. "Is she yours?"

"Oh no," said the boy. "She belongs to the ship, but I've borrowed her for the afternoon. I'm in the Navy, you know – midshipman."

Christopher goggled at him. "You can't be," he said flatly. "You're not old enough."

"I'm sixteen, the boy retorted. "There's plenty younger than me, and I went to sea before I was twelve. It's the usual thing, after all."

"Is it?" asked Christopher doubtfully. "I thought you had to be a lot older than that – nearly grown-up."

"Sixteen seems pretty old to me, especially when you think they can't promote me to Lieutenant until I'm eighteen at the very least. You have to have six years service, you know, and you're supposed to be twenty anyway and you don't necessarily go up at all. Lots of people get absolutely nowhere. That's one advantage of being at sea in wartime! There are so many more chances of promotion. Got to fill the gaps, you know!"

Christopher didn't know, so he decided to try a different line, especially as that last remark sounded a little more gruesome than he really liked. "When you say wartime," he said, "does that mean you've really been to sea on a battleship?"

"Ship of the line," corrected the other boy loftily. "Yes indeed, and she's a fine ship too. My uncle's the captain, which is a grand bit of luck for me because he might be able to give me a leg up when the time comes. Not that he gives anything away on that score! I mean, he doesn't favour me above the others. But then, he's pretty fair to everyone, and the men all like him. Not like some!"

Christopher sat himself down again on the sand and looked

curiously at his new friend.

"It must be fun," he said, "to go on a really long voyage. I've never been further than a cross-Channel trip!"

The other boy laughed, and sat down beside him. "That's something I haven't done myself," he admitted. "At least not right across! I've spent a goodish while tossing about off the French coast, though – mostly in the Mediterranean. High time we had a spot more excitement! It can be a bit of a bore simply hanging about, especially in bad weather!"

"Were you seasick?"

"Devil a bit of it!" the boy said cheerfully. "I'm one of the lucky ones. I can take any amount of pitching. Some people never do get their sealegs, though. Even the Admiral suffers, they say."

"Which Admiral?"

"Nelson, of course! There's plenty of others, but he's the only one that really matters."

"Nelson? LORD Nelson?" Something seemed a little odd, there.

"That's right. Who else? We've been under his command for the last two years, and they say bad weather bothers him, at first at any rate. Now me, I don't care two bits about a blow, which is just as well because we've had plenty. It gets beastly rough in the Gulf of Lyons at times."

"Have you been there all the time?"

"Very nearly – hanging about outside Toulon, waiting for the French to come out of harbour and run for it. The Admiral had us lying just over the skyline, hoping they'd think the coast was clear and chance it, but it didn't do."

"I don't understand this at all," complained Christopher. "What was the idea?"

"Look, I'll explain. It's all on account of this fellow Bonaparte – Napoleon, if you prefer to call him that. Even you must have heard of him!"

Christopher was indignant about that "even".

"Of course I've heard of him!" he retorted. "Who hasn't?"

"Well then, as you must also know, he thinks he's another Alexander the Great, and he wants to conquer the world,

Britain included, and by all accounts he's all set to invade us. Now, there's two things we can do about it; let him come, and hope for the best from the Army, or send out the Navy to stop him coming at all. Are you with me so far?"

"Yes, I see that. So they've sent out the Navy?"

"That's right. England's wooden walls, they call us, and by heaven they're right!"

"And what did you do? Did you have a battle?"

"No. He won't give us the chance if he can help it. What we've done is to wait outside the French ports like a lot of cats at a mouse hole. Napoleon daren't send his invasion barges over without his navy to guard them; and the French ships daren't come out of harbour because ours are in the way. It's really very simple."

"Yes, but wait a minute! Surely, if they're going from France to England they'll have to cross the Channel?"

"Of course."

"Then what on earth were you doing in the Mediterranean?"

"I'm telling you! It's not the invasion fleet itself we've had to stop but the fleet that's meant to protect it. We had to stop the line of battle ships from reaching the Channel, where the barges are. Now do you see?"

Christopher nodded.

"Well then! The French navy has been scattered about a bit. There are some in Brest, some in Rochefort and Lorient, down the west coast of French; some in the Texel – that's right up in the north of Holland! – and some down south in Toulon. There were even some in the West Indies, but Napoleon brought them home again. Not a very bright thing to do!"

"Why not?"

"Because for one thing it cleared our trade routes to America, and for another they'd no sooner got back as far as Spain than some of our fellows turned up and bottled them up tight in Ferrol. Much good that did them!" and the boy chuckled.

"How long has all this been going on?" asked Christopher.

"I told you! Nearly two years, and it hasn't been funny. A friend of mine was nearly wrecked in the storm off Brest the winter before last, and he swears he'd rather be in a battle any day. He says he's not afraid of the French but you can't hit back at Nature when she really gets going!"

"I suppose there's something in that!" said Christopher. "Did you get caught in storms too?"

The other boy sighed. "I told you that, too. Aren't you listening? When the wind blows down there it doesn't do things by halves. We've ridden out many a gale, but if we have to be on blockade duty I'd rather be there than on the other stations."

"Why?"

"To start with, we were with Nelson, and I don't believe there's anything he can't do. In the next place, he had more scope than anyone else. You see, he had to keep watch over the whole of the Mediterranean – had to stop 'em getting out past Gibraltar or over to Egypt – or Turkey either, for that matter! And then, being such a long way from home, their Lordships in the Admiralty couldn't very well interfere with him; he could act on his own initiative, and no one has more initiative than Nelson!"

"What did he do then?"

"Tried to get the French to fight, but they wouldn't have it. I told you, he kept us out of sight of port just to tempt them, but it wasn't any use. Once last summer we thought we were getting somewhere but when they realised we were waiting for 'em they ran back home again. It really was too bad! We were itching for some action. I say, I'm not boring you, am I?"

"I should say not! I wish I could have been there too! It sounds great!"

"Do you?" The other boy looked at Christopher rather oddly. "Wouldn't you be afraid of being seasick?"

"I should think it would be worth it, just to sail with Nelson!"

"You'd do, young 'un" said the older boy with approval. "I really think you'd do!"

"Hey!" said Christopher. "Not so much of the 'young'un,' if you don't mind!"

"Well, you are young, aren't you?" said the other grinning. "It's what you called me, so makes two of us."

"Oh, have it your own way, said Christopher. "Go on. I'm

12

listening."

"Right you are! Where was I?"

"Not being sick in the Med," said Christopher, grinning in his turn.

"So I wasn't! Anyway, round about last Christmas time there was quite a lot of taking sides. Spain chose to join the French, which pleased Napoleon no end. It pleased the Prime Minister too – Mr Pitt, you know –"

"Why on earth was he pleased?" asked Christopher.

"Because it cleared the air, of course; showed him where they stood. But when it looked as if Austria and Russia might come in our side, Napoleon didn't like it at all, because naturally he didn't want us to have any friends. So he wrote to the King and suggested making a peace."

"And the King jumped at it?"

"Not he! He went into a royal huff – he can, you know – at the very idea of Boney writing to him as if he were his equal, and you can't blame him for that. I'd feel much the same way myself, and I'm only a midshipman! Besides, we'd tried it once, and it didn't last long. There's only one thing to be done – we've got to get rid of Boney!"

"Can you?" asked Christopher, doubtfully.

"Well, he's only human, after all, and he's not even an Englishman! Come to think of it, he's not really French, either; he's a Corsican, and so he's a traitor as well as everything else!" The boy gave a crack of laughter. "I never thought of that before! What fun! Anyway, we'll do our best to stop his little tricks for good and all. Besides," (and this was said with great scorn) "he's only a soldier, when all's said and done"

"Now look here and wait a bit! If he's only a soldier, as you put it, how does he come to be top dog anyway? I mean, was there a – what d'you call it? – a military coup or something?"

"Not exactly. You see, the French went mad round about fifteen years ago, and –"

"What, all of them?"

"Most of them; and it wasn't altogether surprising. Must be fair! The people had been having a rough time of it for years, you see, and when you treat people badly, sooner or later they're going to start behaving badly. That's one reason why my uncle's so particular about his officers. He won't stand for petty tyranny nohow! Well anyway, came the day when the French people thought they'd had enough…"

"I know!" cried Christopher. "That was the French Revolution!"

"That's right; and it mightn't have been so bad if they hadn't gone crazy with it, like I said. But there you are! Give 'em an inch, they'll take half a mile. They decided to make quite sure they'd got rid of their aristocracy, and so they murdered them, as many of them as they could catch. King and Queen, too, if you please. Well, anybody could have told them that was a rotten idea. After all, we'd tried it ourselves once, and it didn't work out all that well. Then they started murdering each other. All this was a bit before my time of course; I was only a baby then; but we've had it drummed and dinned into us like anything because naturally it helps if we know what we're doing, and why."

"Yes, I see that. But where does Napoleon come in?"

"I'm coming to that! You see, the French got so carried away by it all they thought it would be a grand idea to spread it a little further; even here if possible. All in the name of Liberty, Equality and Fraternity! Meaning everyone's going to be the same as everyone else. Which is just plain silly, because it stands to reason that someone somewhere is always going to finish up on top. Look at Boney!"

"You still haven't got to him," said Christopher impatiently.

"Oh yes I have! You see the French got so uppity in the end that they more or less declared war on anybody who still chose to have a King, if you please, let alone nobility! That's when they sent their own Louis to the guillotine, poor man, and insisted that they'd fight everyone who didn't do the same. So of course, we fought them! Boney was an artillery captain with a bit of a flair about him, and he certainly got results – on land. Italy – Austria – Switzerland – Egypt – you name it, he conquered it! Then he went back to France, and the next thing anybody knew, he had a brand new job all to himself.

The boy kicked his legs in the air, and went on, "First Consul, they called him then. By that time, everyone was getting fed up with the war, so when he suggested a peace, he got one."

Christopher said, puzzled, "But I thought you said there was a war on now."

"Oh, there is! You see, it couldn't possibly last! Myself, I think we'd have been better off without it, but of course, it wasn't anything to do with me! The peace treaty they drew up didn't do much for us, but it certainly suited Napoleon, and the French were so pleased with it that they made him Consul for life. And I suppose it didn't really hurt us to have a bit of a rest."

"Didn't that go for him too?"

"Unfortunately, yes! Or do I mean fortunately? Depends which side you're on! All this was three years or so ago, and the peace didn't even last for two! Boney's not First Consul any longer. He's the Emperor now, and what he says goes. Only not here if we can help it! Where was I?"

"You'd got to the time he'd made the King angry."

"That's right. Well then, come New Year we almost had some excitement. We'd gone into port in Sardinia to take in stores, I remember, when we got word that the French fleet had come out at last. I don't remember when we worked so fast! All I can tell you is that in no time we were all chasing after them in a filthy gale with Nelson himself out in front."

"Did you catch them?"

The boy scowled. "No, we didn't. They had bad weather ahead and Nelson behind so they simply went home, and we never saw them – we went eastward, because the Admiral was afraid they'd be making for Sicily, and he had to stop that at all costs."

"Why Sicily?"

"Isn't it obvious? If the French landed troops there they'd start running about all over the place, and then the fat would really be in the fire. It's a pity they didn't in some ways; our lads were just ready for a scrap. They should have had us outside Rochefort; some of the French ships actually managed to get out from there!"

He sent a flat pebble skimming out to sea, and Christopher asked, "Where did they go?"

"As a matter of fact, they went to the West Indies, though we didn't know that until later. A lot of others would have liked to do the same, but our ships weren't going to let that happen twice."

Christopher was even more puzzled. He said, "Why the West Indies? Wasn't that rather out of the way?"

"Not a bit of it! You see, as long as we were blocking the way to the Channel, Boney hadn't a hope of getting at us. He had to shift us first. So he wanted desperately to get his ships out to sea without fighting; give us the slip, in fact. If they went over to the West Indies to threaten our possessions there, he thought we'd be bound to go after them. That would be their cue to double back and make for the open Channel. It wasn't so far-fetched as it seems, you see! A few did make it out of harbour, as I said, while ours were taking in water supplies. Of course, it was ages before we knew about it. We were still cruising about off Toulon, and had the most rotten luck."

"How was that?"

"I'm telling you, aren't I?" said the boy impatiently. "The French admiral – Villeneuve, his name is – decided to have another shot at escaping and Nelson tried to call his bluff. He had us put in an appearance near Barcelona, and then we made all the sail we could to catch them coming round to the south to avoid us. Somehow, Villeneuve must have got wind of what we were up to, because he simply vanished."

"Do you mean he sank?" asked Christopher.

"Of course not! Not even a Frenchman could lose a whole fleet that way! He went west after all to collect his Spanish chums out of Cadiz, and we lost all sight of him. Everyone felt pretty sick about it, so goodness knows what it was like for Nelson."

"What did he do?"

"What could he do? He set out to look for then – kept us nearly a fortnight sailing backwards and forwards between Sardinia and Sicily, and we never got as much as a smell of them. Not surprising! They'd gone off to the West Indies too, though we didn't know it then."

"How did you find out?"

"Oh, Nelson heard – quite by accident, mark you! – that the Government were sending an expeditionary force to Malta. Doesn't seem to have occurred to anyone that they might have told him earlier, but there you are! So off we went to westward, to get in touch with that force before Villeneuve did. Am I going too fast for you?"

"Not a bit," said Christopher politely. "Go on."

"Right-ho! Well, to cut a long story short, we've been chasing about all over the Atlantic looking for the devils. But the sea's a big place, and what with the shocking weather – well, we never saw a sign of them. And would you believe it, when we did get a fair wind behind us we missed them by a day. One day! It was too bad."

He picked up another pebble, and sent it hopping over the waves, saying casually "It'll be different this time. This time we really mean business."

"This time?" asked Christopher warily.

"Yes. You see, when he found the French fleet was heading for the Channel again, Nelson sent a fast sloop home to warn the Admiralty and ask for reinforcements. There was a bit of a scrap then, and they say Boney was furious because a couple of French ships were lost."

Another pebble went the way of the first two, and the boy went on, "Villeneuve has got his ships snugly in Cadiz harbour now. He's safe enough for the time being, but he hasn't been as clever as he thought he was, because he can't get out again."

"Why not?"

"Because we'd seen him, that's why! There is a very useful sort of ship in the Navy, in case you don't know, called a frigate. It's smaller and faster than a line of battle ship. Lord Nelson calls them the eyes and ears of the Fleet, and that's a very good name for them. And one of them saw the enemy ships and followed them, to make sure what they were up to. Luckily for us, this one had a particularly clever captain. The Admiral thinks the world of him!"

"Who is he?"

"His name's Blackwood, and he knows his job inside-out! As soon as he was quite certain the French had bolted into Cadiz harbour he was off home to tell the Admiral, and those English ships he met on the way went off down to Spain to make sure they stayed there. And the idea is, you see, that they keep the enemy bottled up until the rest of our Fleet can get down there to reinforce them. Like this. You see that little pool there, under the rock?"

Christopher nodded.

"We'll say that's Cadiz harbour. These red pebbles are the French fleet – and these grey ones are the Spanish – see!"

The boy threw the pebbles gently into the pool one by one. They landed with a splash, sending warm salty water over Christopher's arm, and settled at the bottom in a murky little swirl of sand. "These white ones, here, are the English ships," he went on, spreading a handful in a curving line a little way away. "And these others, right over here, are the rest of us making ready to join then. So there we are. Villeneuve's trapped in Cadiz harbour, there, afraid to come out, and when we've joined the others – like this" – he moved the second group of white pebbles over to the first lot – "we'll be ready to have a go at them!"

There was a silence between the two boys as he finished. He looked at Christopher with one eyebrow cocked. Christopher said, slowly, "You said this time we meant business. Do you mean you're going back to chase the French all over again?"

"Oh no – we're going back to give them a good drubbing!"

"Then what are you doing here?"

"That's a fair question. We came home because the ship needed some attention after two years at sea in all weathers. We're leaving tomorrow; in fact, the Admiral's probably gone already."

"What sort of ship is yours?" asked Christopher, with keen interest.

"Third-rate: Seventy-four guns, two decker: her name's Nonesuch. Would you like to see her?"

"Would I? I should say so!"

"Come on then!" and the midshipman leaped to his feet, holding out his hand. "She's fitting out round the corner, and we can be there in no time. She's a sight worth seeing, I can tell you!"

His grey eyes were sparkling with pride and mischief. "Come on, young 'un, hop in! Oh, and by the way – what's your name? I never asked you."

"Christopher Crown," said Christopher, as he took the outstretched hand. "What's yours?"

"Britten – Richard Britten, midshipman, at your service! In you get!" and Christopher climbed into the boat, scarcely knowing that he did so. His actions no longer seemed to be under his control, and he didn't much care.

"All set? Here we go!" and Richard pulled out to sea and round the point. "You know," he said, as they skimmed over the sunlit water, "I've done an awful lot of talking about myself, but I don't know a thing about you! What do you do with yourself?"

Christopher flushed. "Oh, I'm still at school," he said defensively, "but I can't help it."

"Good lord, you are a young 'un, aren't you?" Richard looked at him "You look older," he said generously, "and anyway, some of us have to be clever. I never was much good at lessons so they sent me to sea instead as soon as my uncle would have me. Just as well. The earlier you start in our line the better. Do you know anything about sailing?"

"Not really," Christopher confessed. "I can row, of course, and I've been out several times in a small sailing-boat, but that's about all."

"Well, never mind. I don't suppose it matters."

Christopher looked puzzled again. "I don't see what –" he was beginning, when they came round the headland, and what he saw took his breath away. They were in sight of the harbour; familiar enough, but somehow strange if only Christopher had thought to look at it. He never noticed that there was no sign of the trim houses on the heights, or that many familiar landmarks had vanished. He never even noticed that the great road and rail bridges had disappeared. He had no eyes for the harbour at all. It was the ship that took all his attention and his breath with it.

She was like no other ship he had ever seen in his life, but he had no regrets for the great grey giants of iron and steel that he was used to. This vessel had a grace and a dignity that could only belong to the days of sail. She was smaller than he had expected her to be, too. From her bows a long bowsprit thrust over the water, and two great holes, like eyes, were pierced through her timbers where the enormous anchor cables ran down into the sea. Across her rounded, arching stern ran a double row of – of all things! – windows, and galleries, too. Three soaring masts rose out of her upper deck, held to her sides by strong ropes, and set at right angles across them at intervals were heavy wooden bars from which the sails would hang. At this moment they were neatly furled in canvas rolls, waiting to be loosed on the complicated rope webs of the rigging. More ropes ran behind and before the masts, and from the foremast to the bowsprit. Sheltered by that jutting arm there rode a gaily painted figurehead – a gleaming white unicorn's head with a jewelled crown set upon its gilded and twisted horn. Christopher looked at Nonesuch, and loved her.

"Like her?" asked Richard softly, watching him intently.

"Like her? She's beautiful – the most beautiful thing I've ever seen!"

Indeed, no one could have blamed him. Gleaming with black and yellow paint, she swung idly at her anchor, spars standing stark against the sky. She was painted black, with broad horizontal bands of yellow, and the lids of the gun ports along her sides were black, too, showing on the yellow like squares on a chessboard. The whole effect was very stylish. "Nelson fashion," explained Richard proudly. "She's dressed to kill – in more ways than one!"

There were men moving about on her decks, and even as they drew near a piping wail was heard, and the whole of her upper works swarmed with sailors, running to the masts and raising the huge canvas sails.

"By George!" cried Richard. "Just in time! They must have come under orders sooner than we expected!" and he pulled harder at his oars. As they came up alongside, a voice above them barked, "Mr Britten! Where have you been? You narrowly miss being marked as a deserter!"

"Your pardon, sir!" cried Richard respectfully. "I've been away on the King's business, and it took longer than I expected!"

"Indeed! You will kindly explain yourself to me in my cabin immediately – IMMEDIATELY!"

Before him, Christopher saw a dangling rope ladder; behind him, Richard gave him a push, and he climbed up and found himself on the deck. He was aware of gold braid and piercing blue eyes in a tanned, lean face: then the same voice said, "What the – who the devil is this?"

"I said I'd been out on Naval business, sir," answered Richard. "This is Christopher Crown, a loyal subject of His Majesty – and I've pressed him!"

2

For a moment there was a stunned silence; then, "I say, look here!" cried Christopher and "I see," said the captain, a muscle twitching at the corner of his mouth. "I think we'd better talk this over quietly together, don't you? Take him to my cabin and wait there until I come."

He turned and made his way to the poop. Richard took Christopher's arm. "Come on, young 'un," he said. "Orders have to be obeyed without question, you know. This is the Navy!" And Christopher, too staggered to argue, went along quietly.

Together they crossed the quarterdeck, and Christopher found that he was being taken along aft. The great white sails were unfurling above his head, and with a rattle and a clank the anchor came home. Someone was singing,

"We'll bid farewell to Plymouth Sound,

Way hay, hay hi ho!

We'll bid farewell, we're outward bound,

We're leaving you for Vigo!"

He sang in a rich, fruity baritone, and Christopher turned to look at him. He had rolled up the sleeves of his jersey, leaving his hairy arms bare to the elbow, but there was no mistaking the man who had chased the boy over the cliff top. So he wasn't a pirate, after all. It was all very mysterious. He looked incuriously at them as they passed by, the deck swaying beneath their feet. Nonesuch was beginning to move, slowly, so slowly, but all the same moving, on her way out to open sea.

Their way took them past the big ship's wheel, and so into the captain's cabin, right aft under the raised poop. Christopher was surprised at the size and comfort of this room; he wasn't altogether sure what he had expected, but it certainly wasn't this. The room was full of light, coming in through the window built into the ship's stern. There was a big table in the middle, and there were several chairs, including the comfortable winged sort. There was a mat laid on the floor, covering the bare planking, and the dark mahogany furniture gleamed in the afternoon sun. There was a handsome leather-topped desk with a silver inkstand and its own round-backed chair. There was a shelf of books with rich leather bindings and gilded spines. There was no sign of any sleeping arrangements; presumably the captain also enjoyed the use of a separate bedroom. Distant shouts came through the thick wooden ceiling: but for that, and the sight of the rippling water creeping past the window, Christopher might have fancied himself in some quiet private house, whose owner had a taste for elegant furnishing and a dislike of fuss. But you wouldn't find a gun taking up space in a private house, and the ceiling was very, very low. There were only a few inches to spare between Christopher's head and the solid timbers; Richard just cleared them. A tall man like the captain would surely have to keep his head bent whenever he stood up here.

The walls were painted a pale ivory colour, to make the cabin seem larger and lighter than it was. Huge and gleaming on its solid wooden platform stood the gun, with its long nose pointed malevolently towards the wall where a closed trap barred the way. In time of action, obviously, the lid would swing open on the ropes hanging from the deck timbers, and gun and platform would rumble forward together on wooden wheels until that ugly mouth stuck out from the ship's side.

By now Christopher had recovered from his surprise, and he turned on Richard wrathfully. "This is a fine state of affairs!" he cried. "What on earth do you mean by it? You've got me in a

22

regular pickle now, haven't you?"

Richard's eyes were brimming with laughter. "Don't say that!" he begged. "It's a splendid lark! I've done you a rare good turn, if you'll only stop to think about it!"

"I don't see that," complained Christopher. "I'd never seen you before this afternoon and now I don't know where I am or where I'm going or – or even who I am, anymore! How can you call it a lark?"

"Of course it's a lark! You said you wanted an adventure and now you're having one, aren't you? As for who you are and where you are, you're Christopher Crown of the Royal Navy, on board His Majesty's ship Nonesuch, and we're off to fight the Frenchies! What more do you want? Why, you said yourself it would be worth being seasick to sail under Nelson, and here you are as good as doing it already. How are your sealegs?"

Christopher glared at him speechlessly for a moment; then he started to laugh. Richard joined in, and when Captain Britten strode into his cabin he found them both doubled up and whooping joyously.

"Now then," he said sternly, calling the meeting to order. "This is no laughing matter! Richard, you will kindly explain yourself at once! At once, do you hear?"

"Yes sir," said Richard briskly. "You see sir, I found myself with nothing particular to do this afternoon..."

"Indeed? I don't know how that might be! We'll enquire into that later! Go on!"

"...so I took a boat out on the off-chance of meeting someone who might be useful to us – and I did! I've heard you say often and often how difficult it is to get a ship manned in a hurry, so I thought I'd see if I could persuade someone aboard myself; knowing we'd be needing every good man we could find!"

"H'm – your intentions at least appear to have been good if a trifle unorthodox! And so you say you have 'pressed' this boy to serve with us?"

"Yes, sir!"

Captain Britten smiled, not unsympathetically, and seated himself at his desk.

"I applaud your patriotism and your – er – initiative," he said, "but I'm afraid it won't do!"

"Oh, sir! Why not?"

"He's too young, for one thing; and I shall be surprised to hear that he has any sea-going experience!"

"He's not much younger than I am, sir!"

"Possibly not, but you are a potential officer. Pressing a seaman is a very different matter and one should stick to the rules – if possible! In the first place, you did not act under the instructions of a commissioned officer; so your impressment is unlawful. Secondly, you should, strictly speaking, be at least eighteen years old, which he very plainly is not; so your impressment is unlawful. And thirdly, he most certainly has not had as much as two years' seafaring experience. Have you, my boy?"

"No, sir," said Christopher. "I haven't."

"I repeat, Richard, your impressment is unlawful. I do wish you would be a little less impulsive!"

But Richard had seen the twinkle lurking in the captain's eyes, and pounced. "Sir," he said eagerly, "they haven't always been to sea before, have they? And you've thought of something; haven't you?"

"Perhaps! The obvious course is to put him in a boat and have him rowed back home; but I must admit I'd rather not."

"Why not, sir?" Richard asked hopefully.

"Because, as you yourself said, every member of the company we can get is precious. And it would take time, and time at this moment is precious, too. The Admiral has already signalled to us to join him down Channel, which explains why our departure has been brought forward. Ajax and Thunderer are already ahead of us, and as you may have noticed, the wind is set at present most unhelpful." Captain Britten paused, and looked intently at Christopher for a moment, balancing a slender paperknife on a long forefinger.

"Tell me, my boy – what is your name again?" he asked.

"Crown, sir; Christopher Crown."

"Very well then, Crown; tell me, would you be willing to sign with us as a member of this ship's company, to sail with us into foreign waters and serve your King and country to the best of your ability, come what may?"

Christopher's eyes sparkled. "Yes, sir!" he cried, without stopping to think of any possible consequence.

"Hooray!" exclaimed Richard. "I knew he was a right one, sir, the moment I met him!"

His uncle quelled him with a look.

"Then, Mr Crown, I propose to enter you on the books as a First Class Volunteer with the prospect of ultimate promotion to midshipman, and you may take up your quarters in the midshipman's mess. Despite your own unusual attire–" and he looked down his nose at Christopher's jeans and t-shirt – "you are obviously used to better things, and I cannot feel," he went on, turning to Richard, "that your friend would be entirely happy on the Lower Deck."

"No, sir; neither do I!" Richard agreed. "That's an absolutely splendid notion, sir; I might have known you'd make everything all right!"

"Your confidence in me is extremely gratifying, but I believe I can do without your compliments just at present! I will inform Lieutenant Scott of this development, and he will see you about initiating Crown into his duties. Now take him to your berth and see what you can do about suitable clothes for him. And don't do it again!"

"Yes, sir! No, sir!" and Richard ushered Christopher out of the cabin.

"There!" He cried exultantly, as he led the new recruit back along the deck. "Didn't I know he'd make everything all right and tight? He's a great gun!"

"I can see why you admire him so much," agreed Christopher. "He needs to be on top of things to keep you in order! I still don't know whether I'm coming or going!"

Richard grinned. "Right now you're coming with me to the cockpit!" he said. "That's where we have our lodgings. We're a lucky lot on Nonesuch; we're all much of an age, with no oldsters to start mollocking about, and so we all keep together. Otherwise we'd most likely have to stow you further aft with the Gunner to keep a fatherly eye on you! This way!" and he led Christopher down below and past the main deck, scrubbed and clean, with great polished black guns stretching along the line on either side. Down they went, and to the right again.

"What is the cockpit?" asked Christopher, meekly following.

"It's an odds-and-ends sort of place, like the mob who live in it," returned Richard. "It's down low in the ship, and we don't count very high either; but then it's aft, you see, because we all hope to get our commissions before too long, and this is the half of the ship where the officers live. We eat and sleep here, and so do the surgeon's assistants, because they work here too when we go into action. The surgeon and the chaplain are down here as well, then, of course, but they're too grand to live here. They're in with the officers."

They reached the cockpit as they finished speaking. It was a dark and stuffy little room, not a bit like the captain's bright and airy cabin. It was a moment or two before Christopher's eyes became accustomed to the dimness after the bright light above. There were forms and benches here, and long tables. The daylight couldn't penetrate so far down in the ship; they were below the waterline now, so windows were out of the question. This meant that fresh air too was almost impossible to be had. A very limited amount seeped down the open hatchways but by the time it actually reached the cockpit it had already been breathed in and out by so many pairs of lungs that "fresh" was hardly the word. Lanterns hung around from the beams to give the light the sun couldn't. There were no guns here. The cockpit was one of the few parts of the ship without them, because it was so low in the water, and in time of battle the cockpit was used as a hospital. Here at least the men were more important than the guns. There was no covering on the floor and no paint on the walls, only the heavy, bare oak timbers of the ship's sides and frames.

The boys came in through a kind of antechamber, where several sea chests held the midshipmen's belongings, and where they slung their hammocks at night. "Snug quarters," said Richard cheerfully, "but we sleep pretty well at sea. And at least you know you're not alone if you happen to be afraid of the dark."

There were only two midshipmen in the cockpit this afternoon, both a little older than Richard. One was reading a book by the light of the lantern; the other was scowling into space. The first looked up as they came in; the second took no notice.

"Hullo," said the one who was reading, and as he put his book down Christopher saw that the two middle fingers of his left hand were missing. "You got back in time, then! We all thought you'd run for it – following the bad example!"

"You don't mean to say Green never did show up?" asked Richard.

The other nodded. "Got clean away!" he said. "At least, I hope he did, for his sake. Not a sign of him anywhere, and they combed the town for him, I can tell you!"

"Of all the pudding-hearts!" exclaimed Richard in disgust.

"I don't know," said his friend. "I'd sooner be in fifty battles than risk what he'll get if they ever find him, but there's no accounting for tastes at all."

"Oh well," said Richard, who never looked at the dark side of things if he could help it, "you should know. We're better off without him, and I've brought in a jolly good replacement! Let me introduce you – Christopher Crown, first class volunteer as from this afternoon – Hugh Stirling, midshipman!"

They shook hands.

"Glad to welcome you aboard," said Hugh grandly. "Where did you find him, Richard?"

"Oh, upalong," said Richard, waving a vague hand. "He's awfully keen to come with us, and the captain took him on like a shot."

"Oh lord! Not another!" burst out the fourth boy. "That's too much, by heaven!" and he stormed out without so much as a look at Christopher.

"What's the matter with him?" asked Christopher in surprise.

"That's only Fellowes in the sulks again," said Richard, with a shrug. "Don't take any notice of him. We don't!"

"He certainly doesn't seem very friendly," said Christopher ruefully.

"Oh, he's like that with everyone!" said Richard. "He's not a bad type underneath and he does his work well, but he's as surly as a bear half the day. Don't let him bother you!"

"Forget it," advised Hugh. "You'll be too busy before long to notice that he's even among those present. Richard my boy, we must get Crown organised! What about his gear?"

"Heavens, yes! I was told to find him some clothes, but I can't think where. I can't lend him any; for one thing I haven't enough and for another they'd fall off him!"

Hugh was surveying Christopher thoughtfully. "He's about the same size as Green," he said, and he didn't take any luggage with him – no time to pack! He could wear some of his toggery – that is, if you don't mind borrowing from a deserter!" he added apologetically. His face clouded.

Christopher said he didn't mind in the least, so his new shipmates started rummaging in one of the chests, and he found himself transformed in a surprisingly short time. He stood up arrayed in a white shirt and a dark blue suit with a stand-up collar to the jacket. The collar had white flashes on it, and the gilt buttons of the jacket had an anchor and cable pattern on them. Shoes like Richard's finished him off neatly, and his companions assured him that he looked as precise as a pin, Richard going so far as to say that he might have been born for the part.

The chest contained another suit like this, as well as several shirts, a couple of hats, two pairs of white kneebreeches and a whole roll of silk stockings. "He did himself well, didn't he?" remarked Richard appreciatively. "Cotton wasn't good enough for Green, mark you! Where on earth did he get the money for it? He must be rolling in it if he could afford to leave stuff like this behind him!"

"Best not to ask! All that matters now is that it all fits Crown as if it had been made for him. Looks like he's the answer to a prayer!"

They were still admiring him when a tall officer appeared – the First Lieutenant. "I'm told we have a new face here," he remarked briskly. "That's fortunate, since we are so regrettably one member short. You will have to work hard, my boy, to pick it all up in a short time. Do you think you can do it?"

"I can try sir."

"Are you a quick scholar?"

"Not too bad, sir."

"Then in the morning you can report to the signal lieutenant and he will begin to teach you the flag system – or try to! You will also stand a watch. You will find the full details of your duties posted on the Watch and Station Bill tomorrow. What you are told to do you will do immediately and without question. Do you understand that?

"You will find that the youngsters are mostly kept pretty busy. You will run errands when required and generally make yourself useful. You will be kept well occupied except on rare occasions." He bent a stern look on the two midshipmen, who were standing respectfully by. "This appears to be one of them. Do you know anything at all of seamanship or the rules of navigation?"

"No sir."

"Do you know how to sling a cot?"

"No sir"

"Everything to learn, haven't you? Very well, Mr Britten shall teach you that right away. It might keep him out of mischief until suppertime at least!" The lieutenant turned on his heel and disappeared, leaving Richard indignant, Hugh amused and Christopher apprehensive.

"I say, he's a tartar, isn't he?" he asked.

"Not he! He's very hot on discipline but I've never known him unfair. Mind you, I think he's feeling sore about Green just now; we've never had such a thing happen before, you see. The men run, yes – that happens in every ship – but one of us deserting is a bit too much for him."

Christopher said, "He didn't go into the town, you know"

Richard stared at him.

"How on earth do you know that?" he asked.

"I saw him," Christopher answered. "But I couldn't make out what was happening. Not until now."

"But you must have heard the gun go off – the alarm, you know! Didn't you realise what it meant?"

"No, I didn't," said Christopher. "I'd no idea. But a boy ran past me going like a hare, up on the cliff top."

"That's funny," said Richard. "The bo'sun's party went up

there while another lot searched the town. I can't think how they missed him."

Christopher said, "He went through the hedge. By the time that man who was singing just now came round the bend he was out of sight – and across the field, I suppose, unless he hid in the ditch."

"Bates? Didn't he ask you if you'd seen anyone? I'm surprised he didn't press you himself!"

"He didn't see me either. I was on the other side of a bush, and stayed there! After all, I didn't know what it was all about, and anyway –"

He stopped, remembering the boy's pale face, and the hunted look on it.

"Anyway what?"

"Oh nothing! I did look through the hedge afterwards, and there was no sign of anyone."

"Whew!" Richard whistled through his teeth. "He must have gone like the wind! Just as well for him he did."

"What would they have done to him if they'd caught him?"

Richard looked at Christopher sideways. "Let's not talk about that, shall we?" he suggested. "It wouldn't be a pleasant topic of conversation, I can assure you. Now then, about this bed!"

For the next hour or so, Christopher was very busy indeed, slinging and unslinging his cot under Richard's supervision until he had the knack of it, and meanwhile learning quite a lot from his talkative messmates about the people who shared this floating home.

"Fellowes you've already met. Nuff said about him!'"

"Isn't he very nice, then?"

"I don't exactly know what you mean by nice. He's a funny sort of mixture; flies off the handle at nothing and he's got a deuced unpleasant tongue at times. Odd when you think his father's a parson. Doesn't seem to have taught him much tolerance of other people"

"He's got a kind of jealous streak in him," put in Hugh. "He hates to think anybody might be getting something he isn't. That's why he said what he did to you; thinks you're a special protégé of the captain, I imagine." He gave Christopher a swift upward glance. "Are you?" he asked directly.

"Me?" Christopher was thunderstruck. "Why, I'd never even met him until his afternoon. It was all his doing," and he nodded at Richard who grinned wickedly.

"Richard! What have you been up to now?" asked Hugh curiously.

"Nothing much. I only told Christopher we were off to sea again and he upped and came along like a good 'un."

"Tell the truth! I never even met him until this afternoon either, and I never dreamed he was going to kidnap me this way."

"Is that what he did?" Appreciative laughter gleamed in Hugh's eye. "I wondered what he was up to, gone away so long."

"I was having a very busy afternoon," said Richard primly, "whatever Lieutenant Scott may choose to think!"

"So it seems! How did you manage to persuade him?"

"I didn't. I just invited him aboard and he fairly swallowed the bait. Dash it; did you think I knocked him out or something?"

Hugh collapsed on a chest and wiped his streaming eyes. "Let that be fair warning to you," he advised Christopher solemnly, when he recovered. "Never trust Britten when he's looking saintly! It always means mischief! Was he looking saintly?"

"Well, now I come to think of it – yes!"

"I knew it! That's when he's most fiendish!" and Hugh started giggling again.

"That's enough from you!" said Richard sternly. "We're none of us angels; not even you!"

"Oh, I'm harmless enough."

"I'll grant you that. Hugh's our scholar," Richard said to Christopher. "When he hasn't got his nose in a book you'll find him engaged in some other improving pursuit. He keeps a regular diary too. Puts us all into it, I shouldn't wonder. What a lot you'll have to put in it today, my lad!"

"Well, my father likes to see it when I go home," said Hugh defensively.

"Where is home?" asked Christopher hurriedly.

Hugh's face brightened. "Bang in the middle of Somerset," he answered promptly. "My father has an estate there, not far from Glastonbury."

"Is he rich, then?"

"Not really. He's comfortably enough off but we're a big family so we can't run to a house in Town or anything like that. Not that we want one. Who wants London when you can live in the country? We're handy for Bath, after all, when we want shops and society."

"How many of you are there?"

"Well, there's me, and my brother – he's the eldest and has a house of his own a few miles away. And I've got four sisters too."

"What made you come to sea?"

"Dashed if I know, really, except that I never wanted to do anything else. Richard has it in the blood; his family's bursting with sailors and always has been. And Fellowes could hardly help himself; he's Devonshire born and just about grew up in a boat, I think. His father has a living on the coast down Exeter way. Actually, he and I get along pretty well."

"Anyone gets along with you, old fellow!" said Richard. "It's a pity Christopher got off on the wrong foot, though I don't know why. The rest of us are a fairly jolly lot, though of course we do have our ups and downs. It's no good being too fussy in your notions; we live too close together to be unsociable. Lieutenant Scott you've met. He's the First Lieutenant; keeps the whole ship running like clockwork or else! Next after him comes Lieutenant Yorke; he'll catch you out if Scott doesn't, so look out for him! Then there's the Third, in charge of signals. His name's Kent, and it sounds as if you might be seeing quite a lot of him."

"Are there any others?"

"Oh yes! There are six lieutenants here. The Fourth is an interesting man; name of Welch. He came up the hard way; promoted from the lower deck."

"Is that unusual?"

"Doesn't happen all that often. He'd spent some time in the merchant service before he came into the Royal, and he's a first-class navigator. Got to be Master in no time, and was given a commission for doing something heroic in action. I don't know the details."

"He's not a young man, then?"

"Bless you, no, but he's most interesting to talk to if you can get him going, and he's the soul of kindness. Number Five is Lieutenant Mann. He's the small arms merchant; teaches the men how to pop off a musket, and so on. It's the Sixth you want to avoid; Lieutenant Ross. He got his commission just a few months ago and can't forget it. Then there's Captain Caldy, commanding the Marines, and two Lieutenants of theirs, but they don't bother us."

There was a sound of running feet, and several other mids came scrambling down into the cockpit. Christopher guessed from the high wailing of pipes up aloft that something was going to happen. It turned out to be supper, and he was soon sitting between Richard and Hugh at the long table, tucking into cold meat, cheese and an incredibly hard kind of biscuit, all washed down with ale. It was strange fare to him, but he downed it all with good appetite, even the ale. It seemed ages since he'd last eaten anything, and he was hungry. Everyone seemed to be in tearing spirits, except for Fellowes, brooding over his beef. From the others, Christopher gathered that this being the start of the voyage, the food was wholesome enough. What it would be like after several weeks at sea was another matter.

"And at the rate we're going," said Hugh, "we'll be a month making Land's End! What a wind! As foul as can be!"

"Sealegs still all right?" asked Richard with a twinkle.

"Couldn't be better," answered Christopher, as he cracked another biscuit.

Hugh nodded at it. "Another six weeks or so and you won't do that," he said. "You'll take care to tap it on the table first to let the weevils out."

Christopher's face was a picture. "What do you mean?" he asked.

"I mean just that. If you bang it first, the maggots fall out of their front doors and you don't eat 'em along with the biscuit. Or you could do what I'm told some of the men do; keep it and eat it after dark so you can't see what you're eating. The cheese gets quite sprightly, too."

Everyone roared at Christopher's horrified expression. Even

Fellowes smiled. "It doesn't do to be faddy over food at sea," he said sweetly. "I do hope you're not a fussy eater. Though if you are, there will be all the more for us when we get down to the rats."

"You must be joking!" Christopher protested.

"I'm not. I never joke."

"That's true enough," growled Richard, "but I'd like to know when you ever had to eat a rat!"

"I haven't, but it has happened before now that a fat juicy rat has been worth a lot to the man who caught it when the stores were running low," retorted Fellowes.

Christopher's gorge rose at the thought. His insides gave a sickening lurch and just for an instant the ceiling timbers seemed to swing out across the room. Then he caught the malicious gleam in Fellowes' eye, and his hackles rose. Stretching out for more cheese, he said evenly, "In that case, I'll make the best of what I can now, while I can!"

There was a murmur of approval, and Richard said, quite clearly. "End of round one! Well done, young 'un!"

"Yes," chirped up another, not to be outdone, "and just wait till you try our best nautical porridge! Burgoo, the men call it. You haven't lived till you've tasted rotten oatmeal boiled in scummy water!"

"And what does it taste like?" asked Christopher, really wanting to know.

"Well, like – like rotten oatmeal boiled in scummy water! Like nothing else on earth!"

Now the seats were scraped back, and Richard offered to show Christopher something of the ship's geography before turning in for the night, "because," he argued, "you're going to have to do an awful lot of running about and it helps if you know where you're meant to be running!"

From the after cockpit they passed through the space where the hammocks were slung at night. They were, Richard explained, on the lowest deck, the orlop, and under that again were the holds and the powder room. Also on the orlop slept the surgeon and the purser, so that they could be near their surgery and their stores. Aft of the cockpit where they had just had their supper slept the Chaplain and the Gunner – handy for the gun room, right aft. On a ship of war, the Gunner was obviously a most important person, and he had a whole little bevy of assistants (or "mates") to himself. When the ship went into action, he would be in full charge of the magazine and the dispensing of ammunition. Down here, it seemed the ship was shut off into a number of different compartments for the accommodation of men and stores. The higher you went, the less crowded it became, until you reached the lonely eminence of the Captain with his comfortable suite all to himself as the reward of responsibility. And in front of the boys now stretched the lower deck, where the big guns vied for space with the seamen. Even without them, the room would have been cramped enough for four hundred odd men. With them, sardines were better off in their tins. The glimpse he had of this crowded, sweaty hotbed of humanity was sufficient to convince Christopher that the captain had been right about one thing at least; he would not have been "entirely happy on the Lower Deck! Yet they seemed a cheerful crew enough if the bursts of hearty laughter and snatches of song were anything to go by. Somewhere in the middle of the crowd someone was playing a jig on a fiddle, the tune almost drowned by the noise of tapping and shuffling feet and the constant drone of voices. The atmosphere was rather ripe, too, for so many ill-washed bodies in this confined space hardly made for sweetness.

"Is it always like this?" asked Christopher, appalled, and thanking his stars for his narrow escape.

"It's never a bed of roses, if that's what you mean, but it's not so bad when the ports can be left open. Of course, that's out of the question at night, or when there's anything of a sea running. It's very near water level here."

"But what a crush!" and crush it was, not helped by the room taken up by the enormous rope cables which stretched down the centre of the deck before disappearing into the depths of the ship. It seemed from what Richard said that there was even more life here than Christopher could have imagined, for hens and sheep to provide fresh meat had to be stowed somewhere, together with a kitchen on the deck above. The guns too had to be fed when the time came for action, and the main magazine had its place down below the waterline.

"But how do they all eat and sleep?" Christopher wanted to know.

"Oh, it's the neatest thing in the world!" answered his friend. "They keep the tables fastened to the deck beams between meals, and when they're needed they're brought down and set up between the guns. And it's the same with the hammocks, though they're kept on deck in the nettings. They make a useful guard against shot when we go into action, there, as well as keeping the deck clear in the daytime. Not much room for them here, I grant you, but it's not as bad as it looks because some of the men are asleep while the rest are on watch – turn and turn about, you see. It does get beastly stuffy and smelly but they don't seem to mind too much."

Christopher shuddered. "But not so good if you don't happen to have good sealegs!" he commented.

Richard looked at him quickly. "Do you feel all right?" he asked anxiously.

"Oh, I'm fine – so far! What else ought I to know?"

"As far as layout goes, not a great deal. You'll see it better in daylight and you'll soon find your way about once you've got the general hang of things. The main deck you've seen, and the quarterdeck; the poop's raised above that aft, with my uncle's quarters beneath it; handy for the quarterdeck, you see. And if you should happen to be there when he appears, get over to larboard as quickly as you can."

"Larboard?"

"Left side. It's easy to remember; they both begin with 'L.' As I was saying, make yourself scarce so that he gets the starboard side to himself, take off your hat, and don't speak unless you're spoken to except when you really must in the course of your duty! Remember, he's the captain and therefore more than human; at least as far as this ship is concerned."

"Does that apply to you too?" asked Christopher curiously.

"Of course it does! I'm not his nephew at sea, remember – I'm just a humble 'mid', lowest of the low! That's about all, I think!"

"Where do the other officers live?" asked Christopher, as they turned to go back to their berth.

"Wardroom, aft of the main deck. You'll probably get a chance to see it before long; they often ask some of us to dine there and we have some jolly times. Strictly off-duty, of course!"

Down in the dimness of the lower deck you couldn't tell the ship's present position, but in fact Hugh's gloomy forecast seemed well-founded. The wind blowing from the southwest was dead against them, and the swell was also surging in from the west, making progress almost impossible. To make a headway at all, Nonesuch had been set to beat on the zigzag course, so that the first one side of her bows and then the other was presented to the adverse breeze; a lengthy and trying process. The quartermaster at the helm swung it round until the ship lay close into the wind on the starboard side then back round again on the larboard tack, beating her weary way down towards Land's End. The binnacle light before him glowed faintly yellow, throwing flickering shadows over his face, intent on his task. In the darkness the men managing the sails worked by instinct, all together, urged on by a baritone voice singing,

"Hey boys, haul away,
Haul on the line oh!
Haul away together boys,
Haul for better weather, boys,
Hey, haul away!"

And as the bows came round into the wind the heavy yards were swung on their ropes to catch the wind more favourably. For a moment the ship hovered, slowly finishing the swing. Then back again in the opposite direction, turn after turn to the end of the weary watch, when a fresh batch of men would come up to take over the monotonous work…

They would take care, as they wove back and forth, to give a wide berth to the rocky Cornish cliffs. Past the sleeping landsmen in their cottages they slowly made their way; it would be some time, at this painful rate, before at least the gleam of the light high up on the Lizard would tell them that England was left behind and all the world was before them. A long night stretched ahead as the men trimming the sails or hauling at the ropes, and the man in charge of the wheel, kept Nonesuch turning first one way and then the other to catch all she could of the elusive breeze. Everyone hoped for a good northerly blow once the Lizard was reached; until then, if present conditions kept up, beating their passage down Channel this way was the only way they could expect to reach the open sea.

Sounds of cheerful laughter came from the after cockpit but Christopher felt unequal to any more that evening after such a long and exciting day. His whole frame ached with weariness; he was, he thought, too tired even to fall asleep, particularly in his strange new bed. Richard's final "Sleep well, young 'un! The night's shorter than you think!" did nothing to change his mind for him, but the gentle swaying of the hammock and the creaking of the timbers overcame exhaustion. Before he had time to think over the events of the last few hours he had gone to sleep, deeply and dreamlessly.

3

He was woken up early in the morning – hideously early in the morning -- by someone yanking his coverings from him and poking him sharply in the ribs. He blinked and gazed blearily about him. For a moment he couldn't think where he was. This dim, crowded chamber with the wooden walls and low wooden ceiling meant nothing to him at all. He concentrated, frowning; and looked straight into a pair of twinkly grey eyes. Then memory came flooding back, and he exclaimed aloud.

"Rouse out there!" cried Richard gaily. "Rouse out! It's tomorrow morning!"

Obediently, Christopher got out of his swaying hammock – or rather, fell out! – and scrambled hastily into his clothes. "Where are we?" he asked.

"Lord knows! Come up on deck and we'll soon find out!"

So trustingly, like a little dog Christopher trotted after, and followed Richard and the other mids up to the upper deck. The men off watch had roused too and hastened to stow their neatly rolled and lashed hammocks, with the straw mattresses and blankets tucked inside, round the bulwarks. The clean fresh air hit Christopher in the face like a physical smack and he gulped it gratefully into his lungs after the fug below decks. He stood still for a moment, blinking in the grey light and trying to get his bearings. Unfortunately, he had chosen to pause right at the head of the hatchway and Fellowes, coming swiftly up behind him cannoned straight into him and made him stagger. The older boy grabbed his arm to steady him. Christopher thought himself lucky, later, that he hadn't left him to fall flat on the deck! Maybe it was simply a reflex action, or maybe better nature did prevail with Fellowes. But not for long. He frowned crossly when he saw who it was in front of him and said, "For goodness' sake! Don't block a man's way like that again, especially at the top of a ladder. If you've got time to stand around staring I certainly haven't. You won't get far if you spend your time getting in everyone's way." He stormed off, not stopping to listen to Christopher's hastily stammered apology.

"Not a very good start, that," he said ruefully to Richard.

"Oh well, it could have been worse," said Richard cheerfully. "Everyone makes mistakes at first – Fellowes included! And that's one you won't make again at all events. Come on!" and he led him along the deck. A faint breeze ruffled their hair but it wasn't nearly enough to fill the spread of canvas above their heads, and in any case it was blowing the wrong way. The sails hung dejectedly from the yards like so much washing put out to dry. There was a rolling swell moving up Channel under Nonesuch's keel, making her lurch as she struggled painfully on her way, but there was the familiar tang in the nose and the familiar salt taste on the lips, and the early morning air was keen on the skin.

Richard stole a sidelong look at Christopher as he stood gazing eagerly about him. His blue eyes were bright with excitement, his cheeks were flushed pink in the sharp early morning air and altogether he was looking almost indecently healthy for a raw recruit after his first night at sea.

"Feeling quite all right still?" Richard asked slyly. "Ready for breakfast?"

"I could eat a horse!" he replied. "When do we get it?"

"When hammocks are stowed and we're all clean and tidy! And if you're feeling like it I'd say the sealegs are holding out well!"

Christopher laughed. "Don't put it into my head!" he begged. "I'll never forgive you if I disgrace myself now! Where are we?"

Richard looked over to starboard, where the coastline was inching past, and pulled a face at the curving shore that could be seen some miles away. "At a guess I'd say we were somewhere opposite Looe," he said. "Looe! We could have swum further in the time! How long since we started? Thirteen – fourteen hours? The wind couldn't be fouler if it tried."

"You might have swum it!" retorted Christopher. "I shouldn't have liked to try. What do we do?"

"Oh, we make sure the hammocks are properly stowed in the netting, and everything shipshape. Then we have to see that the whole of the upper works are spanking clean, and I mean spanking clean! The rule always is, ship first, men afterwards! At least, the bo'sun's mates supervise and we look knowing."

Christopher laughed. "I don't believe that's true! You know how it should be!"

"Of course I do! And I'll tell you – lesson number two for today. Each man has a special place in the netting to stow his hammock – you don't have to worry about that, he knows it better than you ever will. Then they cover them with bolts of canvas and wrap 'em up nice and snug against the weather. Damp beds are beastly uncomfortable; unhealthy, too!"

"But why bring them up at all?"

"I told you; because there simply isn't room for them down below all day. They'd be in the way at the best of times and when you clear for action it has to be done quickly. Think how much time you'd waste rolling a lot of beds about! Besides, up here they make a pretty good barricade. When it's a choice between you or your bed getting ripped up by a musket ball, no one in his right mind bothers about the bed!"

So Christopher again trotted obediently behind Richard and did his best to look knowing. The log was hove, and the result made Richard groan. "Hark at that!" he mourned. "Simply crawling along! At this rate we might make Land's End by Christmas!"

"Oh, come now!" said Hugh, who had joined them at this moment. "I never knew such a fellow as you; all up in the air one minute and down in the dumps before you can say knife. This won't last, and even if it did you're exaggerating."

"You think so, do you?" grinned Richard. "I tell you, I've a good mind to get out and push!"

"We'll remind you of that when we're battling in the teeth of a howling gale! Then you'll wish for this kind of weather again. Try looking at it this way," Hugh advised, "we can't go much slower, so we're only likely to go faster. Being impatient won't help, though!"

Richard's spirits were rapidly rising again; he never did stay down in the dumps for long; that was something! "You're quite right," he said gaily. "If things can't get worse they can only get better. And just now I'm more impatient for my breakfast than anything else!"

"And there it is!" answered Hugh, as the pipes started up. "I'll be glad of some coffee myself. It's chilly up here!"

Breakfast was a merry meal, and as usual Richard hardly stopped talking. He said to Christopher, "We'll go along after breakfast and take a look at the Watch Bill. Then when you know where you're meant to be at any time I'll tell you where to go and if you're stuck at all just ask me," he finished grandly.

"What usually happens?" asked Christopher.

"Divisions next – Captain's inspection," answered Richard, with his mouth full. "And I daresay there'll be a muster today as well, first day out of port. Usually it's only once a week or thereabouts. And of course there are all kinds of jobs to be done as well just to keep the ship going. You never know from one minute to the next what they'll be – all according to the weather, naturally, or what gentry we meet. And lessons," he added ominously.

"Lessons?"

"Of course! Navigation and seamanship and so on. That shouldn't worry you; you're used to school, and it'll make a change from reading, writing and 'rithmetic. In fact, you'll probably start with an unfair advantage, coming straight from one classroom to another!"

"Where do you keep your classroom?" asked Christopher.

"Wherever in the ship you happen to be! Mostly on the upper deck, of course, so pray for fine weather!"

As it turned out, Richard was right and after Captain Britten had been round his spanking clean little kingdom all hands were brought onto the quarterdeck for the call to be taken. They were a pretty mixed bunch, Christopher decided, after a quick glance round. All told, the company numbered some five hundred and forty, including the officers, fifty or so short of the full complement.

"Well, they can't say I didn't do my best to help," said Richard, chuckling.

"I only hope you think it was worth the effort," retorted Christopher.

"You haven't let me down yet! Though of course, you haven't had much time so far, have you? Ssh, captain's starting."

One by one with surprising speed, each man's name was called and checked against the captain's list, and Christopher watched with interest as the mixed bag of men answered their names.

"William Harris, Able Seaman" – and a big burly man was identified; aged thirty, from Hastings. After him came an amazingly thin person with a mournful bloodhound's face. This was Thomas Lewis, also Able Seaman; aged twenty-eight, from Portsmouth. John Peters and Henry Darby followed in the able seamen's list; the first a Suffolk man, the second Cornish from Fowey. "Don't they come from all over the place?" Christopher wondered to himself as the call went on: carpenter's mate, bo'sun's mate, sailmaker, cook, able seaman, able seaman...from Devon, Cornwall, Lanark, Dublin, Devon, Devon...The ship might not be carrying a full complement but there seemed an awful lot of them to Christopher. Captain Britten's crisp voice went on through the list. Then a harsher note crept in. "Edward Green, midshipman, of Whitby in Yorkshire. Aged seventeen. Joined 1801. Run."

Shocked disbelief showed in scores of faces as the captain

went on evenly through the roll. And right at the very end came the name of Christopher himself, volunteer, aged fifteen, joined at Plymouth on September 17th, 1805. Nobody ill so early in the voyage, nobody injured. When everyone had been duly checked, they went back to work again, and Nonesuch carried on beating her way past the Cornish coast.

As it happened, there would be several new names added to the next muster-list. Later in the day, with Fowey still in sight, one of the lookouts shouted, "Sail to the south-west!" Captain Britten raised his telescope and gazed intently through it for a moment or two; then he snapped it shut, saying, "Merchant-man. Lieutenant Welch, man a boat and board her!"

"Ay, ay sir!" said the Lieutenant. He added over his shoulder as he turned to go, "Will half-a-dozen of theirs be enough, sir?"

The Captain nodded. "I suppose so," he said. "We mustn't leave her too short-handed. But mind you press the best! In the King's name!"

Richard whistled softly under his breath. "Copying my lead, by Jiminy!" he hissed.

"Nonsense!" said Hugh. "Just you take a lesson in how it ought to be done! There they go!" And indeed, with the oncoming vessel now within hail, the boat was being made ready and an armed party was all set to go. Bates was one of them, looking more like a pirate than ever, with dark stubble sprouting over his chin and cheeks. "Lower away, mateys!" he bellowed. "Lower away! Steady as you go!"

No sooner had they all piled in than they were off, pulling away strongly over the swelling waves with Nonesuch herself coming up behind. The boys watched the proceedings intently. They were close enough now to see the crew standing about on the other ship's quarterdeck. They didn't seem to be doing anything in particular, but there had been plenty of activity a very short while ago. Their lookout man had seen Nonesuch when she was quite a way off, and the chequerboard paintwork had been enough to alert the captain, never mind the Ensign drooping from the jackstaff. When he saw her bearing down upon them, he knew all too well why. He had sworn a terrific oath, and called all hands on deck. "Press-gang to starboard," he snapped. "You – and you – and you –" he pointed to half-a-dozen or so of the spryest and strongest seamen – "down in the hold and hide there. Move!" It was a faint hope, but worth trying. They bolted below decks like rabbits with a ferret behind them, and dived among the casks and crates at the bottom of the ship, where they lay half-stifled and hardly daring to breath. It was back luck for them that the Lieutenant had been a merchant seaman himself and was up to all the tricks.

The captain turned as soon as they were fairly out of sight and snarled at the rest, "You lot! Try to look useless, damn you! That shouldn't be difficult!"

"Ahoy there!" bellowed a voice from below. Bates was enjoying himself. "Look alive!"

The captain hung over the rail and shook his fist at the boat bobbing about on the swell beneath his bows.

"Look alive and be damned to you!" He bawled back. He was red in the face with fury.

"Lieutenant Welch shouted, "In the King's name! I am coming aboard for the defence of the realm!"

The captain looked him straight in the eyes saw the resolution in them, and decided, now that the big seventy-four was so close, that he'd better give in with a good grace. He could see that the man o'war had obviously only just left port, for she had a fresh and business-like look about her, so it was not likely that she would be able to substitute any of her own crew for the men she took off, and since enough hands must be left on board his own ship to bring her safely home with her precious cargo, he probably wouldn't have to give up very many after all. And the best of them were well hidden, he hoped. So he shrugged his broad shoulders and sent down a ladder. Lieutenant Welch swung himself up and aboard, followed by the eager Bates and most of the others, armed and ready for trouble.

Once fairly aboard the merchantman, Lieutenant Welch looked at the rather unappetising hands standing around and grinned. "I'll take a look below decks," he said to the sullen captain. "Belike I'll find you smuggling forbidden goods, in which case...You two come with me! The rest of you, stay here and watch this lot. No tricks, mind!" and he led two of his own men below decks. Bates and the rest of the pressgang stayed on deck to stop any attempt at rescue. They stood with their cutlasses at the ready, but the look in Bates's eye was enough. The merchant crew stood quite silent, fearing the worst but hoping for the best.

At the bottom of the ladder the Lieutenant paused, his drawn sword in one hand and the other holding up a dark lantern with the slide open. He swung it slowly round. There was nothing to be seen but boxes and bales, but his quick ear caught the sound of muffled breathing, and he went forward, closely followed by his two able seamen. He walked slowly along the deck a few paces; then "Aha!" he cried. "A stowaway! Out you come, my lad!" His keen eye had seen a flash of scarlet between two tall barrels. A sailor, too dressy for his own good, had chosen to wear a bright red neckerchief and reaching in between the barrels, Lieutenant Welch pulled at the neckerchief. There was a choking gasp; the barrels were kicked aside, and the man was landed like an oversized fish, to lie at their feet cursing his captors and his bad luck alike.

Having handed him over to the able seaman, the Lieutenant stood one moment poised like a cat waiting to spring. Those quick ears had caught the faintest possible sound of a barrel being scraped by – a rat? Or could it be an incautious toe trying to make itself comfortable? He swung the lantern round, low and slowly, and sighed. "Aha!" he said again, softly. "Just as I thought! Better be pressed for room than pressed, eh? You'll know better next time!" and he chuckled to himself as a beam of light showed a foot sticking out between the bales. The seamen swooped, and captive number two emerged, dusty, cramped and choking with rage. The Lieutenant didn't so much as glance at him; he was far too busy probing behind the cargo, very delicately, with the point of his sword. It was too much for another of the hidden men. There was a yelp and a clatter, and he burst out, glaring. Three good men were no bad haul; more would have been better, but Lieutenant Welch said, chuckling again at his own bad joke, "Time presses as well as us!" and the captives were shoved up aloft, leaving their more fortunate comrades still concealed among the stores. The Lieutenant chose six more from the second-rate selection left on deck, and they were bundled swiftly down the ladder and into the boat. Their captain fumed helplessly, but at the same time he thought himself lucky to have lost so few, and only three from his best men. As for the pressed men themselves, once the first shock had worn off they were fairly philosophical. After all there was a war on, and all was fair in it, though no one could have blamed them for preferring the higher wages and softer living in a merchant vessel to the tougher and more dangerous life in the fighting fleet. This sort of thing was all in a day's work, and no amount of crying would fill a spilt pitcher of milk. And at least, if the French were likely to knock off their heads at any moment, they might have a chance of getting their own blow in first. Resigned to their fate, they clambered aboard silently and were taken aft to the captain straight away to take the oath on becoming members of the ship's company as defenders of the King's estate against the enemy. And that was that! Declared fit for service by Mr Campbell the surgeon, equipped with bedding and other necessaries they were absorbed into the life of HMS Nonesuch like pebbles dropped into still water, with scarcely a ripple to disturb the surface. Christopher felt sorry for them, if nobody else did. It had happened to him too, more or less. As soon as he could, he tackled Richard about it.

"Isn't anybody safe from you people?" he asked. "How can you just tap a man on the shoulder and take him away from his home and his work and everything else, just like that?"

"But we can't. You ought to know that! You heard what my uncle said to me! By rights he should have sent you home again, only he hadn't got time."

"Well, I still think these methods are shockingly high-handed; not to say rough and ready!"

"Maybe, but you must remember that we've been at war a long time. We've got to keep the ships manned or they wouldn't get to sea at all. And war wastes men, you know." Richard looked stern for a moment. "Battles, illness, accidents – you lose them all the time, one way and another. Not to mention a deserter or two."

"Can't you just call for recruits?" asked Christopher innocently.

"Oh, you can call for them all right, but precious few come. Or at any rate, not enough. So since you have to keep as many ships afloat as you possibly can, and since you have to have crews to do it, what else can you do if they don't come of their own accord? You have to go and fetch them. They don't like it much, of course, but in the end your pressed man turns out no worse than the next and often a good deal better! Never forget that we live on an island – entirely surrounded by water, you know! – and that being so the Navy is the last bastion if the worst comes to the worst. It just has to be kept going at all costs."

Christopher thought this over. "So," he said slowly, "it's a case of 'you might as well come quietly because you've got to come anyway. I should think myself lucky, shouldn't I?"

"Well, and so you are! There's an adventure ready made for you on your very first day! What more could you want?"

"You're changing the subject!"

"No I'm not. I can't see what you're making all the fuss about. Here we are needing more seamen to fight the war – there was a ship carrying more than she really needed to bring her cargo safe home – wasn't the sensible thing to do to help ourselves to a couple? In the King's name?"

"Oh, I give up. All right, it's entirely necessary and patriotic but I still feel sorry for them."

"Oh, they'll be all right! It's no more than they expected after all. Anyway, it'll give old Hugh something to put in his precious diary and he'd have had a blank page otherwise, so it's an ill wind that blows nobody any good. This one," he added, looking up at the limp sails. And Hugh did exactly that.

"Wednesday, September 18th.

This afternoon," he wrote carefully, "we came upon a merchantman making her way up Channel for home. Lieutenant Welch went aboard in search of likely hands to man us, as there is always room for more on board than we are carrying. Tonight the ship's company has been swelled by nine who will surely be able to make themselves useful. We think this a good omen for the voyage and this was needed, as we are still having difficulty in getting to the mouth of the Channel. This will be another long night. We have passed Fowey in calm weather with a swell coming from the west. But we are determined to join the Fleet as soon as possible and it won't be for want of effort on our part if we don't get there in time!

After twenty-four hours everybody is settling down to shipboard life once more and our berth is its usual cosy self; too cosy in some ways! But we are with our old friends in the old life and we get along very comfortably on the whole. Our new shipmate is making himself at home and I think he will be popular. He is eager and willing to learn but doesn't push himself forward unbecomingly. Really, Richard chose very well!"

In fact, Christopher had been rushed off his feet all day. As the newcomer in the midshipmen's berth he was everyone's errand boy. He went from officer to officer with messages, from officer to bo'sun, to carpenter, to everyone, or so it seemed. But he had to admit that it was a splendid way of getting to know who, what and where everybody and everything was. He was really quite pleased about it. He had expected to spend his first day at sea standing about watching other people doing interesting things and generally making him feel useless, but it wasn't like that at all. Lord Nelson had insisted that no one could be an officer who wasn't a seaman as well as a gentleman. Captain Britten, sharing this belief, thought that everyone aboard should know something at least of the seaman's craft, and his officers were particularly knowledgeable. It was his creed that no one ought to order another man to do something he didn't know how to do himself. And if nobody was telling Christopher to do something, they were showing him how to do something else.

"Can you tie a knot, my boy?"

"I can tie a reef knot," said Christopher eagerly.

"Can you now? Then let's see you do it."

Christopher did so, and got an approving nod. "And why do we call it a reef knot, eh? What would we use it for? Think now!"

Christopher thought, and suddenly the answer seemed to

click in his mind. "Why, for – for reefing the sails, I suppose; rolling them up."

"Very good! Know any more?"

Christopher had to admit that he didn't know any more.

"Not so good! You can watch me make a sheet bend, and then you can show me how to do it. That's another one that's easy to let out, although it won't slip. We use it to fasten the sheet to the clew of the sail. That is to fasten this rope – that's the sheet – to the bottom corner. The tautness of the sheet, you see, regulates that of the sail, and by hauling on it or letting it go we can stretch the sail fully, or change its direction if necessary. There's plenty more, but that'll do to be going on with."

So Christopher spent part of his morning wrestling with pieces of rope.

He was pounced on to join the noonday navigation class and was more foxed by the sextant thrust into his hand than by anything he'd ever used in his life before. This business of finding out where you were by fiddling with angles was a mystery, but it obviously worked. He was pounced on by Lieutenant Kent, who sent a midshipman to find him, and he got a cold reproof into the bargain for not turning up of his own accord.

"I believe Lieutenant Scott told you to report to me?"

"Yes, sir."

"Didn't you look at the duty bill?"

"Yes, sir."

"Why didn't you come to me, then?"

"I forgot, sir!"

"You forgot! Forgetting an order would count as mutiny with some officers, and don't you forget that! Remember, nobody in the Navy ever forgets his duty, whoever he is. You don't expect me to go running all round the ship after you, do you?"

"No, sir."

"Very well. This is your first day with us and I'll overlook it this time. Mind it doesn't happen again." Then as Christopher stood silent and downcast before him, the lieutenant smiled, a surprisingly kind smile, and laid a hand on his shoulder. "Come along now. That's a lesson it's as well to have learned at the beginning, and you won't forget again. Let's waste no more time. There's more than enough for you to learn, and little enough time to do it in."

He was pounced on by Fellowes, who seemed to find an incredible number of odd jobs for him to do, as if to see if he were capable of doing them. Christopher took good care to see that Fellowes was out of sight before asking anybody else where to go. It reminded him of the "fagging" in old school storybooks, and if that was the system then that was the system and there wasn't much he could do about it – yet, at any rate. "Only wait until I'm not so much the new boy," he thought to himself. Then he saw the funny side of it. "I'm as bad as he is," he reflected. "He must have gone through this too, and looked forward to the day when there'd be somebody newer still to boss about – just like I'm doing now." All the same, some of it seemed rather unnecessary. Christopher bided his time, and decided to ask Richard's advice at the earliest opportunity. When the opportunity did come, Richard raised his brows and laughed.

"Fellowes tries it on like that with everyone," he said. "Next time, just look frightfully important and say that you've already got something to do – for an officer." It worked like a charm.

Slowly during those first days the familiar landmarks slid away past them – Black Head, the Dodman Point, Nare Head, Falmouth with the twin castles facing each other across the estuary. Then there were the grim and treacherous rocks called the Manacles to be looked for and given a wide berth before rounding a second Black Head and the Lizard, with its farewell light winking away on the high cliff. From there they would make their creeping way out towards the Scilly Islands, leaving Land's End somewhere over to the northward. Land's End, the last of England. When would they sight those cliffs again? Christopher wondered. Ah well, he'd burnt his boats behind him now. There could be no turning back.

4

Four days out from Plymouth they finally cleared the Scillies, and met the fair wind for which everyone had been hoping. With a breeze from the north blowing behind her, Nonesuch was set for a quick run across the Bay of Biscay. To celebrate this crossing of the first hurdle, the officers gave a party, and among those invited from the midshipmen's mess were Hugh, Richard, Fellowes – and Christopher. Christopher was glad that Richard's forecast had come true so soon, and he was eager for this new experience. He brushed his clothes, polished his buttons, and generally tried to make himself as spruce as possible. He should have known that this would fuel Fellowes' scorn.

"Going on the strut?" he asked with interest. "We haven't given you much opportunity to shine up to now, I'm afraid. There isn't a great deal of scope on board for one of the dandy set, but I'm glad to see you do make the most of your chances!"

Christopher kept his tongue between his teeth, and went on brushing his hair. Fellowes, mistaking his silence for discomfiture, went gleefully on. "One thing I will say for you Crown! You do respect other people's property. Green would be so glad to know you're looking after his clothes nicely, and…"

"It's a pity he did not have a bit more respect for them himself!" said Richard angrily. "Why drag him into it? Nobody else would ever mention him if you didn't – and what's more, it's a crying insult to mention him in the same breath as the young 'un! Come on if you're ready and for goodness' sake try to be a little more sociable. This is a party!" and he put a hand on Christopher's shoulder and led him away.

Christopher felt very shy going into the wardroom for the first time, but a kindly welcome soon put him at his ease, and he looked round with interest. The officers' quarters were reached behind a bulkhead separating them from the rest of the deck; after the lantern-lit stuffiness below it seemed peculiarly light and airy. Like the captain's cabin, the room got its light from the windows built into the stern. The long table stretching down the length of the wardroom was actually laid with china and glass. There were chairs ranged along it; a welcome sight after days of perching on a narrow bench at mealtimes. Like the cockpit, the floor was bare of covering, but the plain scrubbed boards were spotlessly clean. The walls were painted, and the general effect was surprisingly comfortable. Widthways, the space was restricted, because on either side there were cubicles where the officers could sling their beds in reasonable privacy. Christopher noticed that these "bedrooms" – and they were small enough in all conscience – were made of the flimsiest materials. This he knew, for Richard had explained it, was so that they could be swiftly and easily dismantled when the call to battle came, leaving the deck bare of everything save the guns. You could never get away from the guns. Nearly everywhere you went in the ship you saw them, enormous and threatening, waiting for the moment which would prove them to be more important than anything else on board – the men who fired them only just excepted! Here they were again, and the officers were obliged to squeeze themselves and their belongings in between them. As it was, only the senior ranks were privileged to sleep here; the junior members of the wardroom were berthed elsewhere on the ship.

Only the captain enjoyed a bedroom all to himself, with a sentry posted outside to guard his privacy. But that was the reward of his rank. It would never do for him to live in such close proximity as a shared dormitory with any other person in the ship's company, however senior that person might be. The captain represented absolute power, and that kind of intimacy would lessen his authority. Besides, just as the surgeon and the purser were housed close to their work, so was the captain, as near to the poop and quarterdeck as he could be without actually spreading a mattress out there under the stars. That was plainly logical! Usually as well as sleeping alone he ate in solitary state; such mundane habits as eating did not go well with divinity, any more than sleeping did. But many captains were naturally sociable and only too happy to invite other people to share their meals: Captain Britten was one of these.

Today, however, he was guest of honour to his officers, and joined the gathering looking relaxed and friendly, despite the air of authority which sat upon him like his clothes.

The meal itself turned out to be a surprisingly gracious affair, with the captain in the seat of honour, servants to wait on the company and unusually good food. This was partly, Richard whispered, because they'd only just left port; the officer's stores were well-stocked with wholesome food which they had bought themselves. On a long voyage with little chance of re-victualling, things would be very different. It was enough, tonight, to enjoy a change from the monotony of ordinary ship's rations. There was wine, too, and toasts were drunk. There was ritual it seemed even about this – Christopher was beginning to think that the Navy ran entirely on ritual! – with special toasts for each particular day of the week. Now, it being Saturday, the loyal toast to the King would be followed by "Sweethearts and Wives." This didn't mean much to the younger guests but nobody would dream of tampering with tradition. Besides, no doubt more than one of the older members of the party would give more than a passing thought tonight to a pair of bright eyes anxiously waiting for his safe return.

They began with buttered crab – a real delicacy. Certainly, the officers had made the most of their marketing time before the ship left Plymouth! Christopher thought it was delicious, and polished off his share with gusto. He had found that the sea air and the hard work gave him a tremendous appetite which wasn't always satisfied in his own mess. Now he was going to make the most of what promised to be an excellent meal and he didn't give a hoot for Fellowes, raising a supercilious eyebrow at sight of his swiftly-emptied plate.

Broiled fowls came next, and were swiftly and skilfully dismembered before being served with mushrooms, green spinach and delicious sauce. The fowls finished, a large and luscious trifle made up the third course, and bowls of fresh apples, pears and peaches were laid on the table.

He would certainly not have been "entirely happy" on the lower deck. For a fleeting moment Christopher wondered if the seamen knew of these delights enjoyed in the wardroom. But even as the thought crossed his mind he remembered that the ship was, after all less than a week out of harbour: that the fowls were carried aboard in any case: that the officers did at other times share the hardships with more than their share of responsibility; and that they were, after all, paying for their party!

For all the enjoyment of his dinner, Christopher felt too overawed by his company to say a word. Luckily for him Richard was busy chatting with his other neighbour, and Fellowes on his other side had chosen to turn away from him, so he was left alone, a silent little island in a sea of talk. As the meal went on he noticed that the captain in an unbending mood was keeping up a flow of conversation with the officers seated on either side of him, and Christopher, straining his ears, listened unashamedly.

"This is handsome entertainment, Mr Scott," the captain was saying to his First Lieutenant. "Are we celebrating in advance?"

"I hadn't thought of it quite in that way, sir, but it makes as reasonable an excuse as any! I'm glad you approve."

"Oh, it puts my own poor efforts quite in the shade!"

"You flatter us, sir."

"I assure you I don't! Don't think I'm carping – we must enjoy such things while we can. It may be quite a while before we get another chance."

"I'm entirely of your opinion. A little more chicken sir?"

"Thank you."

The sign was given to the servant, and a helping of wing was laid on the captain's plate.

"Does the thought please you, Mr Scott?"

"I confess I have found the past months a little – irksome, shall we say? It would give me great pleasure to pay back some of the debt with interest."

"I think we all feel that way. Mr Yorke –" (turning to the Second Lieutenant, seated at his left hand – "does Mr Scott speak for you too?"

"For me and for all of us sir. We only hope we are in time to take part."

"Oh, I don't think there's any doubt of that! We can't be so very far behind the Victory now and unless I'm very much mistaken nothing will happen without Lord Nelson."

"You don't think that the enemy may try to run the blockade again?"

"It's possible, I suppose, but I believe we have shut the door too firmly. No, no Mr Yorke, he will not emerge until we choose to let him. Maybe not even then!"

"In that case, sir, I propose to banish him from my thoughts – at least for this evening! I won't fret myself over a Frenchman at a social occasion."

"Quite right. Let us think no more of him! Lieutenant Scott, you went to London last month. What is the latest news there?"

"Really, sir, I fear I can tell you very little. There was a lot of business to do, as you know, sir, and I hadn't much time for gadding about. Except for taking my young nephew to Astley's! That was an engagement I couldn't dodge!"

"The Amphitheatre?" asked Lieutenant York, amazed. "I shouldn't have thought that was much in your line!"

"It wasn't, but I couldn't break a promise. The whole spectacle is very crudely presented, although the horsemanship is very clever. But my nephew lapped it up – horrible child! His Majesty is not in Town, by the way. He is restoring his spirits at Weymouth."

"It's strange," remarked Lieutenant Yorke pensively, "how Royalty makes sea-bathing resorts so fashionable nowadays. There is the Prince of Wales, for instance, so in love with Brighton that he has built himself a positive palace there! I collect it is something quite out of the ordinary, though I confess I've never seen it."

"I have," said Captain Britten, and a slight shudder twitched his broad shoulders. "A fantastic sight – and it isn't even finished yet!"

Lieutenant Scott laughed. "You prefer a more classic style of architecture, sir?"

"I have no great love for fantasy, I'll admit."

"And yet, sir, the Marine Pavilion is not without its attractions. A summer residence which boasts of a sea view from all its windows has much to commend it."

"What is so remarkable about that? We boast a splendid sea view from all our windows – better, I don't doubt, than any his Highness has!"

Lieutenant Scott raised his hand in acknowledgement of the point. "But each to his own taste," he insisted. "And if the Prince is satisfied, who are we to cavil? I daresay he would think us very strange, to prefer our own way of life to his own."

The captain chuckled. "There I'm quite sure you're right!" he agreed. "The difference is most – er – pronounced!"

Lieutenant Yorke hurriedly turned the conversation into less dangerous channels. "His Majesty's presence apart," he said to his colleague, "did you find Town very thin of company?"

"It wasn't crowded, certainly, as far as Society was concerned, but then that doesn't concern me particularly! No doubt they are all having a rest before another hard winter attending balls and rout parties."

"Oh come! You're too severe!"

"Not a bit of it, and I wouldn't change places with any of 'em!"

"A seaside holiday holds no charms for you?" asked the captain, with a smile.

"What need, sir? You said yourself that our life here is always that!" and the three men laughed together over the joke.

Christopher was amazed. Clearly this was an "off-duty" occasion, but – such idle chitchat on board a man o'war? A little further down the table the Captain of Marines was having a spirited argument with Mr Campbell the surgeon about their favourite actors, another pair were discussing prize-fighting, and Hugh was earnestly defending Mr Walter Scott's latest poem against an unimpressed Lieutenant Kent. Scraps of conversation floated in the air and bounced off Christopher's ears as the medley of talk flowed on.

"I maintain that Kemble is the finest of tragedians. He has such a stately air."

"I don't like his declamations. He'd do better addressing an open-air meeting. He can't hold a candle to his sister."

"Ah, Sarah! Yes, indeed!"

"I'll stand to it against any argument, Jem Belcher's the

greatest of them all."

"Too good in some ways – fight's all over before a man's fairly in his place. People want to have a bit of a show, after all."

"Cribb'll master him before he's done, you wait and see. Beautiful style! Staying-power too."

"He's a true patriot, sir, you can't deny it!"

"Hmm – I'd think more of his patriotism if he were out here fighting for his country instead of writing about it."

"But he's a cripple!"

"There's at least one notable cripple among us."

"This young man Kean will rank among the greatest, I'm convinced of that."

"Never saw such a fighter in my life – always on the dance!"

"But a slow starter; don't know where you are with him."

"All the better! Gives him time to size up his man."

"The man lives in the past. It's the future that concerns us!"

"But it's the past that gives us hope for the future, sir; don't you see? Isn't it because of the past that we're fighting this war at all – to preserve what we've made?"

"But such a jingle! 'The way was long, the wind was cold, the minstrel was infirm and old' – you see, I have read the thing!"

"What we want now isn't great actors, it's great playwrights. There haven't been any really good new plays for years."

"Ah. There's too much drama these days in real life. The theatre can't match it."

"He's young yet, though. Given the choice, I'd plump for Jackson – after Belcher!"

"Ah, there's style for you! And I never saw a man so sweet-tempered in the ring or out of it. Pity we couldn't have seen more of him."

"'Vengeance deep brooding o'er the slain!' That's us! There's fire in it, sir, and rhythm – it – it just sweeps you along with it! And the description – you feel you're really there too!"

"Well, well! You'll grow up, and so will he – I trust!"

Then the covers were removed, the chairs were pushed back, and the captain thanked his officers graciously for their hospitality and went back to his own cabin. The talk became general. Christopher, rather to his dismay as he was following a policy of seeing all, hearing all and saying nothing, found Lieutenant Scott himself was speaking to him, but that officer's tone was so surprisingly human in this "off-duty" hour that he could have answered perfectly well without the helpful nudge he got from Richard, seated beside him.

"Tell me," the Lieutenant began, "how are you settling down? Don't feel quite so strange, eh?"

"I'm quite happy, thank you, sir," he replied. "I seem to have been at sea forever!"

Lieutenant Scott smiled faintly. "If the wind hadn't changed when it did there might soon have been some justification for that remark!" he said. "Do I take it that the pitching hasn't troubled you?"

"Oh no, sir, not at all!" and "He's got splendid sealegs, sir!" came the answer at once from both boys. Richard was giggling, and the lieutenant, scenting a private joke, smiled tolerantly.

"I'm glad to hear it," he said. "Even the best of men can be poor sailors in that respect. If you're not unwell, you'll have all the more time to learn your trade, though Lieutenant Kent tells me you're surprisingly quick with the signal book. That may very well be useful to you if we get into action."

Christopher flushed with pleasure. Fellowes, on the edge of the group, scowled and turned away.

"Perhaps some disappointment in that quarter?" suggested the Lieutenant. "If so, I'm sorry for it."

"I think, sir," said Richard hesitantly, "that Fellowes would have liked to do signals himself. He feels that it's something really important; and of course it is. He was put out when Green first did that job, you know."

"No, that wouldn't do," said Lieutenant Scott decidedly. "I can make better use of Fellowes in other ways. He has the makings of a first-class officer and I can give him more scope for his talents elsewhere. Besides, Crown here is obviously a quick learner, and since he seems to have come to us in Green's place, he might as well be trusted with Green's duties. If he continues to shape as well as he has begun, I shall be happy to leave him with Lieutenant Kent. If not," warningly, "I shall have to change my ideas. I hope it won't be necessary." He caught sight of Richard's sceptical face. "I know you and Fellowes are apt to rub each other up the wrong way," he said. "Don't think I haven't noticed!"

"Sometimes, sir," said Richard daringly, "I think you notice everything."

Lieutenant Scott's mouth twitched. "I do," he said, "and don't you forget it! It's my job to – and one day you may well be glad of the same ability! I have noticed your frictions, I admit. They don't surprise me; but you might well find yourselves surprised in each other. I notice other things too, you see! I could wish you got along better, but as long as you don't let your personal quarrels affect your work I shan't interfere."

"Sir," said Richard proudly, "I've got other things to think about than Fellowes; and he doesn't bother me much anyway."

"Don't let him bother either of you," the Lieutenant advised. "Just keep your minds on those other things. You'll soon be too busy to do anything else."

"We are going to have a battle, aren't we?" asked Richard eagerly.

"I believe so. I don't think the enemy will give us the slip again, as long as this fair wind holds. It would be too much to go chasing him about half over the world again like so many Flying Dutchmen!"

"I've never been altogether certain," ventured Christopher, "about who he was or what he was doing."

"Then you should ask Lieutenant Welch. He's the man to put you right about that and plenty of other sea legends as well. Mr Welch!" Mr Scott raised his voice slightly. "Come and tell these lads about the Dutchman!"

He pulled up a chair for the other officer, "What makes you bring him up?" asked Lieutenant Welch, sitting down heavily on it.

He was a middle-aged man, sturdily built, with a weather beaten face and knotted hands that told of years of toil in all climates. His voice was gruff, but the kindly twinkle in his eyes belied the bark.

"He simply cropped up in conversation."

"Ah! And there's no saying where he may crop up," said Mr

Welch, solemnly. "He's not the safest subject for good sailor-men, I can tell you!"

"Why not, sir?"

"Because he's evil fortune, that's why! And those who see him come to certain destruction. If ever you meet him, turn your head away and make all the sail you can to escape. The Dutch-man's no safe company."

His deep voice rumbled on, and everybody moved closer to listen. Mr Welch was always sure of an audience.

"And he never was safe company for the likes of you! He was the sort of man your dear mothers would hope you'd never meet, though it's ten to one you'll come across more than one of his sort, come to think of it! But he was the worst of the lot!"

"But who was he sir? And what did he do?"

"Is – not was!" said the Lieutenant firmly. "That's the worst part of his punishment. He can't even die, and so he has no way of escape. His name is Van der Decken, and he lived hard, drank hard and swore hard, till even the Devil himself grew tired of his antics and condemned him to sail the seas for ever, because he once defied him. His crew weren't a great deal better – all tarred with the same brush – and that wasn't surprising, for with his wicked ways no decent man would step on shipboard with him. So he went from bad to worse, giving good seamen a bad name among those who met him, until one day in his cups he declared he would round the Horn in any weather though Old Nick himself should bar the way."

He paused for a moment, and rubbed his chin reflectively. "Don't know what made him say that, mind, but bear in mind that he was drunk at the time. Why he should think the Devil would want to go to those parts beats me! The winds from the south there are piercing cold to cut a man to the bone, and from all I've heard the gentleman in question likes his surroundings on the warm side."

"You've been round the Horn yourself, then, sir?" asked Richard with respect.

"More than once, my boy, and I'll tell you this! If that old Hollander had been rounding from the West he'd have had small need to boast, given the wind behind him. But coming round that gaunt old Horn outward bound with the wind in your face – ah that's a different tale again! To be up on the yards with the hail beating on your head and your hands, with the heaving sea below, and a howling wind that's been round the world and back again – why, the man was mad as well as drunk to be wishful to do it, that's all I can say!"

"But did he do it?"

"I'm coming to that! There he was, you may suppose, lolling back in his chair and muttering defiance in his black old beard – black as his black heart! – When behold! He had a visitor – and who do you think that could be?"

"The Devil himself!" Richard answered readily.

"Right enough! There he stood as plain as I see you now, and "So!" he said, "sail in despite of me, will you?" 'Ay' answers the Dutchman, "I'll do it, if I sail till Doomsday!" 'Then sail and be damned to you,' says the Devil, and that's the way it's been with him ever since, and his wicked crew with him. You can tell his ship at a glance. She has black masts with sails the colour of blood, and never a ship sailed as silently as she! There's no creaking in her timbers and no flapping in her sails, and the sailors hauling on her sheets are bent old men with long grey beards. Only Van der Decken stays the same – never getting any older – not any better behaved! It's an ill thing for the man who's first to spot the Dutchman's vessel; he's doomed from the moment. Nothing can save him – and only one thing can save the Dutchman."

"What's that, sir?"

"The love," said Lieutenant Welch, looking down his nose, "of a faithful woman."

"There's not much chance of finding one at sea!" grinned Richard.

"Well, even the Devil plays fair – sometimes. Van der Decken's allowed ashore once every seven years to look for one, but he hasn't found one yet and I don't believe he ever will."

"You have a poor opinion of women!" commented Lieutenant Scott.

"I'll admit I'd rather trust a ship any day," said the older man. "A ship has a strong personality, with everyone is different. Now

I once heard tell of one, and a sweet-tempered ship she was who never refused to obey her orders but once. Then one day when the man at the wheel tried to swing it around – wouldn't budge – wouldn't shift and inch – no matter how hard he tried. And if it had, that ship would have holed herself on a submerged rock and drowned every man Jack of 'em. How did she know? How could she tell? I say her spirit was in charge of her – ay, and of her crew, too!"

There was a pause which no one cared to interrupt. Then, "I'll tell you something else," he went on. "The sea's a vast amount of water and it's full of mystery. No one knows what goes on down there in the dark, or what strange monsters live at the bottom and never see the light of day. Maybe it's as well not to enquire too closely. There's no one can keep a secret as well as the sea can! There's many a fine ship has sailed out from her home port into nowhere, with not so much as a floating spar to prove her foundering. Who takes them? And how? The sea will never tell you." He drained his glass. "The strangest sea of all," he went on, "is the one they call 'Sargasso' – from Bermuda to the Virgin Islands, or thereabouts, and half across the Atlantic as well! If you fear the Horn for stormy weather, beware the Sargasso for a deadly calm! There the sea is covered thick with seaweed and the hot sun beats down without mercy. It hardly ever rains, and there's scarcely a wind to speed you on your way. Many's the good seaman who's died there of thirst or madness, and very likely both. It wouldn't be the first time a ship has been found there with everyone aboard stone dead, and only their spirits left to keep her sailing on among the seaweed. Some say there's a fair burying-ground beneath, where the spirits of the sea bring the wrecked ships to rest."

Lieutenant Scott was looking at Christopher's face.

"Come, come!" he cried, clapping Lieutenant Welch on the shoulder, "enough's enough! There never was a man so full of superstition, and heaven knows most sailors have plenty!"

"Hark at you!" returned the other, good-humouredly. "Who wasn't fit to live with until we made a safe harbour once when we set sail on a Friday – though 'twas but one home port to another?"

"Touché!" cried Lieutenant Scott. "That I'll admit I did not like – and if I have my way I'll never do it again. Nor was it, if you remember, a trip entirely free from mishaps! But come now, away with these gloomy thoughts, and let's have another glass all round. These boys will never sleep tonight if you feed them any more grandfathers' tales."

Lieutenant Welch acknowledged this friendly hint with a smile. "You started it," he said, with mock reproach. "You brought up the subject in the first place! And sure, our boys are made of sterner stuff than that!" They're not going to be scared out of their wits by tales of Dutchmen – or Frenchmen either, come to that!"

"I should just think not!" cried Richard. "The Admiral says an Englishman is worth three of the French – and I'm not afraid of any Englishman I know of – so a fig for the froggy and I don't care how soon we meet him!"

"What a young fire-eater!" drawled Lieutenant Welch's deep voice. "I don't mind admitting that I do. Let's wait until we're really ready for him! If there's any surprising to be done, let's be doing it ourselves, not t'other way about! How say you, boy?" he asked, turning to Fellowes.

"I agree with you, sir," said Fellowes, in a thoughtful voice that Christopher hadn't heard him use before, and made him think that perhaps Lieutenant Scott did notice everything. "We've waited so long to catch up that it really would be too bad to muff our chance by jumping in feet foremost now. Another two weeks' patience won't hurt us. I hope the enemy does keep safe in port until we're all gathered together – then we can think of fighting; unity being strength, after all."

"Cow-hearted!" said Richard under his breath; but Fellowes had heard him.

"Far-sighted!" he returned hotly. "If you had your way you'd go off hunting for the whole French fleet and die happily and gloriously against the odds – and much good that would do anyone! Myself, I'd rather meet them in my own time and on my own terms. That way, if I should finish in that graveyard of the Atlantic, at least I could say I'd brought some of them along too!"

"Then may I suggest," put in Lieutenant Scott quietly, "that you both keep your belligerence in check until we do find the enemy on our own terms, and then give him the full force of it?"

"I beg pardon, sir," said Richard stiffly, and was silent, while Lieutenant Welch helped to pour oil on the troubled waters by asking Christopher how he liked his new life.

"Not sorry you joined, are you?" he enquired.

"No indeed, sir; but there is a great deal to learn, isn't there?"

"There is – and none of us ever stops learning."

Soon after that, the party broke up, and the boys made their way back to their own stuffy berth. The hands too had been enjoying their Saturday evening leisure. There was a sound of stamping feet over their heads, and the cheerful din of laughing and singing.

"Are sailors always as happy as this?" asked Christopher.

"No," said Richard. "Of course they aren't. They fall ill, they're badly paid, they get rotten food and then never know when or if they're likely to see home again. But on this ship they're lucky. They've got a decent captain and the officers are pretty fair to them. And they're not a bad bunch themselves; no really hard cases among them that I can think of. And when your shipmates are right then you're all right! There's a kind of camaraderie on board that they'll never find ashore, I'm sure of that. If you'll pardon the pun, they're all in the same boat together and so they make the best of it. Besides, they have no worries – no responsibilities once they're at sea – it's all taken out of their hands entirely."

"In fact," commented Fellowes, who overheard, "what can't be cured must with patience be endured."

"If you like to put it that way," agreed Hugh, mildly. "Myself I like to hear them happy because there's nothing like a happy crew for a pleasant voyage. When the seamen look sullen, watch out!"

"Besides," said Richard, "they've got a real job of work ahead now, and that always helps."

"Shocking row, though, isn't it?" asked someone else.

"Oh well, it's Saturday! And anyway it won't go on for long. Middle watch'll be wanting to grab their sleep."

Christopher's good opinion of Fellows soon reverted to normal. For they hadn't reached their own quarters when he said, in his usual sneering fashion, "Don't take too much notice of the Lieutenant's bedtime stories, sonny. You won't really hear anyone moaning – it's just the wind in the spars: and if you should see a white shape flit along the deck you can be sure it's just a trick of the moonlight on the sails."

"I should be far more likely to think it was you scampering about in your shirt," retorted Christopher tartly: but later he whispered privately to Richard, "I know I shall dream tonight. Too much wine and too many spooks!"

"As long as you don't shout out I shan't mind," was his cold comfort. "You wake me up and I'll really give you something to be scared of!" And the evening ended in a friendly scuffle before both boys flopped into their hammocks. Christopher needn't have worried. He slept like a top, and woke early to find the fair wind holding and Nonesuch scudding before it across the Bay, anxious to make up for lost time.

5

The first ten days or so of the voyage were the busiest that Christopher could ever remember. There was so much going on that there was no time to feel homesick. In fact, Christopher had almost forgotten about home – it seemed so far away in time and space – and he gave himself up to this new world, so strange and so self-contained.

Life on board, he thought, was like a big jigsaw-puzzle, made up of people instead of cardboard pieces. Everyone from the captain down had his special place and his special job to do – sometimes more than one – but each falling neatly into place. There were ranks and grades, too, throughout the lower deck, with hands divided into sections, so that whenever anything needed to be done, and the men went scurrying about their business the job was done as smoothly and quickly as could be, since every task had its own men appointed to do it. And everyone, even the very humblest, knew that his own job had its own importance, and that without his efforts the whole complex machinery would stop in its tracks.

"You know," Christopher said thoughtfully, "it's just like the old rhyme about the horseshoe-nail!"

"I don't know that one," said Hugh. "How does it go?"

"For the want of a nail the shoe was lost," repeated Christopher,

> For the want of a shoe the horse was lost,
> For the want of a horse the rider was lost,
> For the want of a rider the battle was lost,
> For the want of a battle the kingdom was lost,
> And all for the want of a horseshoe-nail!"

"Yes," agreed Richard. "That hits the nail on the head exactly! I'm sorry," he added hastily, above his friends' chorus of groans, "that was a ghastly pun but quite unintentional! You see how important even you are on board! Not that we need to fear any lost nails here! We mean to win our battle!"

Below the commissioned officers and above the rest of the crew came the Standing Officers and other warrant officers. The Standing Officers were the Boatswain, the Gunner and the Carpenter, and the boatswain was a man of power! It was Mr Bull who passed on the orders, and whose mates' shrilling pipes could be heard at all hours. As yet the calls sounded all the same to Christopher but the men knew them all apart, and would sprint off at once when the wailing notes were heard. Wherever they might be, when those silver tubes were raised to the lips the men would come up at the double to their appointed place. The oldest, steadiest, and most experienced among them would be up on the fo'c'sle, working at the bowsprit to which the forestays were fastened, or on the foreyards, dealing with the sails. (Christopher learned that the ropes holding the masts fore and aft were called stays; those which gave sideways support were shrouds.) When the ship came to her anchorage or when she set sail, these men would be stationed at the heavy capstan, winding the cables that let down or brought in the anchor. Then there were the "topmen"; cream of hands, and well they knew it, for theirs was a job calling for nerve as well as skill when they swarmed up the masts like monkeys and out along the yards to adjust the sails. High up above the decks, at the mercy of the wind and rain it would be all too easy to slip a hand or a foot, and that slip could cost a man his life. Splendid though his sealegs might be, Christopher felt dizzy whenever he saw these men shinning up to stand on the high ropes and, with their arms over the wooden yards, start hoisting the sails. The acrobats who sat astride the ends of the timbers gave him a specially nasty turn. He averted his gaze whenever he could.

These were the aristocrats of the lower deck, who thought poorly of the "afterguard", regardless of the fact that their own work would be useless without the efforts of those others, hauling on the ropes which swung the yards round and so trapped the winds in the sails. Also, these others were set to work on the lower sails, where a good head for heights was perhaps not so important.

There were plenty of other jobs to be done, too, not directly connected with seamanship as such but essential to the smooth running of the ship. Someone had to keep her clean for a start! Someone had to do the repairs. Someone had to keep the paintwork just so. Someone had to look after the animals, someone had to kill them for the table, and someone had to cook them afterwards. Someone had to look after the stores, and keep the sails in good order. Someone had to help out in the sick bay; and those particular "someones" were very useful in a ship whose main purpose was to sail into battle – and out of it again!

No member of this tight little world could ever complain of boredom, dull though blockade work could be. Spare time was very precious. It was all the more precious because it could be interrupted at any moment, and emergencies could crop up without a word of warning. Perhaps a sudden change in the weather would mean an unexpected burst of activity on the masts and yards; perhaps the enemy would appear over the skyline, and there would be a tremendous bustle as the battle-ship came into her own. No one knew where or when such things would happen. He simply performed his duties and made the most of his leisure time.

Even the most ordinary day was busy. Christopher thought he was lucky to be put down for the first watch, which ended at midnight, so he had a reasonably uninterrupted time for sleep afterwards. When at seven o'clock next morning the midshipmen went on deck, they would find the seamen busy stowing their hammocks in the bulwark nettings, but the seamen had in fact been up and about a long time before that. For the last three hours the morning watch had been hard at work, barefooted on the deck, making the ship fit to be seen. The deck beneath their feet was already clean and almost gleaming from their efforts – washed, scoured and scrubbed. Down on their knees, scraping away with the "holystone" – a soft, porous kind of stone – they would rub sand into the dampness of the deck, scraping off the previous day's dirt. It was a hard and thankless business; but at last the grime and the grease would be gone, the dirty sand collected in the scuppers and so sent overboard, and the swabbing party would dry the wet decks, leaving them white and amazingly clean. Others again had been hard at work polishing the bright metal parts. These men had to be careful to work well in front of the ones who did the scrubbing, so that the dust they raised could be washed away with the rest. And when the midshipmen came up the hatchway the ship's wash and brush-up was complete, and the hammocks were being lashed and stowed for the day. While the spring-cleaning went on, the cooks were busy in the galley, and by the time the call to breakfast sounded the ship's upper works would be as clean as a whistle, the lookouts would already be perched aloft at the mastheads, and the ship's speed would have been noted on a slate. This always fascinated Christopher. With one man holding fast to the reel and another with a half-minute timing-glass in his hand, the officer of the watch threw the log overboard. The log-line itself was marked off at regular intervals, and by counting the number of marks which passed off the reel before the glass had emptied it was possible to calculate the rate at which Nonesuch was moving.

So even on an ordinary run-of-the-mill working day there was much to be done before breakfast. The early morning sea-air and the work together gave everyone an appetite, even though the breakfast itself, when it came, was nothing to write home about. Then as well as the routine work of keeping the ship moving steadily southward to the rendezvous with the rest of the Fleet, there were inspections by the officers and rehearsals for the battles which were the reason for the ship's very existence. The men practised getting themselves and the guns into position for action, and there was much rivalry between the teams to be the first into place. And there was small-arms practice for those detailed to board the enemy vessels. The fighting machine must be prepared to go into action swiftly and smoothly as if by instinct.

Christopher was as busy as anyone. He might as well, he thought ruefully, be back at school after all. He was constantly being taught something by somebody; basic seamanship, the different parts of the ship and their uses, traditional behaviour, odd snippets of seafaring legend. He watched the quartermaster at the helm, with his eyes fixed intently on his task and his ears open only to the orders passed to him by the Master. He watched the hands making yards and yards of multiple plait with rope-yarn, and he watched the sailmakers at their work. He took a turn or two himself pulling on the rough yarns to make chafing-gear, and found it very hard although it looked very easy. Soon the skin was peeling from his fingers and the tang of salt on the sore places stung like mad.

He had, while running his endless errands, explored nearly every part of the vessel. He had penetrated to the galley, where disgusting-looking messes were boiling and bubbling on the big iron stove. Strange that while the food could be none too appetising at times, the pots and pans were always sparkling clean! Whiffs of cooking sometimes came oozing through the pipe on the forward deck, making the men grimace at the thought of the meal for which the sea air gave them such an appetite. There were heavy spits here, too and enormous ovens, and this was the warmest place in the ship. The cook and his mates had red shiny faces as they worked, for they took great care over the fires, of course, for the ship was a wooden one and one stray spark could set her in flames very, very quickly. Christopher got used to scampering along the gangways and up and down the hatchways, and despite the cramped conditions he couldn't complain of lack of exercise. He became acquainted with nearly every part of the ship, from the captain's cabin to the ill-fated animals milling around in the reeking manger: and once he was taken, with great precautions, down to the main magazine way down deep under the waterline. This was a dim and awesome chamber, behind a heavier bulkhead than any other in the ship. This was one which would never be removed, because the ammunition had to be kept carefully away from all danger of chance of explosion. So the magazine had a permanent wall with a thick covering to cushion it from any kind of shock, and no lamps were allowed inside. Together, Christopher and his companions, checking the stores under the eye of the Gunner, removed their shoes outside, put on loose felt slippers, and crept about noiselessly in the faint light coming through a window built into the wall for the purpose. No one was allowed inside until he had changed his shoes for fear of throwing out a spark from the soles. Everything was laid out in neat rows, carefully labelled so that a man could put his hand immediately on what was wanted. There was a strange, eerie feeling about the place as if the war itself were sleeping here. Christopher was glad when the door was safely locked behind them, and they could climb back on deck once more.

Above all, he learned the use of the signalling system with its many-coloured flags. Lieutenant Kent talked with him very seriously on the subject, and found him an apt and willing pupil. He learned from the signal book that there were ten different flags, one for each figure from nought to nine; also substitutes for these, and flags for the words "Yes" and "No". The numbers were arranged codewise to make set sentences. All this was very ingenious and covered a great many situations, but it would obviously be too bad if anyone wanted to send a message other than the fixed signals given in the book. This bothered Christopher. He said so.

"It bothers a lot of other people too," Lieutenant Kent told him. "The Admiral for a start! I have heard that the details of a new and more flexible system are to be given us when we reach the Fleet. Meanwhile we just have to do what we have always done with the old arrangement."

"How will it work, sir? Do you know?" asked Christopher, with real interest.

"I don't know a great deal about it, I confess. But I do know that the flags are coded into words instead of sentences, and you would know if a message were being sent by this method and not by the old one because a special introductory flag would be sent up first – red and white"

"So that you could really say anything that came into your head?"

"Exactly! If anything unforeseen happened you could tell the rest of the fleet just what it was and what to do about it, instead of hunting for the nearest phrase and hoping for the best. If you really felt like playing games and had the time as well as the inclination, you could carry on a regular conversation!"

"I wonder why no one thought of it before."

"It isn't altogether a new idea. It was invented by Sir Home Popham some years ago in a tentative sort of fashion, and he has since expanded it to bring in a lot more words. Actually, a lot of warships have already got copies of the new signal book. We haven't unfortunately."

"Oh well, as long as we get ours before we go into action, that's all right!" said Christopher sunnily.

"I hope so," said the Lieutenant, with a sardonic inflection that made Christopher blush. "Meanwhile, you can concentrate on getting some of the sentence flags fixed in your head – then the words will come all the easier, I hope, for we don't know how much time we'll have once we rejoin the Fleet." He saw Christopher's look of chagrin and smiled. "You won't find it too difficult, I hope; you will simply have to find the flag combinations as quickly as you can in the book and note them quickly down. There is something else you must learn too."

"What's that, sir?"

"Why, if you stop to think about it, there are times at sea when it's difficult to tell what flags are being flown. If the wind is blowing directly in line with you, or if the signalling ship happens to be a great way off, you won't be able to tell the colours of the flags with certainty. So what do you suppose can be done?"

"I don't know, sir."

"It's simple enough. We use other devices as well as flags, and haul differently shaped symbols aloft, as well. The different combinations of shapes have different meanings in the code, and the mast used has a significance, too. You'd better make a point of studying these distance signals as well as the normal ones. No one can possibly tell what conditions we may meet, or when, and a quick and accurate interpretation can make all the difference to your manoeuvres."

"I see that, sir."

"Oh, and one other thing."

"Yes, sir?"

"I shouldn't let Fellowes see you poring over it, if I were you."

Really, was there nothing these officers didn't see?

And so the early autumn days became a kaleidoscope of events and impressions, with incidents standing out like relief carvings against the background of routine; good and bad alike.

✢ ✢ ✢

There was his first climb up the mast. Here his courage had quailed, for he doubted his head for heights on dry land, let alone up above the deep blue sea. The top of the mast seemed an awfully long way away. No doubt the deck, from that lofty spot, would seem an awfully long way away too, if he dared to look down on it. It would seem even more so for not keeping still. Anyone might be forgiven for feeling dizzy while the sea kept up this unending motion so far below. But he had the reputation of his sealegs to maintain; he would have to endure the taunts of Fellowes if he failed; and, more than anything, he could not disobey his order. He could not; and he must not. As it turned out, he found it a lot easier than he had expected. He fancied he could hear Richard's voice saying, "Up you go, young 'un!" and with that he placed his foot firmly in the ratlines (as he had learnt to call the soft tarred ropes fixed across the shrouds for a ladder) and began to climb. Higher and higher he went, hand over hand, not daring to look down; past one heavy timber yard after another and on again past the next stretch of billowing canvas and then – he was safely aloft and could have sung aloud for joy. Here he was king of the world! Nothing to be seen in any direction but the heaving sea, and nothing above himself but the sky! From this height he could see the swell of the waves rolling in under the starboard bow, coming in from miles away across the deep, broad Atlantic. The air up here was clean and pure, filling his lungs and his heart with exultation, and the wind blew strongly here, too, so that he seemed all alone with the swifter elements of air and water. Somewhere far over to his left, out of sight but hardly out of mind, were the ships of Cornwallis' fleet, on ceaseless watch outside the harbour of Brest, where the empty spars of Ganteaume's command were still beleaguered. But they hardly counted now. They could not come to help Villeneuve. Cornwallis would take good care of that! Somewhere to the south, three sail of the line with Lord Nelson himself in the foremost were speeding to rejoin the Fleet of Cadiz: beyond that blockade lay the Combined Fleet of France and Spain, waiting its moment to come out. But for the present there was only the sea, and Nonesuch, a lonely little world, making haste across it with all sails set. Up here on the cross-trees he could feel the drive and plunge of the ship as she surged forward through the water. It gave him a most exhilarating sensation of power! He could have felt himself alone and omnipotent here if it weren't for the sound of orders shouted on the deck below him. He settled himself more comfortably, took his spyglass from his pocket, and set himself to keep good watch.

✠ ✠ ✠

There was the Sunday morning service on the quarterdeck. With everyone on board cleaned and spruced, the captain inspected his men and his ship before assembling them for church. Now the Reverend Dr Wells came into his own. Climbing to his improvised pulpit, his long white surplice and his hair fluttering in the stiff northerly breeze, he gazed sternly over his congregation and briskly announced the first hymn. Everyone sang lustily if not altogether tunefully, before following the chaplain's example and going down on their knees while he prayed. Christopher wished Dr Wells wasn't quite so fervent, for the deck was very hard and the wind was rather cold. But when at last everyone rose with a shuffling and a scuffling and began a second hymn, his thoughts took a more reverent turn. There was really something rather grand about the assembly, so far from any regular church, worshipping together with the vast element of air and water spreading around and over them into infinity. Long sermons would be out of place here with the sea and the sky to do the preaching, and Dr Wells must have thought so too, for the little service was soon over, and everyone went off to spend his Sunday with a little more leisure, perhaps, than during the rest of the week.

✢ ✢ ✢

There was the sailor who was flogged. If Captain Britten was God aboard his ship, the officers were his angels. But one of the hands thought differently, and was unwise enough to say so, and to the officer's face. More. This was only half of his offence, for he had disobeyed an order, telling the officer to do the job for himself and cursing him into the bargain. He was drunk at the time and that didn't help; being drunk meant punishment, too. What had happened was this. Lieutenant Ross, passing along the forward deck on Sunday afternoon, had glanced aloft at the spreading canvas and noticed that the topgallant was hanging crookedly. This would never do! And so he promptly ordered the topmen to climb up and set things to right. The men set off, all but one. John Peters had refused to budge. The day was warm, and he was full of drink, for he had taken aboard some of his messmates' ration of rum as well as his own in payment of gambling debts, and he hadn't had the willpower to spread out his intake. So much rum and water slopping about inside him made him reckless. Slowly he hauled himself upright and propped himself none too steadily on one of the forward guns. He stood there, glaring at the lieutenant, but making no move to do as he was told.

Lieutenant Ross looked coldly at him. "Jump to it, Peters!" he said sternly. "Up you go, and look lively!"

"You want the t'gallant bent?" growled Peters. "Then go up

and do it yourself, blast you! I've been up there twice already today and I'll be damned if I'll do it again!"

"You'll be dammed if you don't! And I don't intend to argue with you! Do as I say!"

Peter spat, and his spittle dampened the planking beside the officer's shining boot.

Such behaviour was only a fraction short of mutiny. A small crowd had gathered and Lieutenant Ross hardly needed to turn his head to give the order before two burly boatswain's mates had come up to grab Peters by the arms. There could only be one outcome to the incident now, and Peters was hauled below, still too drunk to realise what he had done, and filled with rage. The lieutenant superintended the re-setting of the offending sail, but soon enough he would make his report to the captain; too soon for Peters' comfort.

The sail was soon adjusted, and the topmen came chasing down to the deck again, somewhat subdued after the ugly incident. But not one approved of Peters' behaviour, nor ever questioned that he deserved what he was going to get.

"He'd no call to be uppity," said Able Seaman Harris. "The job had to be done, didn't it?"

"That ain't the point," said Able Seaman Lewis. "He should ha' done as he were told even if it weren't necessary – which it were. An officer's an officer if he is only a young one!"

"'Tisn't worth it, anyhow. He should ha' known better. Well, he'll pay for it, right enough."

"Ah, and he'd had too much to drink."

"He should ha' known better than that, too. Let that be a lesson to him," said Harris. There was real feeling in his voice. His own rum ration had gone to swell Peters' cargo.

Captain Britten was a humane man, and floggings aboard his ship were rare. This time, with such a collection of offences, he felt himself bound to order the man to be punished, though many another captain would have called the sentence a light one.

"He must be punished," said Captain Britten decidedly. "Neglecting his duty and insulting an officer! I'm sorry, but I see no help for it. But I think, Mr Ross, we must let him off lightly.

He's a good seaman when he's sober and besides," with a grim smile, "we don't want to be carrying any invalids just now, when every man is sorely needed. Ten lashes!"

And so at ten o'clock one morning the pipes sounded a dreary summons, and the shout went up, "All hands on deck to witness punishment!" The entire ship's company was brought up aft as audience, Marines and all, who, spruce in their scarlet coats and white breeches, swarmed to take their place on the poop. The sailors crowded wherever they could – on the deck, in the rigging, anywhere where they could find a place for themselves to see the spectacle. Anyone would think, thought Christopher, amazed, that they had come to see the King pass by, not to watch one of their own shipmates suffering. After all, it could be any one of them another time. He said so to Richard, as they stood on the larboard side of the quarterdeck, the captain himself with the lieutenants standing like avenging angels to starboard.

"They wouldn't look at it that way," answered Richard, "and in any case they're used to it. They're hard men living a hard life, and this isn't anything out of the ordinary to them. In fact, it would be habit on many other ships."

"Was what he did so very bad?" asked Christopher innocently.

Richard opened his eyes wide. "He can think himself lucky he didn't go so far as to strike Lieutenant Ross," he said. "They'd have flogged him through the fleet for that – if they didn't hang him! Discipline is the most important thing there is in this kind of life and you can't have anybody challenging it, whoever they are! Duty is duty, young 'un, and don't you forget it! Besides, that kind of behaviour is the first stop on the road to mutiny, and you have to stamp on it, hard! When you're living in such tight quarters as we are it only takes a small spark to start a regular blaze, and if people start thinking they needn't obey orders if they don't feel like it we should soon be in a rare mess and not fit for anything. Don't waste your pity on Peters! He asked for it and he's getting it. If he's got any sense at all he won't do it again, and that'll be one good thing at all events."

Christopher was sobered, and said no more. It certainly seemed as if the unlucky Peters were fully in agreement with what was going to happen to him. Two of the grated hatch covers had already been brought, and one laid on the deck with the other securely tied to it a right angles. The sight of the grim preparations did not seem to move the victim or the rest of the ship's company in any particular way. This audience watched with an interest that had nothing of blood-lust in it. This was simply an unusual interruption to routine. Asked if he had anything to say, Peters answered "No, sir," quite quietly. And himself stripped to the waist without a flicker of emotion. There was no sign of fear, no attempt to escape. Christopher could not decide whether this was through natural sullenness or despair. He rather thought it was despair. But now Peters had placed his feet on the flat grating, without any persuasion or force, and stood leaning patiently and of his own accord against the other, and let them tie him to it. Captain Britten recited his crimes, and then – most horrid sight of all, in Christopher's eyes – the hideous cat-o'-nine-tails was brought out of the bag in which it was kept and the bo'sun's mate prepared to apply it to Peters' wincing flesh.

Christopher turned away and looked steadfastly in another direction until it was all over. To his surprise, Peters proved as tough when sober as he did when drunk. Not a groan escaped him as the lash rose and fell, though at the end he was limp against the grating with his head slumped on his shoulder, and his back was red and raw. They untied him and carried him off to the sick bay. The gratings were removed. The ship's company dispersed. Justice had been seen to be done.

Christopher turned, and saw that Fellowes was watching him maliciously. "Couldn't take it, eh?" he said sweetly. "Worse sights than that in action, you know."

"Why don't you leave him alone?" demanded Richard crossly. "He's never done anything to you that I know of and he is only a young 'un!"

"But this," said Fellowes, and he didn't drawl this time, "is a man's world, and those who find it too much for them are better off at home!" and he turned abruptly and left them. Richard stared after him blankly.

✤ ✤ ✤

There was the first time he stood a night-watch. He had come up from the noise and stuffiness of the cockpit into the cool clean air on deck and gasped at the beauty of the evening. The first watch was taking over, low voices repeating the orders as the wheel was relieved and the men took up their places to be ready if wanted to trim the sails. The grey-blue sea was now black under the stars, tipped with curling white crests, and the ship was rolling gently on the eastward swell. The inky blue sky had closed round her like a coverlet, so cosy after the blank miles that stretched about her by day. Dotted thickly overhead the stars flickered, and a pale moon sent a silver shaft across the deck, gleaming whitely in the ghostly light. The silence hit him almost like a physical blow; then the quiet sounds of the night came to him, clear and crisp. The lap of the waves as they smacked across the deck, the tapping of a wooden block on a slack rope – all the little noises that passed unnoticed in the bustling daytime were sharp and reassuring in the quiet dark. The fair wind still held from the north, singing a song in the shrouds that echoed happily through Christopher's veins as he stood at the rail looking out across the shimmering water. Nonesuch was an enchanted ship at this moment, and Christopher himself was a part of the magic in it and of it, his heart quite lost to her.

✢ ✢ ✢

There were the jolly evenings in the midshipmen's mess. Sometimes they would feel like the young boys they were, and a rousing romp would develop, or perhaps a game of skittles, or marbles. There would be crazy competitions, with forfeits to pay; or perhaps, in quieter mood, they would swop yarns picked up from the "old salts". Christopher listened wide-eyed to the tales of horrible monsters and lost treasure which, it seemed, littered the ocean floor. There were tales of exploration, piracy and mutiny on the high seas so blood curling that he would have wondered that anyone dared to go to sea at all, if he could have believed half of them. They told him about the monstrous sea-serpent called the Kraken, whose body measured a full mile round, with horns like a pair of masts on its head, and they laughed when he didn't believe them. They told him about Captain Henry Morgan, the buccaneer who lived to be Lieutenant Governor of Jamaica, with a knighthood into the bargain. They told him about Captain Bligh of HMS *Bounty*, whose mutinous crew had set him adrift in an open boat with such men as stayed loyal to him, and how he came safely to land several months and hundreds of miles later, with not so much as a chart to help him across the Pacific Ocean. And he had fought again another day, at Camperdown and at Copenhagen too; and was still alive to tell the tale. They told him about the unfortunate Admiral Byng who, made a scapegoat for a defeat, was shot on his own quarterdeck for negligence and a cowardice belied by his bearing on that awful occasion.

They told him about the strange St Elmo's lights, the pale blue balls which hopped about in the rigging sometimes at night. Some called them a sign of good; others, of ill omen. If the deathfires, as some called them, were high aloft, good weather could be expected. Down near the deck, they boded a storm. Whether they believed them to be kindly spirits or evil, hardly a sailor could be induced to go aloft if the lights were about, for everyone believed that if he climbed up, and found the light shining in his face, he would very soon die. Sailors were superstitious, and had many explanations. The more hair-raising were that the lights were the spirits of drowned seamen trying to come on board, or perhaps the souls of men in torment. Christopher thought privately that there must be a perfectly natural scientific explanation but he held his peace, and if anybody had hoped to upset him with their horrors, they were disappointed.

They told him about the troubles the Fleet had gone through only a few years earlier, when mutiny spread like a forest fire through the fighting ships. One moment the Navy had been a band of national heroes who only a couple of months before had killed the threat of invasion with a resounding victory. The next, it was a hotbed of traitors ready to leave England disarmed and in disarray. The sailors had been sick and tired of basic pay and bad conditions, and since a reasonable request for better things had met with no response from the Admiralty, they prepared to put their personal battle first. On Easter Day, when ordered to put to sea, nobody moved.

"What happened to them?" asked Christopher.

"They had to be heard, of course," said Hugh. "They couldn't very well flog the lot for insubordination. Why, they'd still be at it if they'd tried, I shouldn't wonder!"

"Mind you," said Richard, "it was all very polite to begin with. They didn't turn nasty. They simply wouldn't set sail. And to be fair, they said they would go out if the French appeared, and go straight back to port afterwards! And in the end they begged pardon and put to sea again, though they insisted on better conditions for all that."

"Were you there?"

"Lord, no! I hadn't joined then. This was all of eight years ago! But I've heard my uncle tell the tale many a time. He always says a lot of officers brought the whole thing on themselves by their brutality."

"You mean the men had had enough of it?"

"Just so – Britons never shall be slaves, and so on. Besides, it's only commonsense, I should have thought, that you can't expect a man to be a hero for you if he hates your liver and lights. But there you are! Some of the commanders were drunk with power and you can't get back at them when you're alone at sea, short of mutiny."

"But you said," said Christopher, really puzzled, "you said when Peters was flogged, that it was all right to punish him when he kicked against authority."

"I know I did, and so it was. He refused to perform a regular duty and a reasonable order and the crew themselves would agree with it. It's when punishment becomes a habit and when the rule on board is intolerable that the trouble is bound to start. Showing one troublemaker that he can't get away with it is very different from stirring up unrest in the first place – do you see?"

"So you think they were right to cut up rough?"

"Lord, no! I don't hold with mutiny at any price. But I do think they had some genuine grievances, even if they did go the wrong way about putting it right."

"But was it the wrong way?" put in Hugh, thoughtfully. "What else could they do? If no one took any notice of their complaints – and no one did – they would have to make some kind of demonstration or else put up with things."

"But what happened?" insisted Christopher.

"Well, the powers that be promised some improvement, but the men wanted to make sure that no one would get at them for it, so they said they wanted a royal pardon beforehand. That kicked up no end of a shindy! But they got their pardon all right, and that was the end of it for the time being. Not for long, though!"

"How long?"

"'Bout a fortnight. Then they got the idea that they weren't going to get their extra pay after all, and it started all over again. Some of 'em got really nasty, too – kicked out their officers and nearly hanged a couple into the bargain! And one of them was an admiral! And it wasn't only at Portsmouth, this time. It happened at Plymouth, too, and the North Sea Fleet."

"How was it stopped, then?"

"Oh, Duncan gave the North Sea lot a good talking-to – and he could do almost anything with them, you know! – and their Lordships of the Admiralty gave in, and sent old Howe out to tell 'em so. And bless his heart, he rowed all round Spithead to tell every single ship in person!"

"Did they like that?"

"Like it? They loved it! Cheered him all round and chaired him home into the bargain!"

For the first time, Fellowes spoke up. "That sounds too utterly British," he said silkily. "Fair play for everyone! Three cheers for all of us! They weren't so polite at the Nore. Why not tell him what a real mutiny can be like? You can't shield him from the seamy side forever. He might as well know the worst in case he ever has to face it. I wonder what he'd do?" he added, half to himself.

"I shouldn't bother," Richard said wearily. "There aren't likely to be two Parkers about and if there were you'd be too busy looking after number one, I shouldn't wonder, to worry about Christopher or me or anyone else!"

Christopher broke in on the argument. "Yes, do tell me," he asked earnestly. "Who was Parker, and what did he do? I really do want to know."

"You tell him then," said Richard, "If you know so much about it."

"Richard Parker," began Fellowes, "started off as a midshipman but not a very good one. He didn't last long, but he came back in when the war broke out. In fact, the man was a regular jack–in-the-box where the Navy was concerned. He left the second time very much under a cloud – after a court-martial. So you see, you 'young'un'," with a sidelong look at Richard, "being a 'mid' isn't, after all, a sinecure, and not everyone's up to it. Anyway, back he came again, third time unlucky. He was in gaol at the time, and jumped at the chance of the Navy instead, especially as they gave him a bounty for doing it."

"Can you do that?" asked Christopher, astonished.

"People come into the Navy in all sorts of ways," said Fellowes pointedly. "One doesn't like to ask too many questions." Richard stirred irritably, but Fellowes went smoothly on. "One must get the ships manned somehow, and Parker was better than most. He hadn't done anything worse than run into debt; he wasn't a hardened criminal, or anything like that. In fact, he was a distinct improvement on most of the gaolbirds. He was intelligent, he'd been to sea before and he knew the ways of the Navy, but this time he had to make do with being on the lower deck. Myself, I don't think he was entirely sane, but there it is. One thing he could do that the others couldn't was talk, and he talked to them about their wrongs and their rights until he made them really wild!"

"Tell me exactly what he did!"

"You really want to know? I warn you, it's all rather nasty."

"That's all right. Fire away!"

Fellowes gave him a measuring look, and fired.

"What you must remember," he began, "is that the men had a genuine grievance. For one thing, their pay had been the same for something like a hundred and fifty years, and it never was a fortune. No man worth his salt will watch his family starve and do nothing about it. Their living conditions were pretty rotten, too. Have you had a look at the lower deck?"

"Of course I have!"

"I just wondered. Would you like to live like it?"

"No, I wouldn't."

"I didn't think you would." There was an edge of malice in Fellowes' voice, "We warned you from the first what the food could be like for us all, but believe me our quarters here are princely compared with the men's. They're crowded on top of each other like cattle and not all of them are over-clean, though they can't help that. A lot of them are seasick. When the sea runs high the waves come in through the hawse-holes. The animals stink. And, of course, you can't open the ports to get some fresh air. Dash it, it's a wonder a mutiny isn't a common-place!"

"Turning agitator yourself?" asked Richard tartly.

"No, I'm, not. I'm trying to point out what a lot of the hands do put up with. Even with all those miseries they might have gone on quietly enough if it weren't for the starvation wages and the brutality."

"Brutality?" asked Christopher.

"Oh yes! You didn't like what happened the other morning, did you? And that was a rare thing on this ship. Tell me, what sort of sights do you expect when we go into action?"

"But he was one of our own men! And it was in cold blood!"

"True – and some captains would flog a man almost as soon as look at him. Not altogether surprising when you think how the prison dregs were getting in among the prime seamen. Some of them, mind, didn't know any other language than the lash; it was a vicious circle. But one way and another they'd had enough, and Parker was clever enough to be able to put it into words."

"Clever?" asked Richard. "He deserved all he got!"

"Oh, I agree, I agree! But I'm willing to believe he started off with good intentions as far as his shipmates went. Besides, he had a grudge against authority."

"I must say, said Richard, "you're beastly sympathetic to the man"

"Oh no, I'm not. But I do have a certain amount of sympathy

for the men. Not," Fellowes added hastily, "for the things they did at the time. And Parker encouraged them, after all."

"But what did they do?" insisted Christopher. "I'm none the wiser now!"

"No, you're not, are you? There was another hullaballoo over at Sheerness, before Howe had finished calming the Spithead lot. And this time they weren't fighting for anything in particular. This was mutiny for mutiny's own sake. By George, to think of the trouble that man stirred up! They hoisted the red flag again and turned the forward guns against the quarter-decks. They made armed demonstrations through the streets. They commandeered gunboats, and they even got Duncan's North Sea Fleet to desert him. They tarred and feathered their officers and left them lying about on the quaysides. Oh they had a lovely time!"

"And then?"

"Oh, Parker got too big for his boots, and his own followers began to get tired of him. It happens with most revolutionaries, you know. People find they've only swopped a bad 'un for a worse 'un."

"They didn't all feel that way," chipped in Richard. "Some of 'em were as bad as he was."

"True, and that stiffened the Government's backs. They stopped the food supplies and wouldn't let the men come ashore, and as the ordinary people lost sympathy more and more of the mutineers drew back too. They began to get really fed up with Parker and one by one the ships got away and left him. He was getting madder and madder anyway. Kept more state among the men, he did, than the Admiral of the Fleet himself! Called himself the President, if you please, and went about with bands playing and flags waving, making speeches at the top of his voice. He would have it that their Lordships were lying when they promised a rise in pay, and he produced a Charter which held, among other things, that the men should be allowed to dismiss any officers they didn't care for. And in the end, you see, the men themselves grew tired of his goings-on. They began to come to their senses, and bit the hand that led them – turned him over to authority and ended the mutiny."

"And what happened to Parker?"

"They hanged him at the yardarm," said Fellowes levelly.

Christopher went pale, and shuddered. "His own friends?" he said, aghast.

"Oh no! Not that they bothered much, as long as their own skins were safe. The authorities did that, and sent some of his closest friends aloft to keep him company."

"But that's all over now," said Richard, "and there's other things to think of," and the talk turned to the wars now raging. Names were tossed to and fro – Hood, Jervis, Howe, Duncan – but one name above all sounded again and again: Horatio Nelson. He was the man who fired every imagination, and made lesser men supremely confident of themselves, as long as Nelson was there to show them the way. Stories of his past successes were told with pride and love; his words were repeated with admiration. To Richard he was almost a god. He didn't really look like a hero, but the scars of battle gave the lie to his appearance. He was a small man, and what there was of him was sadly broken, for he had lost an arm and the sight of an eye in the King's service. But he had a brain like ice to make a cool decision and the courage to act upon it immediately, without hesitation. And if perhaps he was sometimes a little vain, and proud of his honours, who had a better right? He had missed the battle of the First of June eleven years ago, for even then he had been stationed down in the Mediterranean, but he had won laurels three years later at the battle of Cape St Vincent, and though the sight of his right eye was already gone this hadn't seemed to bother him a bit.

"Nobody else would have done what he did," said Richard worshipfully. "They wouldn't even have thought of doing it because in effect he disobeyed an order, or rather, he obeyed it before it could be given because he saw that there was only one thing to be done and so he did it."

"You're getting horribly muddled!" said Hugh, with a grin. "You've got your young 'un looking regularly bewildered and I'm not surprised. Calm down and tell him about it properly."

"I'm trying to, aren't I?" said Richard, wounded. "It was like this. The Admiral wasn't an admiral then. He was a Commodore flying his broad pennant in the Captain, just about the smallest ship there that day. Anyway, there he was, thirteenth in the line, and don't let anyone call it an unlucky number! There was a ding-dong fight going on, I can tell you! We were fighting the Spanish on their own that day, and the odds were nearly two to one against us."

"That didn't bother Jervis," put in Hugh. "He simply said that if there were fifty of them he'd go through them. He did too."

"Will you stop interrupting me?" cried Richard wrathfully. "Who's telling this story, me or you?"

"Oh, you are, you are! Get on with it, then!"

"As I was saying, there were only fifteen of us and twenty-seven of them, so the outlook wasn't too healthy. They had the Santissima Trinidad out with them that day. I wonder if she'll be coming out this time."

"I hardly like to ask," said Christopher, "but why her especially?"

"She's the biggest fighting ship in the world," said Richard succinctly. "Four decks and a hundred and thirty guns! Much good it did her, either. They were all banging away like billyo when Nelson saw that although the Spanish line had been broken, it was going to join together again and there wasn't a moment to lose if that was to be stopped."

"So what did he do?"

"Left the British line and blocked the Spaniard's way. Took on several of them at once, including the Santissima Trinidad, and took two of them prisoner into the bargain!"

"They called it," Hugh took up the story, "Nelson's Patent Bridge for Boarding First-Rates. They'd almost blown him out of the water, so he spiked their guns as it were by getting alongside one of them and leading a boarding party in person. He went in through a gallery window, but when he got on deck he found that one of his own officers had already climbed through the chains and hauled down the Spanish colours. So he left some of his men behind and crossed over to another Spanish ship that had got itself jammed up against the first."

"And took that prisoner too?"

"And took that prisoner too."

Christopher drew a deep breath. "Yes," he said, "that was certainly something out of the ordinary!"

"Oh, that's nothing to Nelson!" said Richard airily. "He's never content with half-measures, you see. Last time he met the French fleet he destroyed it. Now he's after another, and by heaven we'll destroy this one for him, too."

"Tell me!" begged Christopher. "Tell me how he did it!"

"Really," broke in Fellowes again, "for a boy who's presumably keen to be in the Navy you know precious little about it!"

"All the more reason," retorted Christopher, "to ask!" He turned his back pointedly, and gazed intently at his two friends as they took up the tale.

"It was Boney's own fault," said Richard scornfully. "He fancies himself as an Eastern Emperor, you see, and so he headed off for India, or so everyone thought. But Nelson guessed it would be Egypt, and he was right. It was a pity their Lordships of the Admiralty kept him short of frigates, because that meant the intelligence was scanty, so he got the timing wrong. He went to Alexandria, and he got there too soon, and the French hadn't arrived. He'd no sooner left to look for them than Boney came behind his back and captured Egypt."

"Just like that?" asked Christopher, startled.

"Just like that. It's his usual way, you know. That's why he's so furious with US!"

"He wasn't the furious one then," pointed out Hugh. "Nelson was sick as a dog about it, cruising round the Mediterranean looking for the French fleet."

"I know he was, and that made him all the more determined! He left absolutely nothing to chance. The ships even sailed in battle order, ready to start shooting at a moment's notice. He had his reward. When he heard that Boney really was in Egypt, Nelson went back to Alexandria. Not a sign! No French to be seen! And just when everyone felt that everything was against them, someone did see the enemy, just round the corner in Aboukir Bay."

"Who was that?"

"Actually, it was a midshipman! We may not be very exalted but we do have our uses sometimes! He was unlucky, though.

The ship next to his saw them getting excited about sending up the flags, guessed what had happened, and signalled "Enemy in sight." But all the same, he was the first to spot 'em!"

"Where is this place, exactly? What did you call it?"

"Aboukir? 'Bout fifteen miles east of Alexandria. A snug anchorage, if you haven't got Nelson on your tail. There are shoals on one side, and a fort on the other, so I daresay the French thought they were safe. But what a target! Sixteen ships, all lined up for the taking. The French were broadside on to an attack, and that should have been an advantage, especially as their ships were bigger than ours. And it would have been an advantage in daylight. It never occurred to anyone that they would have to stand a night attack."

"And that's what happened?"

"Yes. You don't think Nelson would waste time waiting for the morning when he'd been waiting for weeks already? A little thing like a few sandbanks wouldn't stop him. Besides, he'd taken the enemy by surprise and the wind was with him. He decided to pass between them and the shoals; the last thing they could have expected him to do. At least, it would have been the last thing anyone else would have done."

"But how could he tell he wouldn't run aground?"

"Because the French ships were bigger, and if they had room to swing there was room for him to anchor. I wish you wouldn't interrupt so much, just when I'm getting to the exciting part!"

Christopher grinned, and waved him to go on.

"Thank you! You see, he meant to go all out for their weakest part, which happened to be the van – oh, alright, the front end. It was getting dark and there wasn't much time, but that didn't matter. Nelson had drummed his ideas into everyone so well that they knew to the letter just what he expected of them. You know, we had a peculiar advantage at the time. We had officers who knew what to do and men who knew how to do it. The other side were short of both and that was their own silly fault. They'd gone so crazy over the revolutionary idea, you see, that most of their naval officers went the same road as anyone else did who'd had any authority – the road to the guillotine. Which meant that when they calmed down a bit they found there were precious few officers left in their Navy who had the least idea of how to do anything. Anyone could become a captain overnight then if he only screamed loud enough about equality and fraternity. I could. You could! But with us it was different. And it's always been Nelson's way to see that all his captains are fully briefed and then let them get on with it, because he knows he can trust them to do just what he wants. It'll be the same again – you wait and see! So when he sent up the signal to form line of battle that's all they needed. They got into place like clockwork almost before they'd been told."

Christopher opened his mouth and shut it again.

"What is it now?"

"I was only going to ask," said Christopher meekly, "how they could see which was which in the dark. I mean, it would have been awfully easy to start fighting each other by mistake, wouldn't it?"

"It's a good point, and you can be sure Nelson had thought of it. He thinks of everything! Everyone had to show four lights on the mizzen. Simple! They went round the long way up to the enemy van, because that was the safest spot from the French point of view and so the most unprepared. And half a dozen of Nelson's warships sailed up inside the French and gave them what-for from the shore side. You can imagine how tricky that was! All the rest, with Nelson in front, went up on the other side and there were the French, nicely jammed. It was a terrific battle, I can tell you! and Nelson was wounded in the head, right over his bad eye. In fact they thought at first he'd been mortally hurt but it turned out to be just a very nasty cut. The worst thing that happened to us was that one of our best ships went aground. They must have been half crazy with disappointment on board, watching everyone else hard at it. At least their lights were a signal to the others coming behind, so it didn't happen to them as well; that's one comfort."

"You know," said Hugh, thoughtfully, "it must have been quite a sight for them."

"How d'you mean?"

"Well, just try to imagine it. It would be as dark as pitch all round and behind, and in front there would be tremendous flashes from the guns. And the guns would be crashing away ahead too, but it was probably dead quiet on board those rear ships."

"Why?"

"If it weren't, they wouldn't hear the sounding called," Hugh pointed out. "And if they didn't hear them they'd go aground too."

"I never thought of that," said Richard, struck.

"If I were Fellowes, I'd probably say you never think of a lot of things," Hugh grinned back. Christopher looked round anxiously, but Fellowes had drifted over to join another group, and the three friends were alone.

"The battle went on all night, in fits and starts," Richard went on, "but I think it was really over quite early on when the French flagship blew up. They say that when she exploded she lit up the whole bay, and both sides were so shocked that the fight came to a full stop for quite a while. Anyway, when daylight came it really was all over. Only three of the French ships escaped, and one of them went aground, so they set fire to her themselves. And there was the French fighting fleet – gone!"

There was silence for a moment. Then, "But it didn't teach them a lesson," said Hugh sadly. "We've got to do it all over again now."

"And so we shall," said Richard stoutly. "Don't be such a faintheart! We've got the Admiral in charge again and it isn't as though he hadn't had any practice since."

"Come now," said Christopher. "You just said that the French fleet was destroyed at Aboukir only seven years ago. Even Napoleon couldn't have found time to build two more since then!"

"Oh, he didn't. He said he would conquer the sea by the land instead, and he had a jolly good try. He toadied like anything round the Tsar of Russia – he was mad, you know, which made two of them, come to think of it –"

"The Tsar of Russia!" exclaimed Christopher. "How on earth does HE come into it?"

"Oh, everybody's in it," said Hugh, "and most of 'em on

t'other side, too! They all swallow Boney's tall stories and let him be as chummy as you please until one morning they wake up and find he's swallowed them! Though I'm inclined to think he'll find Russia too much of a mouthful, sooner or later. There's such an awful lot of it."

Richard took up the tale again. "I don't know about that," he said. "What I do know is that the Tsar suggested that the Baltic States should join with him to close the northern trade routes to us. Do you get the idea?

Christopher nodded. "Starve us out," he said.

"You're learning fast," approved Richard. "That was about the time I joined, and all I'd done was sit around outside some beastly port or other, waiting for something to happen. But in the New Year they sent Lord Nelson to us and off we sailed to the Baltic. They gave him a barony after the Nile, you know, but I don't often call him his Lordship. To me, he's the Admiral – then and always!" Richard's fresh, honest face fairly glowed with pride. "He doesn't waste time, once his mind's made up, and he made it up then to get right into the Baltic before the Northern Powers did combine, while they were still divided and reasonably weak. And then somebody murdered the Tsar!"

"Don't see how that helped," argued Hugh.

"Well, it would have done if we'd only known about it in time, because the new one wasn't nearly so keen on Boney!"

"But it hardly mattered by then. This really wasn't the usual style of thing," said Hugh, turning to Christopher. "We weren't actually at war with the Danes, you see, but we wanted to make sure they wouldn't be able to help Napoleon if they did take it into their heads. And we did give them a chance to avoid it; sent a man from the Foreign Office to tell them that if they would quit the Armed Neutrality within two days we'd go home again, but that if they stuck to their guns why, we'd bring ours into action! But the Danes wouldn't have anything to do with our envoy and the other admiral was as blue as he could be about it!"

"Old Vinegar!" said Richard contemptuously. "He always was!"

"Wait a minute," pleaded Christopher, bewildered. "What do you mean by the other Admiral?"

"The one in charge."

"But I thought that was Nelson!"

"Don't you know anything about what's going on?" demanded Hugh. "Where've you been, for goodness' sake? The Fleet was really in the charge of Sir Hyde Parker, and he was a good twenty years older than Nelson. Nelson was only second in command, technically at any rate."

"You mean he really gave the orders?"

Richard chuckled. "What I mean is that he persuaded Sir Hyde to do what he wanted to do in the first place. And then, when the old boy wanted him to do something that didn't suit his book – well, I'll tell you about that in due course. Funniest thing out!"

"You were there too, were you? Christopher asked Hugh.

Hugh smiled. "I should think I was!" he said. "We all were! Every man, every ship that could be spared. Every boy, too! It was a desperate situation, you see."

Christopher sighed enviously. "You're a pair of old hands," he said. "I wish I were too."

"Why?"

"Oh well, you know what to expect. You've done it before."

"I'll tell you what to expect," said Richard bracingly. "You can expect us to win when we come to it because Nelson doesn't believe in losing. So as long as you take care to keep out of the way of the bullets you've nothing to worry about."

"That's easier said than done!" Hugh said ruefully.

"Oh! Was that where you lost your fingers?" asked Christopher apprehensively.

"Yes," said Hugh shortly. "And – well, never mind! But I'll tell you what – before the action started I wondered what it would be like, but once we were fairly in it I didn't care a hang. So there you are."

Christopher looked doubtful, but Richard was off again. "Once Nelson gets the bit between his teeth there's no stopping him," he said. "He carries you along with him too, and that's what happened to Old Vinegar. Though not even Nelson could take him all the way. Nelson wanted to sail against the Russian fleet; half of it had got separated from the rest, you see, so it would have been a golden opportunity. But poor old Sir Hyde couldn't think of the Russians in front, only of the Danes who'd be at his back. Still, he did say he'd fight them at least! I think he was afraid Nelson would think him a puddingheart if he didn't have a battle with somebody at that stage! So there we were, just outside Copenhagen. They'd been expecting us, mind! They'd increased the fortifications. Do you know anything about Copenhagen?

Christopher shook his head.

"It's a tricky sort of place," said Richard. "I'll draw you a map and you'll see then what the problem was. Have you got a bit of paper?"

Christopher fished in his pockets, but there was nothing there.

"Here you are," said Hugh. "Have a page out of my journal."

"Oh, thanks!" Now then, here's Copenhagen itself, you see, with batteries all along the shore. There are shoals everywhere in the Oresund – there's a whole bank outside Copenhagen itself, and a whacking great battery outside the harbour called the Trekroner. The Danish fleet and a heap of floating batteries were drawn up in front of this shoal – and being the middle of the Oresund is a terrific sandbank. Very nasty! The water in between, where the enemy were lying, is beastly deep and beastly fast. Now you can see what sort of vision Nelson has! He wanted to come up from the south with the wind behind him and the current with him. Trouble was, that the fleet was at the northern end of the sandbank, where we'd come down through the Kattegat – so he had to get his fighting division safely down to the south without grounding them."

"He obviously did!" smiled Christopher.

"I should think so! He deserved to, too – he spent a couple of the coldest nights I can remember out in the fog in a small boat taking soundings to help him to navigate between the shoals. He left Sir Hyde with the reserves up north, and took his own ships safely down. They'd been told exactly what to do, and the wind was in the right quarter."

"For all that," remarked Hugh, "when we got up to them and things really got going it was more like a heavyweight prize-fight than anything else. There were the shore batteries against us as well as the ships, and three of our own had gone aground on those horrible flats."

"Poor old Sir Hyde got himself in a state," said Richard. "He couldn't join in because the wind was against him and he was so bothered he signalled to Nelson to break off the fight. He ought to have known better!"

"You don't mean to say," said Christopher, "that Nelson – Nelson of all people! – disobeyed an order? After all you've been telling me about discipline?"

"Certainly not!" said Richard, stung. "At St Vincent he anticipated an order and got away with it, and this time he didn't disobey so much as ignore it."

"Isn't that just as bad?"

"Well, I suppose it would be in anybody else!" Richard conceded. "But the way Nelson did it was sublime! He said to his captain that with only one eye he had a right to be blind sometimes, and he put his telescope to his blind eye and said, 'I really do not see the signal!'"

Christopher laughed.

"Be fair to poor old Parker," said Hugh. "You know very well that his real idea was to give Nelson the opportunity of withdrawing with honour if he really found himself in a sticky position."

"He ought to have known that Nelson would never have done such a thing," insisted Richard. "Back out of a fight? The old defeatist! And suppose we had cut and run? Everything we had achieved would have been so much wasted effort."

"Well, anyway," said Hugh peaceably, "he had the chance, and Sir Hyde was really most frightfully pleased that he did carry on."

"I should think so too! We all but finished them off, didn't we? Funny thing – the enemy flagship blew up there, too. Wonder if we can make it three in a row?"

"I don't know, but I do know that at Copenhagen the fight didn't end before time. You must remember that when they set out to save the crew the batteries kept on firing and that didn't help. Nelson thought it time to call a halt, didn't he?"

"So he did. He sent a note to the Danish Regent to say that if they stopped their fire he'd be generous but if they didn't he'd fire the floating batteries!"

"And did they agree?" asked Christopher.

"Oh yes – and a good thing, too!" said Hugh. "Anyway, the job was done, Nelson got a viscounty, and here we both are in spite of it all!"

"The Admiral wasn't hurt that time, then?"

"Not a bit of it! The ironic thing is that though he's half blind and he's lost his right arm he got both those wounds in stupid little actions that didn't really matter two hoots. Maybe that's what makes him so unafraid in a big battle. If I were him I wouldn't care either. I'd want to get my own back! And I suppose, when you've already been through what he has you feel you know the worst."

"I don't suppose he does look at it that way," said Hugh. "He simply says, after all, that he hates a Frenchman as he would the devil. They were horrible wounds, however he came by them!"

"Yes, but it must make it worse to think you got them almost by the way!"

"What I find more ironic," said Hugh, "is that when he lost his eye he wasn't even fighting at sea – it was on land."

"How come?" asked Christopher.

"It was way back – not long after the French Revolution Terror. We'd a base at Toulon, and we had to get out, quick. All the British inhabitants – at least, all that were left after the massacre – were evacuated by the Navy. And who was in charge of that little lot? A certain young army captain from Corsica!"

"Boney himself?"

"None other. There he was, in – and there we were, out – and although we managed to destroy some of the French fleet on our way there were plenty left. Too many! You can see we needed a replacement base, and Corsica seemed ideal. Another piece of irony, that! And of all things, Nelson and his crew laid siege to two forts themselves. One was at a place called Bastia, where they had to haul the guns up the cliffs, and the second was at Calvi. That was where it happened. Nelson was hit by the debris thrown up by a shell, and his right eye was badly cut. That's why he's blind in it."

"He didn't actually lose it, then?"

"Oh bless you, no! He was luckier there than he was with his arm."

"Ah yes! And when did that happen?"

"Eight years ago," said Richard, "at Tenerife. There was a Spanish treasure ship there, at Santa Cruz, and the idea was to land and take the shore batteries and the money as well. So you see, this wasn't really a sea battle either. In fact, Nelson never got ashore at all. He was shot through the arm getting out of the boat and they had to take him back to his ship."

"Yes, and by Jove! He climbed aboard all by himself and took the salute on the quarterdeck as if nothing had happened before going down to the surgeon."

Christopher drew a breath. "He's certainly a brave man," he said.

"Yes," said Richard simply. "We can't go wrong with him in charge. I want a drink. My throat's quite dry after all that yarning!"

✢ ✢ ✢

There was his first sight of Spain; enemy territory, he realised, with a thrill in his throat. It came up over the larboard as the morning mists melted to another clear day with the fresh breeze still blowing behind and a smooth sea rippling below. Hilly and darkly grey the land emerged beside them out of the grey horizon. "The North Cape," said Hugh softly at his side. "Cape Finisterre. The Land's End."

"There's a Finisterre in France too!" exclaimed Christopher. "And a Land's End at home as well!"

Hugh nodded. "I know," he said wistfully. "It's sad, isn't it? We could have so much else in common too, and be friends together. Instead of which, before long we shall be at each other's throats, and all of us convinced that our cause is the right one!"

"But we are right!" cried Christopher, surprised, and Hugh laughed.

"Of course we are!" he said. "To us, at any rate, because we think so. Because life would be wonderful for everyone if only

96

we could all go peacefully on our own ways. But we can't. Because someone somewhere would always be so passionately certain that there were only two ways of doing things – his and the wrong one – that sooner or later he would try to make everyone else follow his ways, by fair means or foul. It's always been like that, ever since Alexander! Ever since Attila! And I've no doubt Bonaparte won't be the last. It's some thought, after all, to be master of the world! But I don't think it will ever happen, because other people will cling to their own customs and traditions and loyalties; as we are doing now, because we've no intention of losing them. And after all, if a man's way of life isn't worth defending to the last then it isn't really worth having, is it?"

Christopher's gaze was still fixed on the hills slipping away across the sea.

"What about the Spaniard?" he asked. "They haven't defended themselves against Napoleon. They've joined him!"

"I suppose they think that's the best kind of defence," said Hugh, thoughtfully. "They aren't as lucky as we are. They've only got mountain passes in between them and France. We've got the sea! Maybe they think they've got a better chance of fending him off their land if they come in on his side. A big mistake if you ask me. Boney's not the grateful sort. He'll collar them sooner or later if he can, you mark my words! And they're a proud race and they won't like it and they'll be sorry!"

"I wonder if you're right?" It'll be funny if that does happen, won't it?"

"Why?"

"Because if it does, we'll be sorry for them too, and want to help them, while here we are now on our way to do them as much harm as we possibly can!"

"That's their fault isn't it? They made their choice and they'll just have to take the consequences."

Christopher had no answer. He could only gaze thoughtfully at that line of hills to the east. By next day the Spanish seaboard was behind them and they were on their way down the coast of Portugal. By Saturday morning, with the wind coming strongly again from the north-west, they were within sight of the southernmost tip of the land. They were nearing journey's end. Richard stood beside Christopher and pointed out a gaunt and jutting headland.

"Look over there!" he said softly. "Do you know what that is?"

"No, I don't."

"Cape St Vincent, young 'un! You're sailing over historic waters now – do you realise that?"

Christopher looked and looked again, first at that uninviting coastline and then at the ruffling waters all about him with their curling white crests. So this was where the Spanish and English fleets had fought it out eight years ago on St Valentine's Day! Not much love lost there, Christopher thought wryly. This was where Sir John Jervis had earned an earldom, and where Nelson had formed his famous "patent bridge", had captured a Spanish admiral's sword, had gained his promotion to flag-rank and won a Knighthood of the Order of the Bath. Now, on this September morning, nothing recalled the flame and thunder of an earlier day. No mass of tangling ships disturbed the tide – just one, their own, was speeding before the breeze. And now the famous Cape itself was falling away astern and the helm was put over as Nonesuch turned along the southern coast of Portugal. They could hear the voice of the Master giving his directions. "Larboard. Steady – steady!" and now the ship was heading eastwards towards Cadiz and destiny, with the helpful wind dropping.

That evening, Hugh wrote in his diary,

"Saturday, September 28th.

By tomorrow at the latest we hope to have rejoined the Fleet after a fair passage. If this morning's wind had held we might have made our rendezvous already, but the Admiral cannot be far ahead of us. Cadiz is really very near now. This is where Sir Francis Drake singed the King of Spain's beard! What are the French thinking, I wonder, there in the harbour? The English ships on watch will certainly be glad to see us, particularly the Victory, since she brings Lord Nelson to them. But even his skill and courage will be useless if the enemy won't come out to fight. How will he make them do it? We are all certain that somehow he will manage to force an issue. How will he lure them away from their moorings? A siege can be as tedious for those outside as for those inside – we know – we've done it before! I hope we don't have to wait too long, because although a battle isn't the most pleasant way of passing the time, days spent at sea just hovering about have a way of fraying everyone's temper. Better to fight the French than each other!"

And so through the calm of an early autumn night Nonesuch came to Cadiz Bay and joined the Mediterranean Fleet. The sight of so many sail together after the long days alone made everyone happy. There were something like thirty of them, rocking gently on the water. There was the Orion, a seventy-four like themselves, and now a hunter like her namesake. There were other two-deckers too – the Mars and the Bellerophon, as pugnacious as their names suggested, and the Conqueror, whose Captain Pellew, was the famous brother of an even more famous officer. There was the second-rate vessel Tonnant, of eighty guns, captured from the French at the Nile, and now commanded by a Welshman. And there were several first-rates – the Neptune, for instance, commanded by one of the Admiral's friends and colleagues, Captain Thomas Fremantle, and the Britannia, carrying the third senior commanding officer, Rear Admiral the Earl of Northesk. There was the huge Dreadnought, carrying the man who had commanded the blockade, Vice-Admiral Cuthbert Collingwood. And there was that other three-decker, newly arrived like themselves, in whose wake they had made the long voyage from Plymouth; the Victory, with Vice-Admiral Lord Nelson aboard.

Surrounded by friends as they now were, those other vessels, which Christopher had vaguely thought of as the "enemy", could not be forgotten. There they were, no ghost ships but solid timber, and safe behind the harbour mouth the lookouts could see their masts streaking bare into the sky. At least thirty of them. More. Thirty-five was it? More than enough, at all events. Tucked away behind that narrow entrance, spread across that famous and ancient harbour, was the threat to England's future. It was a sobering thought, that only their own slender wooden line stood between French ambition and the sea-roads leading homeward.

6

While Nonesuch was sailing before the wind down towards Spain; while Christopher was learning the basic skills of the seaman's craft; while Vice-Admiral Collingwood's weary ships were waiting for Lord Nelson to arrive; the French admiral was a very bothered man. He was short of food, he was short of money, his ships were in need of repair and his men weren't in good health either. On the Spanish ships they were short of men anyway. They had received fresh orders from Napoleon, himself getting bothered about the little British army which he knew was on its way to Italy. The Combined Fleet, he said, must get into the Mediterranean; and he more or less told Admiral Villeneuve that he was a coward for not doing it. He did not tell him that he had decided to give the job to somebody else. But rumour always travels fast, and impending disgrace made Villeneuve decide to take desperate measures. If Napoleon didn't care about the safety of his fighting ships, then neither would he!

It had been a furious Napoleon who had received the same news which had delighted Lord Nelson; that the Combined Fleet was trapped in Cadiz harbour by Collingwood's vessels. This was more than irritating, and he had also to think of that little army which had reached Malta to join the Russians against him. Villeneuve, the Emperor decided, since he would not come up to the Channel, must get into the Mediterranean to ward off this new menace. Here he was to fall into a pit of his own digging, for he had thought that only a handful of British ships lay outside the harbour where his Fleet was sheltered. He did not yet know that their numbers were increasing daily, and that Lord Nelson himself was on his way.

But Villeneuve knew, only too well. Even while he still tried to put his ships in order and head for the Channel he knew, for he had seen them pass across the bay to join their fellows. And the orders he had, to sail to Italy, did nothing to cheer him up. Only Napoleon, scorning petty detail, would have decided so grandly to send his precious fleet out against a tiny army. For England was far more dangerous to him at this moment on the sea than she was on land; and at sea she was waiting for him. No matter! Even when he did know, he didn't see why he should change his imperious imperial mind. So poor Villeneuve was left with no choice. He must put to sea according to orders; and he knew that when he did he must fight his enemy to the death before he could hope to pass on his way.

Now all he had to do was to decide when the battle should be. The dogged British vessels were filled with dogged British sailors, and the greatest of them all was among them. And on that late September night, Nonesuch caught up with her own admiral and joined the waiting fleet outside Cadiz. No saluting colours were hoisted – Nelson didn't want to advertise his presence to the enemy unnecessarily – but the news of his coming spread through his own ships immediately, and the very air about the spars tingled with jubilation. Still rumour travelled fast, even into Cadiz harbour, where Villeneuve changed his mind again. With Nelson at his throat he meant to sit tight, whatever his Emperor thought.

The arrival of the Victory was heady medicine to the weary men watching and waiting outside the harbour bar. Lord Nelson was in the Victory. Lord Nelson would put an end to all this, sooner or later. Tempers had been running high, spirits had been running low. With so many men of different temperament cooped up in so small a space as a fighting ship provided, on the one spot which a blockade demanded, it was all too easy for one to rub another up the wrong way even if he didn't mean to. Action of some kind – any kind – was the tonic everyone needed and wanted, and now maybe they would get it! Nelson had arrived to lead, and the men were ready to be led. He set to work straight away to gather the threads in his fingers and weave them into the fabric of a force to be reckoned with.

The day after their arrival was a Sunday. It was also the Admiral's birthday. He was forty-seven. He celebrated it by giving a party for the flag officers and captains of the assembled fleet. Captain Britten emerged from his cabin resplendent with gold braid, white kneebreeches and a black bicorne hat. He wore a high black stock and spotless white silk stockings. The bullion on his shoulders shone in the autumn sunlight, and his long sword hung at his left side. He strode across the deck, and with all ceremony he entered his boat to be rowed across to the towering three-decker flagship, brave with its black and yellow paintwork, flying a vice-admiral's flag from her foremast; white, with the red cross of St George and the Union Jack in the top quarter of the hoist. The officers and mids who were on the quarterdeck at the time sprang to attention and removed their hats as the Captain was piped over the side and down into the waiting boat. It carried him over the sunlit waters and Christopher, watching, saw him climb the ladder and disappear through the entry-port on Victory's middle deck. From there, he supposed, the Captain would mount the ladder through the hatch to the upper deck, and make his way aft to a cabin not so very different, perhaps, from his own.

He was right. Lord Nelson was seated in just such a room to welcome the captains of his fleet, and they greeted him in their turn, with special warmth on his birthday. When everyone had arrived, Lord Nelson explained the plan of action he had formed, and it was thoroughly discussed so that every ship in the British fleet would know exactly what part it was expected to play. It was a brilliant plan. The idea was not new; and yet so obviously the right thing to do!

Lazing away the quiet Sunday afternoon in the sun Richard, glancing towards the flagship, suddenly sprang to life. The captains were leaving to return to their own ships, and Richard's quick eye had spotted someone on the Victory's deck bidding them farewell. He tweaked Christopher's sleeve urgently.

"Quick!" he hissed. "Look over there! The Admiral! That's him! Have you got your glass handy?"

"It's in my pocket," answered Christopher. "What's the matter?"

"Take a good look at him now you've got the chance!"

Christopher obediently looked. A short, slight, shattered figure was standing by the Victory's rail. The heavily starred and decorated blue coat carried an empty sleeve pinned up across the breast; there was a tired face crowned by a shock of white hair. The scars of war and suffering made the Admiral look older than the forty-seven years he was celebrating today, but even at this distance a strange magnetism surrounded him. Despite his lack of inches he carried himself with the air of one born to command. Christopher wondered what it felt like to bear on one's own narrow shoulders the tremendous weight of responsibility which Lord Nelson carried. It gave him a strange feeling of awe as he gazed across the water at that lonely little figure. How did it feel to be a man of destiny? Christopher had no idea, but he understood in that moment what put the pride into Richard's eyes when he spoke of his hero, and the reverence into his voice. Perhaps Lord Nelson was not, after all, as lonely as he seemed; not a demigod, but a man, with the love and trust of his fellows to support him and their willingness to obey to give him strength. The captains were approaching their own ships now, the small slender figure turned away from the Victory's rail, and the spell was broken. But it was enough. Christopher had caught the infection and now he too would follow blindly where Nelson led. Richard, watching the expression on his friend's face, was satisfied.

Now Captain Britten was coming back on board, and must be welcomed home with more saluting and more ceremony. Again the pipes whistled as he came aboard, and everyone waited for him bareheaded in the sunshine. He paused and touched his own gold-laced hat in acknowledgement of his return "home". Then he strode briskly aft to the airy room under the poop where the marine sentry guarding the door presented arms as he went in. His face seemed all aglow with barely suppressed excitement, and Richard was almost beside himself with curiosity, itching to know what the Admiral could have been saying to evoke this reaction in his unemotional uncle. Much later, the senior officers went about with the same light in their eyes that he had seen in his uncle's; and much, much later still, when the instructions percolated down to the cockpit, they all understood. "The Nelson Touch!" Richard exclaimed. "That's what he called it, and so it is! No one else would have thought of it, but it seems so obvious!"

For like all Nelson's decisions, it had been reached after all possible angles had been considered; reached and then determined. The Combined Fleet, he saw clearly, had to be completely destroyed NOW, while the chance held. Their numbers were superior, their ships were bigger, and they were manned by – indeed, commanded by – desperate men. But if they were not destroyed the only prospect for England's own precious Navy was blockade, blockade and yet again blockade. That had been bad enough outside the Channel ports; on this wild and rocky coast the dangers would be fantastic. What's more, ships had to be kept supplied – and how to do that? The minute they withdrew to friendly ports the Combined Fleet would be out, and either the Mediterranean or the Atlantic – possibly both – would be at risk again. No doubt they would head first for the Mediterranean. They must be stopped at all costs; and the only sure way was to wipe them from the face of the water. A tall order; but still Nelson believed it could be done.

The first problem – to get the Combined Fleet out of harbour – did not rest entirely with him. Only Villeneuve himself could decide when to put his neck into Nelson's noose. The second problem – the weather – was again no concern of his. He must simply deploy his forces as best he could to overcome difficulties like mists and adverse winds. The crux of the matter was time; not a moment must be lost once the enemy were sighted. Swinging the sailing column into a line of battle was the greatest time-waster, so the best thing to do was to keep the great ships still in column formation as they went into action. It was a new idea in naval warfare – but why not? Better still, if the fleet attacked in two columns, and broke the enemy line in TWO places, not just one, the centre of that line would be completely isolated from the rest, and one end of the line could be overwhelmed while the other was cut off and unable to help. What was more, the flexibility of the column formation meant that the ships could reform in broad line if necessary, but it was not so easy for a line abreast to change itself into a column sailing astern.

And so the Fleet would sail into battle in two columns, one under the direction of Nelson himself and the other under Vice-Admiral Collingwood. It was characteristic of Nelson that once the broad intention was made known he had no more to say to that second division. Collingwood's instructions were to break the enemy line somewhere about the twelfth ship from the rear and overwhelm that part of the fleet. How he was to do it would be up to him, and those ships under him would follow where he led. The other column, Nelson's own column, would aim to break through a little in advance of the enemy centre, where the French admiral's flagship was certain to be. The capture of Villeneuve himself was an important consideration.

It was clear that if all went according to plan, the centre and rear of the enemy line would be very heavily engaged. What about the isolated van? It would take them some time to get round to help their own comrades, and Nelson was counting on decimating the rear before the van needed to be tackled.

The rest of the Admiral's instructions were loose, because he wanted no rigid adherence to rules to ruin this chance of annihilating the enemy. The British ships were to follow their leaders until they came to close quarters with the enemy; after that it was up to their own captains to position them where they could hammer away at any Frenchman who came within their range. It was the number of ships captured or destroyed that mattered. Nelson was determined on a free-for-all. This was to be a fight to the death, so the orders were in the broadest terms, the captains being told that as long as they placed themselves against any of the Combined Fleet and gave it to her hot and strong that would be all to the good. The two lines of ships would be independent of each other, keeping out of each other's way as far as possible, and the ships in each were to look to their own particular commander for instructions. Nelson believed in giving his officers scope to act on their own initiative, so long as they kept within the framework of his orders. The end, in short, would justify any means they chose to use during the course of the battle.

The only drawback to this bold scheme was that while the oncoming British columns would be exposed to the full fire of the enemy's broadsides as they approached, they would be unable to use their own long rows of guns until absolutely level with the French; nor would they be able to fire their own forward guns for fear of damaging the ship immediately in front of them in the column. But this was a minor detail, and the danger not so great as it might seem except to the foremost ships; and they would count the risk an honour. Only the bows could be expected to suffer greatly, not the sensitive flanks; and as it was usually the practice of the French to aim high and cut away the rigging the crews would not be open to such danger as it might seem from the broadsides. If the French chose to expend precious ammunition to relatively little purpose, so much the better! This was the chief difference between the two nations when it came to naval battles. The French fired their broadside guns on the upward roll of the ship, calculating that with the masts and spars wrecked their opponents would be crippled and unable to escape. The British, on the other hand, fired as the ship rolled downwards, and sent their shot crashing through the enemy hulls. So they not only stood a greater risk of taking the sea through the shot-holes and sinking, but the carnage among the crews was greater. This might seem cold-blooded, but it stood to reason that a ship without a crew to sail her would be even more helpless than one without her masts and sails; they could be replaced with a little time and ingenuity. And this, after all, was war! Certainly the strict training of the British crews had made them fast and accurate, with little time wasted between one shot and the next, and the effect was more devastating in the long run.

But all this was nothing if the Combined Fleet refused to leave the shelter of Cadiz. The east wind blowing fairly should have tempted them, but still they lurked out of sight and unattainable. Many aboard the British fleet, officers and men alike, despaired of any action. Only Nelson was sure in his bones that leave they must for want of provisions. If necessary he would play Napoleon at his own game and starve them out!

There was another problem which kept Nelson's mind occupied. Two months earlier, Sir Robert Sadler had met the elusive enemy and tackled them in a heavy mist. He had captured two Spanish ships and blocked the way back to safe harbour, but he had not followed up his advantage. Afraid that the ships now blockaded in Ferrol would escape and come to the rescue, he had let them escape. His captains had ground their teeth in frustration, but there was nothing they could do about it. Now the unlucky Sir Robert was called to pay the price of prudence at a court martial. Three captains who had been at that inconclusive battle were asked to return home with Sir Robert to give evidence on his behalf, and though he could ill spare such a large and powerful ship Nelson allowed him to sail home in the first-rate Prince of Wales. Those ninety-eight guns would be sorely missed, but Nelson's generous nature would not let a fellow officer suffer the indignity of being transferred to a smaller and less worthy vessel. That would be judging him guilty before the trial, and poor man, he had sorrows enough – expecting praise for a victory he had found himself as good as charged with cowardice. It was perhaps lucky for him that one of his witnesses flatly refused to go, for Captain Durham of the Defiance was so sore about the whole affair that he would have done him more harm than good. So the Prince of Wales had gone back to England, and six other ships had been set off to take in fresh stores. It could only be hoped that they would return in time, though other vessels were arriving in dribs and drabs to swell the numbers of the English fleet.

A week after Nonesuch had arrived, the wind changed. It was blowing now from the east, straight off the Spanish coast; just perfect for any fleet waiting to sail away from Cadiz harbour and out into the Atlantic. Troops, by then, were embarking onto the ships of the Combined Fleet. Villeneuve must move soon! But still the days dragged on, and slowly Lord Nelson's forces grew. On Monday, October 7th, the Defiance arrived, another useful two-decker ship of the line carrying seventy-four guns. Next day came the newly refitted Royal Sovereign, a first-rate of a hundred guns like Victory herself. She would be Collingwood's flagship. The watchful frigates never took their eyes off the enemy for a moment, and hopes were raised when the French hoisted their top gallant sails and fastened them to the yards so as to be ready to unfurl them and set sail at any moment. More disappointment! Villeneuve changed his mind, and stayed put.

All this was very frustrating to the English, especially to a certain Richard Britten, midshipman, who was fairly biting his nails to the quick.

"It really is too bad," he mourned. "Why can't a Frenchman be more like an Englishman? All this shilly-shallying! It's so inconsiderate! Our Admiral doesn't change his mind every other minute!"

Lieutenant Scott, who happened to hear him laughed. "I doubt if the French admiral is concerned with your state of mind," he said mildly. "No doubt he has his own reasons for not wanting to force an issue."

"I can't think what," said Richard, aggrieved. "It's his job to fight us, isn't it? Then why doesn't he do it?"

"Always so bloodthirsty!" sighed Fellowes, under his breath.

"I'm not! But when everybody knows there's got to be a fight sooner or later then let's get it over with sooner. No point in hanging about!"

"So impatient!" said Fellowes in the same weary tone.

The lieutenant's mouth twitched, but he only said, "Keep your differences for the enemy, if you please! Fellowes is right to preach patience in a situation which can't be helped; Britten is right to wish to bring the issue to a head while we are at full strength. If only we could stir you two well together we might make one good officer some day!"

The two looked sheepish, and Lieutenant Scott went on, "The secret of being a good strategist is to try to get inside the other fellow's mind. Put yourself in his place! Try to think how the situation seems to him – then try to imagine the best way out of his difficulties. Do either of you play chess?"

They shook their heads.

"A pity! It's an excellent training. If you did, you would learn how to plot your game several jumps ahead of your opponent's moves, and then to make your own moves decisively. Now, you know that Lord Nelson had already decided how he will make his attack. Villeneuve doesn't know just how it will be, but naturally he knows that some sort of action is inevitable, and he must know that we want to destroy his fleet as completely as we can. Now try to think yourselves into his place. On the one hand, he must be running short of supplies so he needs to set sail. No doubt his master is clamouring for action – that would be an even greater incentive." He stopped for a moment, and looked at the two serious young faces, watching him intently. "But – he knows we are here, though he probably doesn't now our exact numbers. I imagine he most certainly knows that Lord Nelson is here – the French have their sources of information too, you know! – and until now the wind has been against him. All these things are sufficient to influence him the other way."

"Well sir," burst out Richard, unable to contain himself any longer, "the wind isn't against him any more and if I were him I'd come out and have a go!"

"Are you sure you would? Remember, you're a little English bulldog, not a Frenchman. The French don't lack vision, you know, and this particular Frenchman knows it's no ordinary Englishman who's waiting for him over the skyline. He's in an unenviable position. I'm almost sorry for him!"

Fellowes remained silent, digesting this, but Richard went on gnawing at the point as if he were indeed a little bulldog with a particularly tough bone. "But if it's bound to happen and he'd made up his mind to come out, then why didn't he stick to it? He's as bad as my sister, sir! But you expect it from a girl – not from an admiral!"

"Why not?" countered the lieutenant. "He's had plenty of time to consider, true, but we can only imagine what an agonising decision it must be for him. He's a naturally cautious man; at least, so it seems to me. He knows he would get only a short distance before meeting us, and some of his ships, if the reports we have are right, are in poor shape. Goodness knows what their crews are like. It may be that while we are lying out here, trying to tempt him into the open, he is riding at anchor trying to tempt us to attack him in the harbour itself, which might make things a lot easier from his point of view."

Richard was staring at his superior. "I never thought of that!" he said, impressed.

"Try thinking of it now," said Lieutenant Scott as he turned away. "It will give you something to do, if you really can't find any work requiring your attention."

"There was a nasty sting in that tail," said Richard apprecia-tively, "but I really never did think of that possibility."

"You never think of a lot of things," said Fellowes sharply.

Richard looked at him, startled. "That's a funny thing," he said "Hugh said only the other day that that's what you would say – or something like it."

"Muddled, but I follow you. You could try thinking about that for a start," advised Fellowes. "Meanwhile, I should do as you're told! Find something useful to do, and leave the strategy to someone better qualified."

Not for the first time, Richard was exasperated by his fellow mid – but by the time he had thought of a suitable retort, Fellowes had disappeared, and the opportunity was lost.

The days passed by. Autumn was slipping soundlessly away, and this was worrying, for the stage was ready set, but with winter waiting in the wings it began to seem as if the curtain would never rise. Not that this was a problem to Christopher. The weather was pleasant, he had enough work to keep him occupied and enough leisure to add daily to his store of knowl-edge. He had two very good friends among the mids; the volatile Richard and the quieter, steadier Hugh. Cramped as their quarters were, he would have enjoyed life there to the full if it hadn't been for the constant pinpricks handed out by Fellowes. And for the life of him he couldn't think why. He racked his brains to puzzle out what he had ever said or done to anger the older boy, but it wasn't any use. No explanation presented itself. He had been ready and willing, more than willing, to be friends with everybody else in the mess, and he had succeeded, more or less, with everybody else. Only Fellowes rejected every friendly advance with a cold shoulder and a colder eye. The very first sight of him seemed to have filled Fellowes with loathing. Why, Christopher couldn't imagine. He didn't look that bad, surely! There had been moments when

Fellowes had spoken nicely to him; he had even been almost kind sometimes, telling him things the others didn't. But looking back Christopher realised that these were almost always unpleasant things. Strange, that. It was as if his friends were trying to keep the nasty bits hidden away in a dark corner so that he saw only the fun and the sunlight, while Fellowes seemed determined to throw ugliness in his face and – frighten him, could it be? It seemed a pretty odd sort of thing to do but then some people were like that. And in a way he supposed he should be grateful to Fellowes for showing him the other side of the coin. What was it he had said about being boys in a man's world? That made sense, he supposed, but all the same it was a queer sort of kindness that showed itself in constant pinpricks and refined bullying. No – Fellowes didn't mean to be kind. Fellowes didn't like him, never did like him, and didn't care who knew it either. True, he was like it with everyone else, but not nearly so much, and he's known them longer, anyway, thought Christopher savagely. Whatever the reason, he was the older boy's target from the time they all rolled out in the morning, and while Fellowes didn't actually go out of his way to make an opportunity for being unpleasant he certainly never let the opportunity slip. When they sped up the ladders to the newly scrubbed deck it was Fellowes who begged him to mind in case he should fall. When they tumbled down again for breakfast, it was Fellowes who sneered at his healthy young appetite, wondering how any gentleman could find room for so much fodder (and I don't tuck away half as much as Richard does! thought Christopher indignantly) and speculating on the home which encouraged such habits. When they assembled on deck for the captain's inspection, it was Fellowes who asked if he'd remembered to wash behind the ears and then begged pardon for forgetting his reputation as a dandy. (And he started that one, too!) At the noonday navigation class, it was Fellowes who watched his struggles with the quadrant and his laboured calculations with a malicious gleam in his eye. Well, we can't all be good at the same things, reasoned Christopher, and maths never was my strong point. Whenever there was work to be done, Fellowes seemed to be close at hand, watching for him to make a mistake, waiting to point it out to him. And when he climbed into his cot at night it was Fellowes who sweetly reminded everyone that little boys had to go to bed early. In the end, Christopher took his troubles to Hugh, who always managed to soothe wounded feelings, his own or any else's.

"Does he really bother you all that much?" said Hugh, surprised and anxious. "If he does, for goodness' sake don't let him see it."

"Oh, I don't. At least, I hope not. But I do get fed up with it sometimes, and I suppose just now there's plenty of time to brood."

"Can't you ignore it like the rest of us?"

"I've tried that, and it only makes him worse. And answering back doesn't have any effect, either. I give up."

"He's a funny creature," said Hugh thoughtfully. "Prickly as a hedgehog, but I fancy he's soft enough underneath – like the hedgehog again, if you like. Do you realise that the hands like and respect him almost to a man? And he's only a mid, after all!"

"Do they? Good Lord!"

"You may well say that. He's just the sort you'd think would go about swanking and bullying – you must have seen that some of them do try that on – but he doesn't. He seems to touch just the right chord in them and they respond to it, though most of 'em are old enough to be his father. Grandfather even!"

"Maybe I should have gone on the lower deck after all," said Christopher ruefully. "He might have liked me then, and I him!"

Hugh was shocked. "You couldn't possibly have done that!" he said. "You wouldn't have liked that at all!"

"No, I wouldn't, and of course I didn't really mean it! There's probably more like him there, if I looked for them, too."

"More than likely. They're a pretty mixed bunch, after all! Hush, here he comes!"

"Nice to be some people," Fellowes observed as he joined them. "Got nothing better to do than nothing?"

"Not today," answered Hugh tranquilly. "Don't think anybody's got anything particular to do, either. Don't you find time hanging heavy?"

"I should say I do!" said Fellowes. There's nothing worse

than having a job waiting and being ready to do it and simply not being able to get on with it."

"I thought," ventured Christopher, "you said it wouldn't do to rush things – that night the officers had their party."

Fellowes looked at him; through him, it seemed.

"It wouldn't," he said at last, "but we've been hanging about here for a couple of weeks now and everybody's arrived. That's hardly rushing things, is it?"

"Are you ready?" asked Christopher directly.

"As ready as I'm ever likely to be," said Fellowes a little wryly. "While not sharing Richard's indecent anxiety to have my head blown off at any moment I do feel that it's what we came out here to do – no, I don't mean to have our heads blown off but you know what I do mean! So the sooner the better." He wasn't looking now at the other two boys but went on speaking almost to himself, gazing up along the deck as he did so. "It's like being suspended in time," he said softly. "Here we ride while the days drift along away from us, and what will be – must be – hangs on the horizon beckoning to us – and yet nothing we can do can bring tomorrow any quicker. We all know what's bound to happen but nobody knows when, and nobody can afford to let up for a single instant because at any moment our whole world could be turned upside down. It's almost like one of those dreadful dreams when everything seems perfectly natural until all of a sudden you realise you're having a nightmare and you struggle to wake up – but we shall find we've been awake all the time and – Man overboard!" he suddenly shrieked, and sprinted off along the deck. "A boat! Man a boat!" while Christopher and Hugh stared after him, horrified.

No one seemed to know quite what had happened. One moment the man was sitting aloft on the yardarm, the next there was a choking scream, a dark shape hurtled down out of the sky, and a terrific splash was heard only a second after that shout of "Man overboard!" Immediately there was a rush to the side and to the masts, and a boat was lowered as quickly as it possibly could be, with Fellowes and a handful of seamen in it. Bates was one of them, of course. Where there was action, there was Bates; but he wasn't singing this time. He was rowing as hard as he could, with his mates taking the time from him, towards the dark bobbing ball in the water that was his shipmate's head. Meanwhile the sailors on board ship were busy shortening sail as fast as they could, to stop Nonesuch's idle progress and keep her from drawing too far ahead of the boat travelling as fast as human arms could manage toward that bobbing shape which had as if by a miracle emerged from the sea. Side by side, Christopher and Richard were hanging over the rail, in danger of going over too if they weren't careful.

"They'll never get there in time!" cried Christopher. "He'll go down for sure before they reach him!"

"I don't know," said Richard watching intently. "He can swim – look, he's managing to keep himself afloat! Lucky for him – not many of 'em can."

Christopher was surprised, but before he could say anything the boat had got within reach of the unlucky sailor, and his shipmates had thrown out a line to him. As they drew nearer, Fellowes leaned over and took hold of him, but to the horror of everyone watching from Nonesuch's decks the man had clawed at Fellowes' sleeve, clutching desperately and pulling him half out of the boat into the ocean with him. Only quick thinking saved them both from going to the bottom together; quick thinking on the part of Bates, who threw himself forward to grab at Fellowes' legs and quick thinking on the part of Fellowes himself, who cuffed the drowning man with his spare hand. Fellowes hung over the edge of the boat with Bates holding on grimly to his legs, and the muscles on Bates' forearms stood out ribbed and hard with the strain. But the punch Fellowes had managed to land on the sailor's jaw had made him slacken his grip, and now the other men had shipped their oars and were ready to haul both the midshipman and the half-drowned topman safely over the side. The rescued sailor lay in a wet and gasping huddle on the boards, and a rousing cheer from the ship encouraged the rowers on their return trip.

Christopher had instinctively thrown a hand up across his eyes as Fellowes lurched down towards the sea, but had as quickly withdrawn it as he heard Richard shouting with excitement beside him. "Oh, well done!" he cried. "Well done indeed!

By Jupiter, they've got him, they've got him, they've got him! Hurray!" and he jogged up and down with delight. "Look at that! What's the matter with you?" He tugged at Christopher's elbow.

"I thought Fellowes had gone overboard too," he said apologetically.

"Not he! He clipped him over the ear and they got them both all right and tight. But what an escape! Someone fell that way a few weeks back on another ship – landed smack on the deck, poor devil."

"Was he killed?"

"Not right away, but he died a week later. Better for him if he'd gone at once. He was one of the unlucky ones. What's more, when they do go overboard it's not often you find any trace of them, however quick you are going after then. Here they come!" and there was a surge of seamen as the rescue team came aboard, supporting their luckier comrade. But Fellowes disclaimed all congratulations. Turning away from Christopher's eager praise he said, "I'm beastly wet. I'm going to change," and went below. The two friends looked at each other. Richard shrugged.

"Well," he said, "he may be a giddy hero but he's a dashed surly brute all the same!"

⁜ ⁜ ⁜

The days were now running well into October, and still the Combined Fleet rocked gently at anchor in its Spanish haven. Lord Nelson may have had plenty to occupy his mind during the wait, but for the crews tossing about fifty miles out in the Atlantic the time seemed never-ending. Sent to bide their time out of sight of the enemy, in an effort to tempt them to make a dash for it, while the vigilant frigates kept in touch by signalling with guns and flags, time hung heavy on their hands. Something had to be done to keep them occupied. Aboard Nonesuch, a dramatic turn had been discovered among the midshipmen, and they decided that rehearsing a play would be as good a way as any of passing the time. Much discussion went on over their choice. Richard wanted a funny play, others were for high tragedy, and it began to look as if the argument alone would take up all their leisure time until Richard had his bright idea.

"Let Hugh write one for us!" he said. "We only want a few scenes and he can do it in less than no time!"

Not quite as quickly as that, but in two days, Hugh writing at white heat, produced a very creditable effort. Drawing shamelessly on every play he could remember he put in everything that could satisfy the would-be actors. There was a foolish dowager, in which part Lieutenant Welch came out surprisingly strongly; a wronged hero; an heiress; and a bearded villain doomed to become thoroughly steeped in evil and come to the sticky end he deserved.

The good ended well, the bad not so well, and everyone voted it a piece to make Drury Lane green with envy. The heroine presented a problem, but as Hugh very reasonably said, you couldn't have a play without one. Eventually Christopher, as the newest and youngest member of the mess, was told that he must perform this part. "Besides," said Richard, "You're not so tall and it would look much better."

"Hugh's short," protested Christopher. "Let him do it. He invented the beastly girl!"

"I've done my bit," said Hugh. "Anyway, I didn't invent her and she isn't beastly either. She's my sister."

"Oh, all right. It's only ourselves, after all."

"That's what you think," said Richard wickedly. "We go on stage on Tuesday."

"What do you mean, on stage?"

"Well, we perform – in the wardroom, anyway. Doors open at seven-thirty prompt, audience to be seated on the deck by a quarter past. Ring up the curtain! Now, today's Friday, so that gives us three clear days to learn our words and practise."

Christopher was aghast, but had to give in with a good grace. For the next three days the cast spent every odd moment muttering their lines to each other and rehearsing in corners in twos and threes. There would be only one full dress rehearsal, on the Monday evening, but nobody minded, and when Monday evening came the cockpit was in a hilarious mood as the bits and pieces were fitted together for the first time. Everybody had something to do, for the mids who weren't acting were roped in as scene-shifters, prompters and odd-job men. The carpenters had built a splendid scene for them, whose chief feature was a wall with a balcony on which two people could sit in safety – as long as they didn't wave their arms about too much. The low roof didn't allow them to stand. The man who was so often to be heard playing a lively fiddle had been called aft to act as an orchestra, and with Lieutenant Welch, Lieutenant Kent, Mr Campbell and a lieutenant of Marines amongst the cast, law and order were bound to be kept. The costumes were works of art, for everything had had to be fashioned out of their ordinary clothes and belongings. And when Lieutenant Welch appeared, his bald head crowned with a fantastic wig made of old rope and an enormous canvas cap with a vast frill to it there was a roar of delight. He had borrowed blankets from his friends to make his flowing skirts, and an absurd little fan of pleated paper was lost in his massive fist. The villain who in private life was the marine lieutenant, took one look at this vision and collapsed on a chest, helpless with laughter.

"La, sir!" Lieutenant Welch simpered, and hid his jowls behind his ridiculous little fan. "To be sure, I ever had an effect on the gentlemen, for I've been a beauty in my day – yes, I was a Toast! – still, it's gratifying to a lady not perhaps in the first blush of youth to find so grand a gentleman susceptible to her charms!" and he fluttered his eyelashes, The marine lieutenant wailed helplessly. His own sense of gravity sorely tried, Lieutenant Kent bent a stern gaze on the lady. "Come, madam!" he said severely, "Allow the gentleman to recover, if you please, or we shall be all night! Now, Mr Lester, pull yourself together, and we can start!"

The villain gulped, and rose to his feet. "And I am to begin," he said, and strode into the middle of the cockpit, glaring evilly upon the company. He wore his own boots and a heavy boat-cloak, and his sword hung at this side. He patted this significantly, and launched into his opening speech.

The rehearsal proved to be in the best tradition, for all kinds of accidents occurred. The heroine tripped over her skirts and would have fallen headlong if a robber hadn't caught her in the nick of time – unladylike behaviour which earned her a grave reproof from the dowager. The villain was hard put to it not to relapse into mirth whenever the elder lady spoke to him, and more than once was rapped over the knuckles with her fan. The wall collapsed under the combined weight of two people and landed them in a heap on the deck. Everybody kept putting things down and losing them, and everybody forgot their words. The dowager made up half of hers as she went along, which was confusing, and only three people finished the evening really satisfied. One was Lieutenant Welch, who was always good-tempered and anyway was enjoying himself hugely: one was Hugh who having done his part by writing the piece didn't care a button what they made of it as long as they didn't expect him to act in it as well: and the third was the fiddler, who should have been on watch and was very happy to be sitting down instead – and by orders, too! But, as the ever-optimistic Richard said, these were all trivial matters. Everything would be fine tomorrow. The audience would come prepared to be pleased, and the only thing that could spoil the performance would be the emergence of the enemy. That would be so splendid in itself that it would more than make up for the disappointment.

But nothing did happen to stop the first and only appearance on any stage of "The Outlaw's Return: or, Revenge is Sweet". Tuesday passed as uneventfully as the past fortnight had. Although on the day before word had come that the enemy were at the entrance to the harbour and likely to come out before many days were past, no sudden alarm drove thoughts of fun out of their heads. Still the French hung back, and still the number of the English fleet was growing. Two days before Sir Robert Calder had left them, but in place of his flagship the Agamemnon arrived, of sixty-four guns, commanded by Sir Edward Berry. On her way to join the fleet she had done something the others had not – she had come in sight of the enemy! Not Villeneuve, skulking in Cadiz, but Admiral Allemand, who had slipped out of Rochefort with a small squadron of four sail of the line. Ranging about in the Bay hoping to waylay supplies coming to Nelson from England, the French had spied the Agamemnon and given chase. But Agamemnon was a very fast ship, and Sir Edward Berry was a very fine seaman who could keep a cool head in an emergency. Squeezed between two huge enemy vessels, both much bigger than his own, he had sacrificed a boat and some stores to make his ship lighter, crowded on sail and sped away. The French had chased him for many uncomfortable miles before giving up, but the Agamemnon had escaped unmarked to fight another day. Yesterday, the little battleship Africa had come up with them, and the English force was complete. All they needed now was opportunity.

But the day limped away without excitement, and that evening Captain Britten duly took his place in the front row of the audience on the maindeck, where the bulkhead between it and the wardroom had been removed and a row of lanterns placed across the deck instead between the audience and the performers. The fiddler, perched on one of the guns, played a sprightly little tune to warn the audience into silence, and the play began.

The whole affair was a great success from the word go, when Lieutenant Lester strode almost into Captain Britten's lap, rolled his black eyes, and made clear his very evil intentions – how, having thrown the blame for his crimes on the hero, he would worm his way into the good opinion of the heiress's foolish guardian, and so become master of lands and fortune not his own. Some of his audience might have murmured that they didn't think this would take much acting ability, but Lieutenant Lester's villain was hugely popular for all that. But the dowager was everyone's favourite. She minced about the deck as if she had never trodden on anything but the softest carpet, she giggled away as if she had never roared an order above the shrieking of a gale, and she made fluttery gestures with hands that had surely never hauled hard on a slippery rope that bit into her frozen fingers. Her long curls – you had to look closely to see that they were made out of frayed-out rope – dangled roguishly about her cheeks, and altogether she was the silliest creature you could hope to meet, even going by her own well-known views on women!

Nobody could have asked for a better audience. They cheered the hero, hissed the villain and laughed at the comics in all the right places, and to a man they clapped Lieutenant Welch to the echo. If he had been a success at the rehearsal, he was a riot on the night. Captain Britten laughed until the tears ran down his face as the "dame" simpered and sighed and fluttered her way through her part. And she carried the rest of the cast along with her, for with a real live audience they lost their nerves and self-consciousness. Even Christopher forgot to feel silly, and swung his skirts with an air. He even managed to drop a graceful curtsey without falling over.

"We ought to do this more often," said Richard afterwards, as they put away their disguises back in the cockpit. "It's all the rage on the Britannia you know – I'm told they're frightfully good." He clapped Hugh on the back as the proud author came in. "No fear of you ever languishing on half-pay," he said. "You can make a living as a playwright any day, I'm sure of it. Why, with you in charge of the writing and myself as actor-manager we'd make our fortunes!"

"Ever the modest Richard!" said Fellowes, behind him, removing his false moustaches with a grin of agony. "Wait till you've tried your luck with a really critical audience! We're easily pleased at sea, remember – no standards of comparison! Especially when it comes to the ladies," he went on smoothly as Christopher, free now of his petticoats, came to join the group. "When you haven't seen a pretty face for weeks and aren't likely to either, it's easy to be satisfied with the next best thing. In fact I doubt if many people even noticed the difference!"

Richard's face was stormy. "Just what do you mean by that?" he demanded. "I imagine you're getting at the young 'un again – not even an able seaman would mistake Lieutenant Welch for his mother not even if he's been at sea for as many years as his own Dutchman!"

Fellowes was all amazement. "I'm not getting at anybody," he said. "I'm all admiration. Who couldn't admire such big blue eyes? So expressive! But a little out of place, don't you think on a warship?"

Richard stepped forward, but Christopher, a hand on his arm, pulled him back. Cold fury filled him. The cockpit was very quiet now; everyone was wondering just what would happen next. They didn't have long to wait. Christopher's voice was steady, but his pulses were racing as he said, "I've had enough of this. From the moment I set foot on board you've disliked me for some reason. You've every right to, I suppose, but I wish I knew why! Nothing I say or do seems to suit you and I'm past caring. I've turned the other cheek long enough. But I'll tell you now that I find you a beastly nuisance and I'll jolly well teach you to behave in future!"

Richard gasped, and a joyous shout of, "A mill! A mill!" went up from some of the mids. Fellowes curled his lip. "In fact, a regular challenge!" he said. "Very well then, I'll answer you in form and I'll meet you when and where you like! Say the word! It's up to you – blue eyes!"

"I'll fight you here and now," said Christopher calmly, taking off his jacket as he spoke. "This quarrel's been boiling long enough. It won't wait any longer."

Richard was trying vainly to keep the peace. "You can't take him on!" he said. "He's bigger than you are and heavier! It won't do, young 'un – it won't do!"

"Why not? The French are bigger and heavier than us, come to that, but if that's a reason for not fighting them what are we doing here anyway?"

"That's not the point!"

"Why not? There's nothing like practice!"

"Oh, for goodness' sake! Why don't you both admit the wait's got on your nerves and forget it?!"

"No! He thinks I'm a baby and I'll jolly well show him I'm not. If I back out now he'll despise me more than ever – and with reason!"

Fellowes had already taken off his shirt. "Come on, if you're ready," he said. "Or have you thought better of it?"

"No, he hasn't," said Richard, "but I'd think better of you if you'd picked on someone your own size – you hero!"

Fellowes flushed angrily. "Let him stand on his own feet for once!" he said. "This was his idea, remember – not mine!"

Richard glanced anxiously at Christopher, who only smiled and shook his head. Richard gave up. "Oh well, come and get it over!" he said. "Take your shoes off, both of you! You don't want to slip about and there's no point in making more row than you must. And you!" He turned to another of the mids. "Just shift that lantern along forrard a bit, will you? Must have fair light for both of 'em. Now then – in you go, young 'un, and may the best man win!"

For a moment the two antagonists moved warily, sizing each other up. Fellowes was a goodish bit taller than Christopher and heavy in proportion, with long arms and legs: but Christopher was quicker on his feet, full of bounce, and full of grievance too. Fellowes had made his dislike plain from the first moment of setting eyes on him – why, he still couldn't imagine – and all the slights and digs he had suffered from him during this past month were boiling up inside him. Carefully they circled each other, poised on tiptoe; and then Fellowes struck out hard with his right arm. But Christopher had seen it coming, ducked under Fellowes' arm, and danced up on one side of him, just out of reach. The uncomfortable thumping of his heart had stopped now that the fight was on – he felt cool and calm, and skipping in close again he hit out at Fellowes first with his left, then with his right, before backing out of range again. But this time the bigger boy was ready for him, and sprang after him, making contact with a swift blow over the ear that made his head sing. He shook it, saw Fellowes standing close and jabbed fiercely at his chin. Fellowes jerked back his head, as a mid whistled with his fingers in his mouth, and both boys backed away panting, glad of a chance to recover their breath. Honours, so far, were even and each approached the other respectfully as the second round began. Again Fellowes clipped Christopher over the head, but he had seen it coming and tipped away in time to lessen the force of the blow: then he swung back and landed a beautiful punch to Fellowes' body which made him back away gasping. When he came in there was an ugly light in his eye. And slippy though Christopher was, this time he wasn't slippy enough, for Fellowes got his head into chancery and pummelled him unmercifully, and all he could do was to thump back in hope of making the other boy release his hold.

When they came up for the third time, each had acquired a healthy respect for the other. Now they were exchanging punches in a lively fashion, and with all the force of his long arm behind it Fellowes hit Christopher fairly and squarely on the nose. He felt it beginning to puff up as the blood spurted and trickled down into his mouth. It tasted quite horrible, but there was nothing much he could do about it. Involuntarily, he tipped his head back; and saw the next one coming just in time. He rode it on his chin, but it made the teeth rattle in his head and perhaps it was lucky for him that the round came to an end just then. "Had enough?" hissed Fellowes as he turned away for the moment's break. "No," he panted, and left it at that. Breath was too precious to waste on talking. Richard was looking anxious, but all he said was, "Keep your temper, young 'un, and watch your chance!" and with that advice fresh in his mind, Christopher waded in again. Some of the spring had gone out of his feet, but he was waiting for the moment when Fellowes would drop his guard for an instant. The moment came. That long right arm came shooting out, but like a fencer parrying a thrust and lunging at the same time Christopher dodged even more swiftly, nipped up inside and hit Fellowes full in the face; then, as his head snapped back, he hit out with his other hand on the point of the chin, and Fellowes went staggering back. His knees buckled, and slowly he sagged to the floor, where he slumped, leaning on his elbow. Christopher's breath was coming painfully now, tearing hotly out of his chest; his knees felt like water, and he leaned thankfully on Richard. But he was up and Fellowes was down and that was enough. Someone thrust a rolled-up handkerchief at him, and he held it gratefully to his swelling nose to staunch the blood still welling out. His nose felt the size of a cannonball; his chest and hands were damp with sweat and he had a headache; but there was a satisfied glow in him that grew still warmer as he looked at Fellowes, sitting on a bench with the skin around his right eye already puffed up and changing colour. It would be a beauty by the morning, he thought contentedly.

"And that's that!" he said to Richard. "I'm going to bed."

"Has your nose stopped bleeding?"

"Yes."

"Sure?"

"Of course I am." The two turned together to the sleeping berth, leaving a confused and noisy crowd behind in the cockpit.

"Your 'blue eyes' sprang a surprise on you, didn't he?" one of the mids was asking Fellowes.

"He did, rather," admitted Fellowes, putting on his shirt again.

"Bit of luck, that!" chimed in a third. "Luck for him, I mean – not you!" he added hastily, as Fellowes' head emerged. His right eye was closing rapidly now; it certainly would be a beauty by the morning.

"It wasn't luck for him, either!" he said.

"You don't mean you're going to take it out on him?"

"No, of course not! It wasn't luck he hit me – he deserved to. Game little fighting-cock, he is!"

They stared at him, and Fellowes laughed. It was a peculiar sound, because his face was tender and it hurt him to open his mouth too wide.

"He's not the child I took him for and I'm glad of it. He's tougher than he looks and that's a good thing for all of us. Where is he, anyway?"

"Gone to bed," they told him.

"Good idea! I think I'll follow his example. Goodnight!" and Fellowes departed to rest his bruised face for a few short hours. The other two looked at each other.

"Well! I wouldn't have believed he could be so generous!" exclaimed one.

"Nor I! Wonder if it'll last?"

"Shouldn't think so – 'twouldn't be natural! Wait till he's brooded on it a bit."

"All the same, it was a grand fight! Long time since we've had any fun like it."

"Fun's over for tonight, anyway. Best go to bed too!"

So the spectators followed the principals' example. Very soon there was no sound to break the silence of the mids' sleeping quarters but an occasional sigh and the constant creaking of the timber frames.

7

The next day, Wednesday, they came up on deck to find a fresh breeze blowing from the west. Still no hope of any action, then. The usual routine went ticking on, and everyone fell in for the daily inspection as usual. The only features to mar the spruce look of the ship's company were young Mr Crown's puffed-up nose, and Mr Midshipman Fellowes' right eye, completely closed and ringed with some very pretty colours, from black through purple to a beautiful dark blue. Lieutenant Scott, seeing these phenomena, held his own counsel, but Captain Britten stopped short when he saw them.

"Our cockpit is well named, it would seem," he said. "No doubt the result of getting into trim, but there is no need for quite so much enthusiasm in practice. Keep something in reserve for the enemy, won't you?" But there was a curl to his lips as he turned away. Once out of earshot, he said to his senior lieutenant, "Does this mean more trouble among the midshipmen?"

"Oh, I don't think so, sir! All this hanging about is enough to try the patience of a saint, and goodness knows these boys don't qualify for that! Besides, it was bound to happen sooner or later."

The Captain cocked an eyebrow.

"Like that, is it? In that case the sooner it's over the better!"

"Why, so I think, sir! and they'll be all the better for it. There's nothing like getting it out of your system."

"As long as they don't make a habit of it!" remarked Captain Britten. "High spirits are one thing, but rowdyism I will not tolerate!"

"Oh, no fear of that, sir! They're a pair of good lads, both of them, in their different ways."

"H'mm. I hope they're both satisfied now. I don't want them sparring up at the sight of each other just now."

As it happened, the two combatants hadn't had to face each other that morning; an embarrassment both were grateful to be spared. They had been seated at breakfast at some distance from each other on the same side of the table and as the morning turned out after all to be a very busy one they were both too much occupied in their own duties to spare a thought for each other. Lord Nelson was by now convinced that Villeneuve would leave his lair at the earliest opportunity, and since not a moment must be lost in unnecessary manoeuvring he had determined to draw his fleet up ready in their columns. Once they had come into line, they would need only to clear for action and advance whenever they should come upon the enemy in a suitable position. And so one by one the ships were signalled to fall into their places, while they had plenty of time to perform the movements and while the enemy was too far distant to see what they were doing. Only those vessels detailed to maintain contact with the watching frigates were left alone. They would take up their positions when at last the French were ready and waiting for them, and so each one of these "link men" had been chosen for its fast sailing qualities. The final battle stations had been appointed in Nonesuch and Christopher was particularly satisfied to see his name among the signals party. Hugh too would be on the quarterdeck as aide-de-camp to Lieutenant Scott, and so would Fellowes, for to his intense pride and delight he was appointed aide to the Captain himself.

Shortly after the daily inspection, Christopher read off the signal from the flagship to form the order of sailing, and everyone sprang up, glad of something fresh to do and even more glad to think that things would probably liven up soon. Like dancers in a cotillion the great ships moved gracefully into their places, and by the time hands were piped to dinner the fleet was poised in two long columns, bowsprit to stern. At the head of each was a proud three-decker, Victory leading one line and Royal Sovereign the other, for she was now the flagship of Vice-Admiral Collingwood. From every ship flew the white ensign of the Commander-in-Chief. Strictly speaking, Collingwood's command should have shown blue flags for he was a Vice-Admiral of the Blue, but the change had been made in order to avoid any confusion. Christopher had been puzzled by this, but the patient Hugh had willingly explained it to him some days earlier.

"What's the difference?" Christopher had asked. "I thought they were both Vice-Admirals? Shouldn't they fly the same flag?"

"Collingwood's one rank below Nelson," said Hugh. "He's what they call a Vice-Admiral of the Blue, while Nelson's a Vice-Admiral of the White. In the old days, you see, there were three different squadrons in the Navy, and each sailed under a different colour – red, white or blue. When you first get your flag – if you ever get that far! – you'll be a Rear-Admiral of the Blue. Then you go up to Rear-Admiral of the White, Rear-Admiral of the Red, Vice-Admiral of the Blue, and so on. If you get to the very top of course you're Admiral of the Fleet, but I don't think you need worry about that; there's only one of them at a time! And if you ever do reach those dizzy heights you'll be pretty ancient by the time you get there because there's a whole lot of people ahead of you. That's how flag-officers move up, you know – dead men's shoes. It's a hideously slow process, except when there's a general promotion for some reason or other."

"I'm surprised anyone gets any higher at all, at that rate!" said Christopher, with feeling.

"Well, it does have one great advantage – you can't be passed over in favour of anyone junior to you!" said Hugh, throwing him a quizzical look.

"I see!" said Christopher. "Yes, I see! That does explain a lot, doesn't it?" He was thoughtful for a moment and then he said, "Well, who's Admiral of the Fleet now?"

This really did stagger Hugh. "You're a complete mystery to me!" he complained. "Here you are, actually sitting in the mids' berth, marching about the quarterdeck half your working day, so keen to join in the Navy you let Richard get you aboard on the flimsiest pretext – and you truly don't know the first thing about us!"

Christopher coloured. "You couldn't always have known these things," he countered. "You had to learn them too some time or other!"

"Yes, I know, but when I joined I did have some kind of notion of what it was all about! I did at least know who was in charge of everything! It's Sir Peter Parker, of course, and between you and me and the mainmast he's a living example of a faulty promotion system!"

"Why so?"

"Because when it was his turn for the job he was already far too old! He's into his eighties now, quite useless for any kind of command, of course – and here's Lord Nelson, who's far and away the finest flag-officer we've got, only a Vice of the White! You can see what a long way he's got to go to get to the top! But there you are! to be the Admiral of the Fleet is just – just a long-service award, when you look at it. Their Lordships wouldn't dream of giving the job to Nelson! He's got the brains and he's got the ability but he's not even fifty yet! Couldn't have a youngster like him ordering everyone about, could you?"

"Ah!" said Christopher. "He's just another young 'un!" and Hugh had to cool down and grin back at him.

"Exactly so! And if you do half as well as he has you'll do all right. Anyway, now you know why Nelson and Collingwood have different coloured flags and while I'm at it I'll tell you something else. You can tell at once what rank of flag-officer is aboard by the way he flies his flag as well as by its colour. Rear-Admirals fly them from the fore, and a full Admiral flies his from the mainmast. All very logical, and so you know at once what to expect!"

"I'm beginning to think," remarked Christopher, "That the Navy's a very logical service in many ways."

"Of course it is! When you're so confined for space, you see, you have to be, or you'd soon get in a frightful muddle. That's logical, too."

Just then, footsteps came down the ladder, and Richard joined them. They both looked up eagerly but he shook his head before either had time to ask a question.

"No!" he said. "No sign of life yet. What a business this is! I almost wish they had slipped away again! At least another chase would give us something else to think about. You should have been with us in the spring," turning to Christopher. "That race across the Atlantic was something like, I can tell you!"

"You don't really mean that," said Hugh gently. "Then we'd no idea where Villeneuve was, and now we've got him cornered. You must cultivate repose, Richard, and patience with it. You'd be much happier!"

"Ah, and a pretty dull dog I'd be, too! Own it! You enjoyed that cruise as much as anyone."

"Yes, I did, but I'd have enjoyed it more if we'd had something to show for it."

"But it wasn't entirely wasted effort," Richard reminded him. "You all say I never think about things but this I do know – because we arrived in time we saved the sugar plantations and because we frightened Villeneuve back home he bolted into his rabbit hole and that's why he's cornered now. There!" he finished triumphantly.

Hugh laughed. "Calm down, old fellow! I didn't mean it that way and you know it! You may be spoiling for a fight but you won't get one with me."

"Tell me about the West Indies," put in Christopher quickly. "What was it like out there?"

"Didn't see much of them," said Richard, restored to himself. "We weren't out there two minutes and didn't set foot on shore. Ours was a quick tour of a couple of islands, then home again!"

"Well, and that's more than plenty of people have done!"

"Oh, true, and I wouldn't have missed it. June 4th it was when we reached Barbados – remember it distinctly. Well, I ought to – it was my birthday! What a whirl everything was in! The Admiral sent word ahead by sloop to say he was coming, we got there late in the afternoon and soon after breakfast next day we were off to Trinidad."

"It was a busy night, too," put in Hugh, "taking in troops and finding room for 'em!"

"Yes, by Jove! And then after dinner we cleared for action – we were as close as that, but that Frenchman's as slippery as an eel. Let's hope and pray he doesn't get through the net this time – I wouldn't put it past him. They told us to get right up against an enemy ship and stay there but you've got to find one first and we never did. There we were sailing all round the islands with the guns ready and no one to fire them at! Might as well have been on a stage-coach as a man-o'war! Take your places on the Highflyer, gentlemen – stops at Barbados, Trinidad, Tobago, Grenada and Antigua! Tickets valid for a return trip!"

Christopher laughed. "Not as bad as that, surely!" he protested.

"Very nearly – no worse! A stage-coach does let you get off occasionally along the way. No but I'd rather be at sea than on land. Beastly stuffy things, coaches. Even standing still at sea is better than being cooped up in one of those things."

"Stylish, isn't he?" remarked Hugh. "Always goes inside, mark you! Wonder he doesn't travel post and be done with it! What's the matter with the outside, sir? Tell me that!"

Richard grinned and ignored him. "Where was I?" he demanded.

"Ports on the waybill to Antigua!"

"Oh ah! That's right! We had a ten days' cruise round the islands and back almost before anyone knew we'd been there; isn't that so?"

"Almost," agreed Hugh, "but we'd done what we needed to do and it was delightful out there, after all."

"I thought you said you didn't see anything of the islands?" said Christopher.

Hugh smiled. "That's not entirely true," he said. "You can't spend days cruising round and see nothing at all, even if you don't go exploring. There was the harbour at Antigua, for instance. It's very secluded, you know – hills all round with fortifications on top of them – splendid defences! They do a lot of refits and so on there. And we had wonderful sunshine and glorious colour all round us. I never saw such green green or such blue blue in all my life."

"That is so," agreed Richard. "Must go back some day and have a good look at it all. The Admiral spent some time there at one stage, you know," he told Christopher.

"Did he? When was that?"

"Twenty-five years ago or so – more! I believe they sent him out to Jamaica when he first got his lieutenant's commission. He got his captaincy out there too so it was a lucky port for hm."

"I wouldn't say that," argued Hugh. "He had a bad go of fever, remember, and had to be sent home again."

"And was that the only other time he'd been to the West Indies?" asked Christopher.

"Oh no! This last game of hide-and-seek was over old territory for him – almost home waters, you might say! He was there again four years later, and had a couple of years' service out there, I believe."

"Yes, but you know, I don't think the West Indies have ever been a lucky spot for Nelson," said Hugh thoughtfully.

"Why not?"

"Well, the first time he was ill, the last time he was hunting for Villeneuve and missed him by a whisker, and things weren't entirely smooth for him on that second tour of duty, or so I've heard!"

"Ah," said Richard, "you're thinking of the Navigation Act! But then the Admiral never shrank from doing his duty, even if it were unpleasant – any more than he will now."

"What did he do? And what was the Navigation Act?" asked Christopher curiously.

"Why, it meant that no one could trade in the Colonies except in our own ships, and since the Americans seceded that meant they weren't allowed. But they came all the same, and Nelson impounded them – quite rightly, though it made him very unpopular with the merchants."

"And that wasn't the only nastiness," added Hugh. "There was also the little matter of the deserter."

"What happened to him?" asked Christopher. A sudden thought of the midshipman whose place he had taken came into his head and he felt unusual interest at this point.

"He was a seaman who cut ship in Antigua," said Richard slowly. "They didn't find him for a couple of weeks and when they did of course they took him prisoner and there was a court martial. The Admiral was in charge of that. Cut-and-dried case, of course, so he was duly sentenced – the seaman, I mean."

"Sentenced?" Christopher said. He had a horrid feeling about the meaning of that – and he was right.

"To death," said Richard. "That was the price of desertion – and this wasn't even in wartime."

"Was he hanged?"

"No; he was lucky. He was saved by the peace and Prince William. The Prince was a captain out there at the time, and because it was peacetime he asked specially that they wouldn't execute the man. Of course the Admiral wouldn't go against the Prince's wishes, and I don't believe he would have wanted to. In time of war of course there'd have been no question of a reprieve – desertion in the face of the enemy, you know – cowardice!"

Christopher was still thinking of Green. He remembered his white face, and his desperate look of a hunted animal.

"You said that death was the sentence for desertion," he said. "Is that what will happen to Green if they ever catch him?"

"Shouldn't be surprised – if they ever catch him. What's so particularly bad about his case is that there is a war on and we were about to sail looking for action – so his going off when he did looks remarkably like cowardice, doesn't it? In fact, it would probably count as treason at a court martial. I don't know, but I fancy it would. In which case –" Richard shrugged his shoulders expressively.

"You know," said Hugh, "I'd really like to know how he managed it."

"Why? Thinking of having a go yourself?"

"What do you take me for?" asked Hugh indignantly. "I'd like to know just as a matter of interest. I mean, there were people about all the time, walking about the decks and so on, and the harbour was crawling with them too – officers going backwards and forwards into the town – you'd have thought somebody would have seen him and asked what he was up to. Perhaps he swam ashore."

"That won't do," said Christopher. "Remember, I saw him and he certainly wasn't wet. Besides, the shantyman was chasing him, so somebody saw him run for it. You said yourself they'd looked for him along the cliffs as well as searching the town!"

Richard nodded. "Yes, that's quite true," he said. "But that was after they found he wasn't aboard when wanted. He must have crowded into the liberty boat when no one was looking. Depend upon it, he's skulking in some back street den in Plymouth! Or else he's far away by now in another part of the country. I say – you've come in for all his clothes and things – was there any money there?"

Christopher shook his head.

"Then that proves it! He must have taken his ready cash with him! He can't have been penniless, even if he did do himself well for tailoring. And even if he had to leave everything else behind he obviously wouldn't get far without any money, would he?"

Christopher shook his head again.

"There you are! I'll say it again – it'll be a good thing for him if they never find him."

Christopher swallowed uncomfortably.

"And if they do?" he asked hesitantly. "Will they really – hang him?"

"I really don't know," said Richard honestly. "It would all depend on the court martial. They might, because of the state of emergency we're in – and then they might not, because he's only a boy, when all's said and done. I just don't know. But either way, he's been an almighty idiot. He's ruined for life of course."

"Perhaps he was simply afraid he'd be killed," said Christopher.

"Then he shouldn't have joined in the first place. What sort of life will he have now? His career's ruined at the start and he daren't show his face anywhere. He'll finish up a highwayman, like as not!"

"And end up being hanged in any case," finished Hugh. "I don't believe he'd be brave enough for the High Toby, anyway. What a morbid conversation this is. Do change the subject, somebody!"

"Right!" cried Richard, "and let's get out of this frowsty hole while we're at it and go and see what's happening."

"Nothing's happening," said Hugh. "They'd have been hollering down the hatchway long ago if it had been."

"I want some fresh air anyway," said Richard. "Might as well do nothing in the open air as down here. You two please yourselves, of course."

"I'm coming," said Christopher.

"Oh well, so am I then!" and all three clambered up the ladder and came up into the daylight. All around them the great ships were floating like immense seabirds on the waves still wrapped in the air of watchful expectancy that had held them for the past week or more. There were men moving about on the decks, alert but not urgent, as there were on Nonesuch herself.

That had been a few days ago. Now the atmosphere was changing. This morning, instead of standing idly at the rail talking with his friends, Christopher was at his place beside the signalman and Nonesuch was in her place too, in one of the two columns of ships ready to sail into action almost at a moment's notice. The fighting machine was ready to go to work. Instead of dreary afternoon, this was wide-awake noonday. The breeze was ruffling through the rigging and gaining strength as it came in from the west. Behind and before them stretched the rest of the column, and over to starboard a similar formation was the rest of the English fleet. All they needed now was opportunity. Would it ever come?

8

When it did come, they could hardly believe it. They had waited so long to no effect that they had come to think that the Combined Fleet had rusted into their moorings and would stay in Cadiz harbour for ever as a memorial to caution and indecision. They did not know that Admiral Villeneuve, with disgrace knocking at his door, had decided to risk everything and rush upon his fate. The threat of being replaced in his command, with the stigma of being unfit to hold it himself, urged him powerfully. If he got out to sea before his replacement arrived he could hardly hand over, could he? He had brooded so long upon his situation that it seemed to him that he had a fair chance of defeating his dreaded enemy. After all, he had more vessels

134

The Battle of the Nile 1st August 1798

to command, and they were in any event bigger. Sheer weight of size and numbers could be sufficient to cross a foe weary of blockade. And he knew so much of Nelson's strategic genius that he even guessed that the Englishman's aim would be to separate the members of his fleet from each other. Villeneuve had seen Nelson in action before. From the rear of the French line at the Battle of the Nile, cut off from the rest of the fleet by the English manoeuvre, he had watched helplessly as the fleet was destroyed and had thought himself lucky to have escaped. So let it be now, and over the sooner! Besides, his honour, no less, was at stake; and Villeneuve was a Frenchman, and touchy on that point. Right or wrong, his mind was at last made up.

It was now a month since Christopher had been swept breathlessly into the adventure; three weeks since Nonesuch has joined the anxious fleet watching and waiting off the Spanish coast. It was Saturday morning, October 19th, and everyone was going through the routine after-breakfast work when, all unknown to them, a sudden scurry of signalling was started by the frigate Sirius, nearest of the fleet to Cadiz. A string of flags went up on her halyards to be relayed from ship to watching ship until the news reached Victory herself, way out on the grey Atlantic. "Enemy have their topsail yards hoisted," ran the glad message. Everyone waited, alert and eager, for more news. They had been teased this way once before; it wouldn't do to be more hopeful. But an hour later it came, sent through the hovering frigates under the command of Captain Blackwood of the Euryalus. From them a tenuous thread stretched to the main fleet – first the Defence, then Agamemnon, then Colossus, and last of all Mars. The wind was now blowing steadily from the east, and with this favourable breeze behind the Combined Fleet there was no reason to doubt the second message – "The enemy are leaving port". For, clear to the keen-eyed Captain Prowse as he stood on the deck of Sirius with his telescope practically glued to his eye, the sails of those alien masts, so long bare to the view, fell smooth and taut from the yards. The harbour fell away behind them as at last, at long, long last the Combined Fleet moved slowly on its way out from Spain, out to sea to meet Lord Nelson. And as each frigate took the message, she set off in the direction of the next, firing guns to attract attention and with those welcome scraps of bunting fluttering importantly in the breeze.

Already, with the wind veering as he had hoped it would, Lord Nelson had formed his fleet into his two columns, so that no time would be lost. Nelson himself headed the line to the north, nearer the wind, while Collingwood was stationed on a parallel course to leeward. The wind was fair, the sun was shining, and far away towards Spain a flutter of flags ran to the masthead of Mars. "No. 370" flashed back from the Victory – "The enemy are leaving port". For the first time Christopher, with his signal book and slate, felt that he was really a part of the Navy. The red and white flag first – this was the new, elastic code. Blue with a yellow saltire – three; white and blue vertical stripes – seven; blue and white slantwise halves – nought. "No. 370. The enemy are leaving port!" he cried, his voice trembling with excitement. Then, almost immediately, a fresh hoist went up from the flagship which cancelled all others, including the invitation to dinner which his lordship had been issuing. This signal was "General Chase" – and with all sails set to trap every puff of wind, the fleet set off to the south-west in order to reach, if possible, the entrance to the Mediterranean before the French did.

One by one the look-out ships between fleet and frigates came speeding up as best they could to take their places in column. It was not easy; that first, fresh early-morning breeze had died away, and the canvas hung sadly overhead. At least things were the same for the enemy, crawling out to sea. If the English had been hampered on their way, so that they were still some twenty-five miles outside Cadiz, the Combined Fleet had been brought almost to a standstill before it had fairly started. Some still clung to their anchors in the harbour and of those which had got outside several were strung out north-west-wards. The long afternoon limped away and still the enemy proved elusive. The shiny promise of the morning too had ebbed, and flecks of white spangled the sky, making the weath-erwise shake their heads and declare that somewhere behind them a great storm was brewing. "Ah well!" said Lieutenant Welch philosophically, "maybe Nature will do the business for us, though I don't suppose that would be so satisfying. Provided she doesn't drown us too while she's at it!"

Richard was full of the fidgets, prowling about like a caged animal until even the mild and tolerant Hugh rounded on him.

"For goodness' sake, if you can't find anything useful to do, sit down and keep quiet!" he said. "I want to write my journal and I can't think straight with you padding about all the time."

"Oh, you and your everlasting journal! I don't know why you bother – who's going to read it, anyway?"

"Somebody might, some day. Don't you realise we're making history?"

"We're jolly well not doing anything at the moment. I think I shall go mad if something doesn't happen soon."

"Meanwhile you're driving everyone else mad instead. I warn you, if you don't exercise a little patience something very exciting will happen sooner than you expect!"

Richard glared at him; then he flopped down on the bench beside him and laughed. "Sorry, old fellow," he said. "Here, let me see what you've written. Then you'll know somebody's shown an interest in it!"

Hugh went pink. "It's not particularly interesting," he said shyly. "I've only been trying to sort out how I feel about things now it's coming to the point. I feel as if I'm a different person, standing outside myself and watching me doing things. It's an odd sort of sensation, when your body's acting on its own. Myself, the real me, isn't doing these things at all. And then, when we do go into action, at last the two pieces that are me will click together again and I'll be a whole person once more. I know – it's happened before."

Richard looked startled. "I say, you are keyed-up!" he said.

"Of course I'm keyed up! We all are. I daresay Lord Nelson's keyed-up, though I don't suppose he's a bundle of nerves about it. But at least he isn't going about making everyone else dizzy."

"I stand rebuked," said Richard meekly, "or rather, I sit. Here, let me see the great work, won't you? I'd like to see how it all strikes somebody else."

Hugh pushed the scribbled sheets towards him, and sat back in silence as his friend started to read.

Wednesday, October 16th.

There is still no sign that the enemy intends to give battle, but it can't be long now. We are lying fifty miles west of Cadiz out of their sight and at present the wind is coming out of the west. If it would only change! The French will never be able to get out comfortably with the wind in their faces even if they want to. Our chief problem has been to keep ourselves supplied. Some of us have already been sent to take in stores. We can only hope they will return in time, for their sakes as well as our own. It would be too bad if they were to be cheated out of their opportunity at the last. I suppose it is just possible that the French will stay snug in harbour all winter but that is hardly likely; and if they do intend to come before the winter weather is upon us then they must come soon. They can't wish to stay in such an uncertain position when the cold weather comes; if they are to escape the storms they must up anchor soon and make for the Mediterranean."

Richard broke off and looked at his friend. "Well!" he exclaimed, "you'll make an admiral yet!"

"Don't make fun of it, please!" begged Hugh. "Remember, it's only me trying to set things down as I see them."

"I'm not making fun. You obviously see the position much more clearly than I do." And he turned back to the diary.

"Lord Nelson must think the time is drawing near, little though we may realise it. This morning we were signalled to form into the line of sailing, which is to be our order for going into battle. This took a little while, but now we are all in our places. We ourselves are towards the rear of the column which has Lord Nelson at its head, but if, as we hope, a general mêlée is achieved during the action, I don't suppose we'll stay there long!"

"Hmmm! and why not, pray?" asked Richard.

"Oh, come! You've been in action before, the same as I have!

You know very well that something must be left to chance. For one thing, the French aren't so many puppets to be pulled about as we fancy. They won't stay in one place all the time and neither shall we."

"That's a point, I suppose. You do brood on things a lot, don't you?"

"I don't know about that. I suppose the difference is that you take things as they come – I don't. I like to know why I'm supposed to be doing something, and what's likely to happen after I've done it."

Richard pulled a face. "What you mean is, I haven't got a sense of responsibility! So many people tell me that in so many different ways I begin to think it must be true," he said ruefully.

"Oh no, no," said Hugh quickly. "That isn't so at all. You're quick enough to see the point of things, and don't pretend you're not! It's just that you're too busy doing things to sit down and think about them. That's why you don't keep a journal – I do!"

"You do indeed!" Richard went on reading.

"The wind is stronger this evening. In fact it's blowing a gale, but still off the sea. Useless – quite useless! We dare not come in closer towards Cadiz, for the shore is right under our lee, and is as rocky a coast as we could wish to avoid. Nor do we dare be blown down to the Straits, and let the French escape into the Atlantic. We must bar their path at all costs, whichever way they choose to run. But tonight they must stay at home while we ride out the gale. We are hove to with our topsails reefed, waiting for the morning."

"I should just think we were, too! You haven't mentioned how I got drenched to the skin, have you? Put it in for posterity, my lad – they might as well know about the discomforts as well as the heroics!"

Hugh giggled. "It was your own fault, you know," he said. "Comes of not keeping your eyes open!"

"Oh, it's always my fault! All the same, you might as well tell the whole story while you're at it." What had happened was that out there in the Atlantic with a strong westerly wind blowing, the seas had been flowing in smoothly and evenly, lifting the ship and letting her down between the waves as if she were an enormous cradle rocked by a watchful grandmother. Until like most old ladies the sea grew a little tired and forgot to keep up that rhythmic rocking motion to which the crew were becoming accustomed. Or was it that the sea intended to keep them on their toes? At any rate, she sent up one great roller, and only one, that smacked up against the rail in a drenching spray that came showering down on Richard, standing with his back to the side and his face upturned to watch the men adjusting the foresail. Up on the creaking yard the men were balancing on the ropes, battling with the heavy, flapping canvas. Richard's anxious eyes were fixed on the man teetering astride the end of the arm, swaying in the rising wind and looking to be swept off his perch at any moment. It said much to the boy's credit that he never moved or exclaimed aloud but stood rigid where he was, intent until the job was done. He had taken the resulting teasing from his companions down below in the happiest fashion, and admitted that he ought to have known better than to stand just there in that sort of weather. "But it wasn't even a thorough-going gale," he protested. "Who'd expect a sea like that just because the wind had freshened up? It was the only one, too – especially for me!"

Now he turned again to Hugh's record.

"Thursday, October 17th.
There has been no change in our position, although the wind has dropped and come round to the northwest. We have been marking time all day, for the enemy still lingers in Cadiz – how monotonous this becomes! – and we pass the time as best we can.
Friday, October 18th.
Even as we slept, the wind has changed. The fates have relented, and it is blowing fairly on a fine morning, straight off the Spanish coast. Pray heaven it will prove strong enough to blow the French clear out of their lair, whether they want it to or not! Things on board are so calm that I feel it must be the lull before the storm, which

cannot break too soon for many of us."

"Hum, you can certainly say that with confidence! The strain is getting to be almost too much for me!"

"Yes, I realised that!"

Richard aimed a friendly kick at him and went on.

"Saturday, October 19th.

All our hopes, it seems are to be crowned. The wind holds fair, the sun is shining, and this morning we had the news from the flagship that the enemy is at last stirring from his sleep. Wearisome though the night may have been for us, they will have been busy on board the frigates. We have had five, together with a schooner and a brig, spread between our advance ships and Cadiz, tacking and wearing patiently backwards and forwards, watching for the least sign of activity. By now it must be so much second nature that I think the ships would perform the manoeuvres by themselves, if only the crews would let them try. The men must be working automatically after so many days of going through the same motions – over the wheel, let go sheets, come into the wind, haul round yards on the other tack, over the wheel – backwards and forwards, backwards and forwards. To them it must seem incredible that at last they should have other work to do and so much of it. Imagine the men racing aloft to pile on canvas and send the message speeding over the waves for fifty long miles to us! It was a splendid feat to get the news to us so quickly, and now the first part of their work is done. We are now sailing south-eastwards, in hopes to come up with the French and cut them off. We expect hourly to be drummed to quarters, but it is doubtful if we shall meet them today, for the wind is dropping and we are making little way. The tension on board is acute...

... and there I interrupted you. Never mind!"

"Oh, I don't! My thoughts were getting too confused to set them down properly, anyway. What a long afternoon this is!"

"Deadly, isn't it? Shan't I be glad when it's over!"

At this moment Fellowes came briskly in. "Gentlemen of

leisure, I see!" he said. "How nice for some of us to have time to spare! Don't let me interrupt, will you?"

"Where's the young 'un?" asked Richard, ignoring this jibe.

"Oh, glued to Mr Kent's side just about. I will say this for him – he's very conscientious. He doesn't intend to miss anything."

"That's the nicest thing you've managed to say about him since he joined!"

"Well, credit where credit's due. I think he's wasting his time, mind. There's no wind at all now and not a sign to be seen of the devils from our masthead though I've nearly squinted myself blind up there!"

"But we can't just do nothing!" cried Richard in anguish.

Fellowes' eyes began to twinkle. "I intend to do something," he said "and that's have my supper."

"But it isn't time!"

"It very nearly is, you know. And what can't be cured must be endured."

"Oh, don't be so beastly trite. You're always saying that. What I really meant was we the fleet, not us personally! What's the fleet going to do – or don't you know?"

"As a matter of fact I do. There's an advance squadron sent out between us and the frigates to make sure we don't lose contact. Captain Duff commands."

"H'mm – that's the Mars – a fast goer. How many others?"

"Seven under him. They're to burn lights all night, of course."

"It'll be a long night, won't it?"

"I'm afraid so. They won't risk a night action – not after the pepper they got at the Nile. There's bad weather on its way, too. But we're taking down some of the bulkheads – just in case!"

They needn't have bothered. The long night slipped uneventfully away, and everyone tipped out of their hammocks to find that the wind had veered again and was blowing from the south. At least that would be against Villeneuve if he tried to make for the Straits! It was a dull and heavy morning, with low massed banks of cloud too dense for the sun to break though. The main part of the Combined Fleet was still battling its way out of harbour and having some trouble in doing so, for the weather was growing steadily rougher. The wind was rapidly gaining strength, there were sudden stinging showers of rain, and heavy seas were running. The hope of the French were putting out to sea in a confused straggle. To add to their troubles the wind had altered and was set fair to blow them straight back again. After all their trouble that would have been too much! Their only hope was to track about and steer for the south with the gale blowing from the starboard side. Hovering on the skyline, the English frigates observed these muddled manoeuvres like keen-eyed owls marking the scuttling of mice along the hedgerows.

On board the English ships, patience was wearing very thin. Stormy weather had come with the morning, and the sheeting rain meant that strain as they might, the saturated lookouts could see only for very short distances. The French must be desperate indeed if they continued to try to sail in this weather; at the very least they might expect a battering from the elements if not from the British. What was more, the English fleet itself was in none too happy a position; they were far too close to the shoals of Cape Trafalgar for comfort, with a strong wind blowing before them and the driving rain drastically reducing their vision.

They had been too eager, and had over-reached themselves. They had reached the spot where they should have met the French sailing southward far in advance of them. Villeneuve was still to the north, trying to get all his vessels out into the open sea. But that advance squadron had proved itself worthy of its trust. The grey day was still young when Lord Nelson had the news from them that the enemy was still to the north of him and still trying to leave port. Quickly the order was passed along to wear ship and head for the northwest, back the way they had come.

The master was passing the word to the intent man at the wheel; "Up helm!" The men on deck were standing ready at the ropes. As the great wheel swung steadily over, the sheets attached to the lower edges of the sails were released, and the wind no longer filled them. The ship was turning, turning, and now the wind was smacking crossly at the edges of the flapping canvas. Still the wheel turned Nonesuch's head round before the wind, and the crisp order came – "Haul!"

The men clinging to the braces pulled together, and the yards swung round. The men on the sheets were pulling too, and as the yards turned the sails drew taut once more and the ship had worn round in her tracks and was heading once more north-westward. The wind now was slanting on her starboard side, screaming up from the south, as she struggled on before the gale. Nothing more could be done until the enemy was sighted, and the ship fell back once more into the usual Sunday morning routine. The hammocks, swathed in canvas to protect them from the driving rain and the drenching spray, were neatly lashed behind the netting. The upper decks had had their daily cleaning, although in such conditions this was a thankless task and would soon need doing again. A piping hot breakfast had been downed, tasteless but warming to the heart and stomach alike after the misery of being out in the open. Captain Britten with his solemn train of attendant lieutenants had inspected the lined-up ship's company, ranged in long rows and tidied up for his approval as if there was no such thing as a Frenchman to be thought of in the whole wide world. But the inspection of the ship was a little more perfunctory. With the rain lashing down in sudden bursts it was hardly possible that the upper works, at least, could be kept spotless between one moment and the next. After that, everyone trooped aft where, shivering on the quarterdeck, they stood lurching with the roll of the ship while divine service was held. Mercifully, the reverend gentle-man felt the discomfort as much as anyone, and kept his congre-gation as short a time as he could. With the wind whipping his surplice and the scurries of rain turning his bands limp, he knelt bare-headed and prayed.

"O God of Battles, our enemy is close at hand. Help us, we beseech Thee, so to conduct ourselves in the conflict that none need blush before his countrymen hereafter. Bless the King's fleet with victory over the opposing forces, that the threat of slavery may be withdrawn from our country and from the world, and that peace may crown our efforts for evermore. Amen."

"Amen," murmured the crew. Then, rising from their knees, they joined lustily in a hymn, before Dr Wells began his brief address. Taking his text from the first book of Samuel, he gazed sternly upon them and said, "And David said to Saul, 'Let no man's heart fail because of him; thy servant will go and fight with the Philistine!'" The Philistine, he reminded them, was the giant Goliath of Gath, of whom everyone was afraid because of his size and his boastful ways. Such a one was Napoleon Bonaparte, who had ridden to power on the back of the great Revolution and sworn to conquer the world. "We have a little word to say about that!" declared Dr Wells. "We are not children to be frightened by a bogey man. We shall go forth into the battle determined and unafraid, for we are not impressed with his conquests. Napoleon has never vanquished an Englishman and God willing never shall! Let his power be never so great, we shall overcome – by courage, determination and faith in the Almighty, as David before us delivered Israel from the might of the Philistines. And now may Almighty God bless us and be with us in the heat of the battle."

A suitable solemnity held the ranks in their places; then the Captain dismissed them and they turned gratefully below decks, where they toasted each other in grog drunk from tin mugs before sitting down to dinner. Everyone fell to heartily, for everyone was damp and cold and no one knew but what it might be his last meal for some time.

"I'll tell you what," said Able Seaman Harris, gulping his thick pea-soup with relish. "I don't suppose Johnny Frenchman's got much appetite for his dinner today if he knows we're creeping up on him!"

"He won't have no dinner," asserted Able Seaman Lewis beside him. "You don't find frogs in salt water. That's why he don't like leaving harbour!"

This jest was greeted with acclaim.

"Poor souls! It's a dreadful thing to have a finicky stomach. Now, mine's as tough as – as tough as this here piece o'pork I'm chewing, I reckon if we put it in that old gun and shot it out it'd tear a hole clean through the Frenchy and come out the other side, it's that heavy."

"Carve your name on it then, and send it with your compliments when we meet him!"

"Too late now – I've swallowed it!"

Able Seaman Lewis was chewing thoughtfully. "I suppose this time we shall have a set-to," he said. "We've been chasing them about so long I get to wondering if they're real."

"They're real enough," Able Seaman Darby assured him. "Though they mayn't be as real when we've finished with them."

"Aye," agreed Harris. "His Lordship seems to be mainly set on sending 'em to the bottom so we're bound to see 'em off. Can't let the little man down, can we?" His rough voice was full of affection.

"Why should we?" demanded Darby. "We never have as I'm aware of. He knows he can trust us, just as we know we can trust him. We wouldn't have got him to the Indies when we did, else."

Lewis chuckled. "Ah, we were one too many for Johnny that time, I reckon," he agreed. "Wonder how he felt when he found we were on his heels?"

"Pretty scared, I should think – he took to 'em again quickly enough."

"Yes," said Darby sorrowfully, "and we never caught him after all. Just wasted effort, that's what it was."

"'Tweren't the Admiral's fault," said Harris quickly. "The luck was against him, that's all, and if Frenchy had half as much in him as he thinks he had he'd have stayed and fought it out like a man then, 'stead of leaving us all this work to do again."

"Can't blame him," said Lewis tolerantly. "No one wants to die before his time after all. We had a pleasure trip and he had a few months extra to his time, so it's probably all turned out for the best."

"You're very certain," said Darby with a grin, "that he won't give us the slip again! And you're very sure we're going to best him!"

Harris grinned back. "Ay, I'm certain sure," he said "and what's more, so are you!"

Darby laughed aloud. "Right you are!" he said. "I'm as sure

of all that as that the sun will rise tomorrow – and the day after that as well. Only wish we could all be sure we'll be here to see it happen."

Harris grunted. "I don't dwell on miseries," he said. "I'm just thinking we'll pepper him twice as bad now to show him what we think of being here 'stead of peacefully at home."

"What d'you mean, home?" asked Lewis. "This is home for you, matey – you got any other?"

"Come to think of it – I haven't!" was the answer. "But we could still be peaceful here if it weren't for Johnny out there." He jerked a vague thumb over his shoulder. "Only let me get at him, that's all I ask!"

"You won't have long to wait," his shipmates reminded him; and then the whistles sounded, dinnertime was over, and the mess had to be cleared away, leaving no more time for chat.

Much the same sentiments were being repeated all over the ship. And although they did not know it, as the hands were piped to their dinners the last stragglers of the Combined Fleet managed to clear the harbour. Now there were only twenty-five miles between the opposing forces, and as the French Admiral thrust his painful way to the west Nelson was coming up as fast as he could to bar the way. In Nonesuch's wardroom the mood was one of suppressed excitement. The captain had invited his officers to share his dinner, and after the covers had been cleared they allowed themselves the brief indulgence of a friendly chat. His Lordship's orders had been so detailed and yet so concise that each one of them knew exactly what would be expected of him and had no need to ask for confirmation. The main responsibility of course rested, as always, with the captain, who would fight his ship as he thought best within the outline laid down for him. But Captain Britten was a supremely confident man. He knew his ship and he knew his men, inside out, as well as he knew himself: and he knew, too, that he could rely on everyone even as Lord Nelson relied on him. Everyone had received his orders and digested them; now they only waited for the moment when they could put them into practice. Sailing in their due place in the column, they would smash their way through the enemy line and if no immediate victim presented herself they would join a colleague in attack. Two to one not fair? No – but neither was revolution and tyranny and there was no room for gentlemanly behaviour in an ungentlemanly war. The order was "smash and destroy". So be it. The only drawback to the plan so far as could be seen was that it would of necessity be some time before the rear ships could get into action, while those in front would have to bear the brunt alone.

"We shall go on with the work of stowing away bulkheads this evening," announced Captain Britten. "We cannot run the risk of being caught unprepared after all this time."

"As you say, sir," said Lieutenant Kent, "but I cannot even now believe that an action is really imminent."

"Why not?"

"I mislike the weather, sir. Things are so rough now that I think it more than likely that the enemy will after all turn and run for shelter."

"Permit me to disagree with you! The very wildness of the weather is an indication to me that the French are determined to get out this time at all costs. Otherwise they would never have made the attempt now, having passed by more favourable chances. I think them far more likely to be sent about by the sight of us than by the weather! We must be careful not to get too close and frighten them away again."

"Do you think they're aiming for the Atlantic, sir?"

"More likely the Mediterranean. I believe we shall soon have news that they are standing for the south and therefore hoping to reach the Straits!"

"This uncertainty is a hideous strain!"

"Certainly, but there's nothing we can do about it. I don't think anything is likely to happen before the morning, for Villeneuve won't risk a night action and we don't want one. This isn't the Nile, after all! This time it is to be a free-for-all; quite hopeless if everyone were to be milling about in the dark."

Lieutenant Yorke chuckled at the younger lieutenant's discontented expression. "You must learn patience and philosophy," he said. "Ten to one you will find the watch below stretched out between the guns and snoring away the time while they can."

"I hope you're not suggesting I snore!"

"Lord no! But sleep's a grand tonic for nerves on the stretch."

Lieutenant Kent sighed. "Mine certainly are! I can't help wishing we'd crowded on canvas and got in sight before now."

Captain Britten shook his head. "I've just said," he pointed out, "that that would have sent them back again. We must possess ourselves in patience until they are well out to sea and too far from port to return to it before we meet them. And the gap between us is narrowing, believe me. Meanwhile, our orders are clear, we know what we have to do, and there is nothing left, I hope, to discuss. Gentlemen, I am now going on deck."

And so the party broke up and the captain mounted to the poop, where he spent the remainder of the afternoon watching the rest of the ships in company and most particularly the Victory. Christopher was having a busy time reading off the many signals that were relayed back from the flagship, and passing them to Lieutenant Kent and so to the captain. The latest message flashed from the frigates was that the enemy were still making their way westward. The fleet held grimly on its course through the dreary afternoon, determined to prevent this at all costs. Quite suddenly, there came a dramatic change. The clouds parted, the sky lightened, and a watery sun was beginning to go down in the west, from which direction the wind was now blowing, having switched with disconcerting suddenness. At this time the fleet was about twenty-five miles southwest of Cadiz. And somewhere just over the skyline, the chaotic bundle of the Combined Fleet, scenting their presence, was frantically trying to form itself into a line of battle instead of the three ragged lines in which it had been limping along. Sailing southwards now, it hoped to evade Nelson's clutch before reaching the Strait of Gibraltar. As darkness fell, lamps were lit throughout the French fleet to guide each ship as she struggled into her place. The English made all safe for the night, but the men on the frigates would not sleep. They would keep unrelenting vigil on those pinpoints of light, making regular signals of their own to mark the enemy's direction. Two blue lights were to be shown at hourly intervals if the southerly course were maintained. If the Combined Fleet turned to sail to the westward, three rapid gunshots would give the alarm.

Now the trap was in a fair way to be laid. As the guiding lights were lit among the French fleet, the English columns brought their vessels round on the starboard tack. The first watch was newly come on deck when the order came to wear ship and sail back to the south, parallel with the French. By now the fleets were a scant ten miles apart. Then, shortly before dawn, Nelson would bring his fleet round again. When dawn broke, they would be in sight of each other, and there would be no escape.

The two fleets, with destiny hanging over both of them, were sailing now in opposite directions with those guiding lights to mark their way. Fifteen miles or so out from the rocky coast of Cape Trafalgar the Combined Fleet was making southwards for the Straits, with Captain Blackwood and his frigates marking their trail. Fifteen miles or so further out into the Atlantic were the ships of the British fleet, heading north. The French were the uncomfortable centre of a sandwich with a dangerous shore under their lee and an eager enemy on the weather side. The blue burning lights and the occasional bang of a signal gun brought them cold comfort, while they warmed the spirits of the British crews. Lord Nelson was as certain now as he had ever been of anything that things would come to a head tomorrow. Bad weather or no bad weather, his enemy had stayed at sea – good! British fleet or no British fleet, his enemy was shuffling southward – better! So first he dogged their steps, and then part of the way through the long black night he turned his fleet again to take an opposite direction; no point in frightening them away at the last moment! Now he was asleep, gaining what strength he could for the coming day, when he and everyone else would draw on every ounce they possessed. The larboard watch had taken over, and were keeping up that slow, steady progress. Again a blue flash lit the night sky, and Able Seaman Harris watched it flare and die away with grim relish.

"Still aiming south, he is," he observed. "More fool him! Does he really think the Admiral will let him go?"

Beside him in the darkness Lewis shrugged. "Must do," he

said shortly. "Wouldn't try, else."

"I don't know, though. Maybe he's just fed up, same as we are, and he wants to get it over with one way or the other. Don't suppose he'll be sorry when it's this time tomorrow." He paused, and added reflectively, "Come to think of it, neither shall I!"

Lewis said nothing. He shivered slightly; but not so slightly that his friend didn't notice it. "What's the matter?" he asked. "Scared?"

Lewis was indignant. "Who me?" he demanded. "Watch your tongue, matey! Chill in the air tonight, that's all."

"'Spose it is a bit nippy," admitted Harris. "Be hot enough below decks, though. Me, I'm glad of some fresh air, I am! Be hot enough tomorrow, too. Let's get it over with, say I! Same as Frenchy does."

"Him? Want to fight? Not him!"

"Course he does! Else why doesn't he run home again?"

"Don't ask me! I say he doesn't want to or he'd have been out long ago, 'stead of keeping us hanging about like this."

"Oh, that's just his nasty spite, that is!"

"And I say not!" Too busy thinking of his own comfort to bother about ours!"

"Not much comfort out there, I don't suppose. He's not living off the fat of the land any more than we are. Less, probably. What I say is, if you're a sailor you ought to be at sea, not skulking in harbour on your behind all day!"

"Well, he isn't in harbour now. He's over there somewhere. We'll be seeing him before long."

"Can't see him too soon for my liking. There goes the flare again!"

In the cockpit, the evening had been peaceful. Everyone ate his supper with a good appetite, and the early preparations for action were welcomed. As bulkheads were taken down and hidden in the holds, to save time tomorrow, relief was uppermost in most minds. To be doing something definite was a help. And Hugh even found a quiet moment to bring his precious diary up-to-date before rolling into his hammock to grab what sleep he could.

"Sunday, October 20th.

Today has been a horrid day all round. We began with every expectation of bringing the issue to a head, but it was not to be. This morning the enemy were still some way to the north of us, and to speak truly, one could not be altogether sorry, for the weather was so wild that I believe an action fought today must have been inconclusive. Heavy seas and squalls would have done nothing to decrease the obvious discomforts of being under fire. We had so misjudged the position of the enemy that we were obliged to retrace our steps to maintain contact, but now we are so close that action tomorrow must be a certainty. We are standing off just a few miles away from them and once more heading south with a fair wind. We are all calm and cheerful, and resolved to bring the day to a fair conclusion. Indeed, I do not believe there is a man aboard who considers the possibility of defeat. If there is one, I have not met him. We are ready and confident.

I expect to be particularly busy, for I shall be in a position to judge what course the battle is taking – should there be time to look around and take stock! Poor Richard is to be below decks in the first instance. I am sorry for him, for he will have little opportunity of seeing how things are going unless he should be sent above during the course of the day. But he insists that his is the better part as he will be on the spot when the guns are fired and can feel himself to be doing something really con-structive. Of one thing I am quite certain – neither of us will fail."

Then, satisfied, he clambered into his cot and slept soundly until the dawn.

9

That Sunday night was the longest and darkest Christopher had ever known. It was also one of the hottest, the sticky, heavy atmosphere in no way lightened by the presence of so many human beings packed into so small a space. Occasionally, those on watch would see the frigates guarding the line of the Combined Fleet washed in the weird light of the blue flares which they sent up to mark the enemy position. Still the fighting ships sailed steadily on, and every sound was magnified in Christopher's sleepless ears – the creaking in the yards, the dull flapping of the sails and perhaps a sudden snore from one of his companions, would set his nerves on the stretch.

He tossed restlessly until, longing for human contact in the darkness, and thinking he heard a movement from Richard, he whispered his friend's name.

"What is it?" came the drowsy answer.

"I can't get to sleep."

"Then you'd better go on trying. We've a heavy day ahead."

"That's why I can't get to sleep."

Richard was wide awake now and fully aware of what was going on in Christopher's head. He had been at sea long enough himself to know what might lie in store for either or both of them, but he came of a naval family and both by conditioning and by training he had learnt to discount fears for his personal safety in the interest of his duty – and indeed to "hate a Frenchman as he would the devil." Beating the enemy was what mattered most in the world! Richard was frank and fearless, but he did not lack imagination; all the same, he would not or could not, spend time fearing what might happen. He preferred to think about what was happening. And there was no room for gloomy thoughts when his chances of survival were at least equal, bringing with them the prospect of early promotion, not to mention a share of prize-money. Besides, it would be something of a lark to boast of having been in such an action! Christopher was different. He was younger, softer, unused to danger, thrust into the adventure by the scruff of the neck altogether unprepared. What was more, he was Richard's own find and protégé and must be helped to do him credit. He didn't lack courage, Richard knew that; but no one could tell what the impact of a full-scale battle would be on him. Richard set himself to the task of reassurance.

"You're not worried about this battle, are you, young 'un?" he asked.

"I can't help it," said Christopher apologetically. "I know I shouldn't, but you know I've never been in battle before and I can't help wondering…"

"There'll be nothing to it," said Richard bracingly. "You know what will happen as well as I do. We sail in among 'em, pour in a broadside or two – and then home with Johnny Frenchman in tow – what's left of him!"

"We are going to win – aren't we?" asked Christopher anxiously. "It sounds simple enough, but I can't help thinking your Johnny Frenchman will pour in a broadside or two on his own account!"

"Oh, he's bound to do that! But he won't be a match for our boys, you wait and see!"

"I'm not afraid of the fight – at least, not much – I think – but I am afraid of making an ass of myself."

"Why should you? You've only got to do as you're told – straight away – and do it properly. Nothing difficult about that surely?"

"No-o, I suppose not. Only I might get muddled."

"No you won't! You've come through one battle against the odds already – this will be just the same, you'll see. Only on a larger scale, that's all – and this time there'll be several hundred of us in it. All friends together! Makes a world of difference!"

"Yes I s'pose it does. All the same – it's a pretty terrific prospect, isn't it?"

"Look," said Richard, more seriously than Christopher had ever heard him speak. "Of course it's terrific. But so is anything that's really worth doing at all. If it weren't terrific there wouldn't be any point. Surely you've seen enough and heard enough now to know that the most important thing for us and a whole lot of other people is putting this fellow Bonaparte in his place? Not just for ourselves but for all the people back home, and all the people he's conquered, and a whole heap of people who haven't even been born yet. Life won't be much fun for them if they come into a world that's under one man's rule. Just imagine it! And I think if only Napoleon can be put down, then people a hundred years from now will be thankful to those that did it. I truly do."

"But we can't hope to do all that tomorrow – just us!"

"No – but every little helps! Doesn't it?"

"I shall be a very little, I'm afraid," said Christopher ruefully.

"That doesn't matter! Remember that thing you said yourself about the horseshoe-nail? Think of yourself that way, if you like – just remember you're terribly important and what you do is terribly important and everybody's counting on you! That goes for me, too; and Hugh, and my uncle, and the gun-captains and the powder-monkeys and – and everybody! And after we've all of us done our little bits we'll talk it all over in the evening! Of course, it may take us a little while to pull the thing off, but then, we've got Nelson up there in front and they haven't – that puts us on top before we've started, now doesn't it? And I'll tell you what – he'll be sleeping sweetly tonight to be in fighting trim tomorrow, so suppose you try again and let me drop off too, eh? There's not too much time left for sleeping as it is."

"All right," said Christopher. "I'm sorry if I was a nuisance, but that's your own fault, you know. You got me into this. Goodnight!"

There was no reply. Richard was already asleep. Christopher sighed, envying his friend his lightness of heart, but nonetheless he did feel strangely comforted, and even managed to fall into a fitful sleep in which dreams of horseshoes, admirals and cannonballs jostled one another higgledy-piggledy.

The long dark hours passed. As the eastern sky lightened to grey the pipes sounded, and in a trice hammocks were being lashed and stowed in the netting as a cushion against shot. The dawn of Monday, October 21st, 1805, had broken to a beautiful morning with the sea calm in the sunshine. With daylight, confidence returned, and the sight of everyone going about his business in so matter-of-fact a fashion pushed fear into the background. The fleet had already received Lord Nelson's first orders of the day, and was forming into the appointed battle order of two columns, steering eastwards now. The signal "Prepare for Battle!" had been received, and the screeching of the pipes following the call "Clear for Action!" had set every man on board racing to prepare the decks and himself for the occasion.

At the head of the northern line sailed Nelson himself in his flagship Victory, and a mile away to starboard Collingwood, flying his flag in Royal Sovereign, was making for the enemy's van. There had been other signals, too. As well as tightening the columns now that the enemy was well within sight, Lord Nelson had another subtle manoeuvre to make to get that enemy exactly where he wanted him. He must keep the wind behind him to help his own movements; he must cut off the French from any hope of running back into harbour before he caught up with them; and he must keep them wondering until the very last minute just where he would deliver his attack, when it would be too late, he hoped, for them to do anything about it. And so, early on this lovely autumn morning, the windward column was set to sail tight up towards the enemy, to cut them off. Then came, at last, "Prepare for Battle" – that signal which had set Nonesuch so busy as the whistles screeched. The work of clearing the decks had hardly begun before another change of direction was ordered, and the helm was put over as the ship swung slowly round to starboard, until she was heading eastward. It now seemed to outward view that the column was sailing for the enemy's rear; the lee division was heading, it appeared, for the van; and anyone might have been forgiven for assuming that as the two converged they would form themselves into the conventional line, side by side as they faced their enemy. The enemy themselves still had to get sorted out after their muddled night.

Down on the main deck, Lieutenant Scott was busy sending parties of seamen to dismantle the bulkheads and to remove everything – and he meant everything! – down into the hold that could possibly be shifted. The captain's elegant furniture was taken down the ladders to the bottom of the ship – table, chairs, desk, books, everything. The long wardroom table joined the other furniture, as well as the chairs that usually stood along its sides. The plainer furniture of the lower deck went as well. The benches went below, and the tables were unhooked from the ceiling timbers. In fact, everything that could possibly get in the way was put out of sight and every movable wooden article which could possibly send out a murderous splinter was put safely out of harm's way. Anyone might have supposed that the men would slip on the ladders with their burdens and go crashing to the bottom; but long practice up aloft in all weathers had made them as surefooted as cats and they never did. And when the tedious work had been completed, far more quickly and neatly than Christopher would have supposed possible, the decks were bare as they had come from the shipwrights' hands, and only the guns remained. Now they had come into their own and everything else had given place to them.

Big and bare on the empty decks, they stood solitary and threatening. The gun crews themselves were already at work. They had let down the heavy curtains which would be soaked with water to act as fire screens, and round about each gun were stood the casks of water which held the slow tapers. These were stuck through holes in the top, and if the flintlock of the gun failed it would be easy for the men to use one of these tapers to kindle the powder. There were smaller tubs too, for drinking water, for manning the guns in a close sea action was hot and thirsty work. Others again were to clean the sponges, which in their turn were used to clean out the guns. At the third gun on the starboard side of the main deck, Able Seaman Darby was already a very busy man. He was captain of that particular team, and he had to make sure that his gun would be quite ready whenever it should be needed. Carefully he looked to see that everything was in its place. Then he tested the heavy, strong rope which tied the gun to the ship, so that when the shock of its own firing sent it rolling backwards it wouldn't go further than it should and he tested too the other ropes which would pull the gun back to the open port to be fired again. The rest of the team were busy fetching up supplies of shot, and setting them to hand in their racks. Seaman Harris paused to wipe away the sweat which was already running down his face. "I'm mortal hungry," he grumbled. "I hope Frenchy gives us time to have breakfast before they douse the fires. I could eat a horse, so I could!"

His friends laughed. "There he goes, always thinking of his stomach!" cried Lewis. "Eat a horse, he says. We haven't come down to that yet, lad."

"Not quite," agreed Harris. "Though I sometimes wonder. So I enjoy my vittles – that's all! There's a deal of me to keep going, there is!"

This raised another laugh against Lewis, who was a little man, and Harris went on, "I've known my innards a long time now and I like to look after 'em. Don't believe in letting down old friends." He disappeared and came back shortly with another armful of shot. "There!" he said. "Frenchy'll feel the weight o' that more than I do and that's my comfort." He was interrupted by a shrilling from the hatchway. "There!" he cried. "Here comes breakfast and my old friends and I don't care how soon we come upon 'em afterwards! Off you go!" and away went Peters to the galley forward to collect their breakfast. Today they ate their rations sitting picnic-fashion on the bare planking between the guns; porridge, biscuits and bitter coffee. The talk went on cheerfully, and Christopher would have been amazed to hear the laughter of Peters, whose back still showed the angry red scars of the lash, as he talked with the rest of his mess beside the gun. For Peters was his proper self today, sober as the next man; and Peters lived each moment as it came. For him, the past was past and the future took care of itself. He hadn't forgotten his punishment and would take care not to bring it on himself again if he could help it. But it had happened, and was over, and he wouldn't trouble about it again; certainly not now of all times, when there were more pressing problems. Besides, today's problems were ones he could share, and would share, with the messmates who had welcomed him back from the sick bay without comment. He had been shy of meeting them again afterwards, but they never mentioned it, and he was grateful. So now the morning meal was as usual as it could be on this unusual morning. After all, it was a beautiful day with calm waters, a gentle breeze, and the sun rising in the sky; a good-to-be-alive kind of morning. So Peters was glad to be alive with the rest of them, friends and shipmates as they were. He sighed contentedly as he pushed away his empty plate and drained the last of the warm wet brew. Harris glanced at him and grinned.

"Make the most of it," he advised him. "The Lord only knows

when we'll get another chance."

"If we get another chance," put in Lewis gloomily.

"Ah, why shouldn't we? You don't think Frenchy can shoot straight enough to kill us all, do you? You've as much chance as all of us of seeing the end of the day and Johnny to boot. Cheer up, man!"

"Well, but somebody's bound to be damaged," his friend pointed out.

"And why anyone more than the next man? I don't mean to get my head knocked off, I can tell you! I'll be here tomorrow chewing another breakfast as bad as this one, you see if I'm not!"

"You're pretty sure of it, aren't you?" commented Darby.

"Ah, I look at it this way, you see. If we come through the day all's well, and if we don't it won't matter, so why worry? I don't."

"Nor I," said Peters. "Today's just a day like any other day only we're going to fight a battle in it. And tomorrow's just like any other day too, only there won't be any blessed battle in it, same as yesterday. That's all there is to it, just about, I reckon."

"Anyway," said Darby, "it'll make a change from sitting about on our behinds half the day and that's something."

He was interrupted by more shrilling from the bosun's whistles.

"You can get off your behind now!" said Harris with a chuckle. "Time's up! Wonder what time we'll get dinner?" and the big man went back to work grinning, with the jeers of his mates following him.

Other people too had been making the most of their opportunity for stoking up. Breakfast-time in the cockpit was merry – more merry than usual. It was more, thought Christopher, like a holiday than what might turn out to be the grimmest day in all their lives, and he could not entirely banish his night fears despite the reassurance of sunlight and cheerful company. He was glad to find Richard at his side, very dapper and trim in honour of the occasion.

"You've got your best stockings on!" he exclaimed in surprise, as he took in the full glory of his friend's costume.

"Oh lord yes," said Richard unconcernedly. "They say one shouldn't wear boots in a battle because if you get hit in the leg it makes things so much more difficult for the surgeons; and I've had to put on my best because I can't find my others anywhere. I only hope I don't get hit! I should hate to have these ruined. They cost a pretty penny, I can tell you! What are you laughing at? It isn't funny, you know!"

"I know it isn't," gasped Christopher as well as he could for laughing. "I was only thinking that I'm worrying about you being ruined – and you're only thinking of your stockings!"

"Oh, I shan't be ruined, never fear! I've got a hide like a rhinoceros and a constitution to match. I'm more likely at this moment to die of hunger, so let me get at that delicious breakfast. What have we got? Burgoo again, and who'd have thought it? Any livestock this morning?"

"Here you are, then," said Christopher, "and no taking more than your fair share, mind!"

"Well, make it a biggish share, will you? I'm hungry as a hunter."

"Fair enough," smiled Hugh. "That's what we all are, after all."

Richard stared blankly for a second, then let out one of his sudden cracks of laughter. "So we are!" he cried. "Tallyho forrard! They're a foxy lot after all – the French – aren't they?"

"So they say," nodded Hugh. "I couldn't tell you – I never met any. Did you?"

"No, and I don't particularly want to – socially speaking, that is. Can't wait for this kind of meeting though!"

"But you have waited – for months. Another hour or so won't matter. Hurry up and get outside that breakfast!"

"Well, let's hope they aren't too foxy," observed Richard, with his mouth full. "If they manage to give us the slip this time I shall burst with – something or other."

"No fear of that. We've got his earth stopped this time, and he'll have to stand and make a fight for it. And it'll be the last time for quite a while, so make the most of it!"

"You sound very certain," said Christopher.

"Of course I am! I trust the Admiral!" said Hugh. "He says he'll pull the thing off, and if he says so, it's as good as done."

"Do you have so much faith in him?" asked Christopher,

wonderingly.

"One must, you know; that's the way to win battles, and we're jolly well going to win this one. We've got to, you see."

"You know him better than I do," said Christopher, "so if you say so, I'll believe you."

"Jolly decent of you," said Richard, gulping coffee. "Is there any more of this going?"

"Just about, but that's the last lot you'll get. Leave some for the rest of us won't you?"

"There's plenty! I don't want all that much."

"Not much you don't! Anybody'd think this was the last meal you were getting."

"Not it! I don't intend to come to grief! But it might be the last for a goodish while! Be too busy for any dinner, I daresay. How about you?" He pushed the pot along.

"No thanks, I've had enough. Time's getting short and I've one or two things I want to do. See you later."

"Much later, most like!" grinned Richard. "Hang on a minute, young 'un; I've nearly finished."

"You'll have to hurry up then. Mr Campbell wants the cockpit cleared," said Fellowes, passing behind him.

"Already? Yes I suppose so," and Richard tore himself away from his breakfast and rose to meet the day's work feeling satisfactorily full.

Now all the bulkheads of the cabins had been stripped away and the long decks stretched clear from end to end. The furniture had all been stowed down in the holds and only the guns remained – hideous, black and brooding – with a line of leather buckets filled with water standing along the centre of the decks for fire-fighting purposes. There were men everywhere, swarming like ants; some grim faced and earnest, some laughing, but all swift in their movements as they set about their business. The firing parties were making as quickly as they could for their places beside the guns, and the Gunner's store was a hive of activity as the smaller weapons were put out ready for the boarding parties to collect before going to battle stations. Others were spreading sand thickly over the wooden decks. Richard was explaining to Christopher that this was to give firm foothold, when a familiar chuckle warned them of Fellowes' approach.

"Don't forget the blood," he said, "or don't you want to frighten him? Blood's sticky stuff," he went on kindly, turning to Christopher, "and there's apt to be a lot of it about in a battle, so they put plenty of sand down to soak it up. I hope the sight of it doesn't turn you faint? Captain Britten doesn't approve of squeamishness."

Richard flushed angrily, but Christopher answered quietly, though his inside seemed gently to have slipped its moorings and vanished, leaving an aching space where it should have been.

"You ought to know I don't mind it, of all people," he said. "The captain won't be ashamed of me. I must go," he added, turning calmly away. "I'll be wanted on deck, and I mustn't be late."

The two friends gripped hands for a moment, and Richard laid a hand on the younger boy's shoulder.

"Goodbye for the present, young 'un – and good luck!" he said. Then he too turned and moved away though the crowd, while Christopher mounted the ladder.

Fellowes was left scowling and discomfited, but his words had not entirely missed their mark. For all his determination not to disgrace himself, Christopher's ready imagination had been stirred by those unkind remarks. Of course, it was impossible that no one should get hurt, but somehow the sight of the sand and the thought of its significance had brought it all nearer to him even than the hot darkness of that interminable night. He shook himself, told himself that Fellowes' spite wasn't worth his notice, and came up into the sunlight into a scene of activity every bit as busy as that below. The red-coated Marines were gathering up here, and the burly figure of Mr Bull could be seen superintending the safeguarding of the sails. The yards, should they be shot away and fall upon the decks, could do more damage even than the enemy fire with the sudden impact of their great weight, and heavy chains were added to the ropes in an attempt to keep the timbers in place. Spare sails and ropes were laid ready to hand, and already the grappling irons were hanging in position to snatch at any

Frenchman who might sail within reach. The top decks too had been cleared of all unnecessary bit and pieces, and the masts were festooned with nets to catch the flying splinters of wood which were to be feared as much as the cannonballs themselves.

As quickly as he could, Christopher pushed his way through the throng to his station on the deck. The signal lieutenant greeted him with a brief nod and a slight smile, and he took his place beside the officer with an answering grin.

In the middle of all the bustle, Richard had come upon his uncle, his mouth set and his tread firm as he crossed the deck. Richard expected him to pass by in the usual way, but his uncle laid a hand on his shoulder and drew him aside. "Go straight to my cabin," he said seriously. "There is something I have to say to you. It won't take long; you can be spared until I have said it. I shan't keep you waiting." Mystified, Richard obeyed, and made his way aft, where Captain Britten soon followed him.

"I want to speak with you a moment, Richard," he began. "Not as your captain, but as your uncle. In case I never get the chance again," he added, with the ghost of a smile.

"Don't say that, sir!" Richard cried. "We'll both come through this like all the other scraps!"

His uncle looked at him steadily.

"I'm sure I hope so," he said soberly. "But anything can happen in any kind of a scrap, as you put it, and I believe that this will be like no other fight we have ever had before. Certainly I have every intention of celebrating a victory, but that shall be as God wills! Just in case, then, I want to say to you as your officer that I have every confidence that your conduct in action will be as praiseworthy as I have tried to train it to be; and as your uncle, I want to beg you not to do anything foolhardy. Do, please, think first of the consequences of anything you may do!"

Richard gave a laugh that broke in the middle. "There may not be time for that, sir!"

"You may not think so," returned his uncle, "but in fact there is always more time than you realise. I know how you idolise the Admiral – please try to remember that however impulsive his actions seem there is always sound reasoning behind them!" He paused and then went on. "You are still young and more than a little impetuous! I should hate to think that your parents could ever blame me for any accident that might befall you. You are in a sort in my charge, although I try not to let that influence me where the running of my ship is concerned. I do ask you, most earnestly, not to run your head into any danger."

Richard flushed proudly. "My parents," he said stiffly, "would never wish me to forfeit my honour, danger or no danger. I shall not hide away, sir, if that is what you are asking."

His uncle's gaze softened a little. "Am I likely to?" he demanded. "Of course you must do what you have to do; no question! But for heaven's sake don't get carried away, in any sense of the phrase!" He looked steadily into his nephew's eyes. "There!" he said. "I've said all I wanted to on that head. Now go to your station, and – God bless you!"

Unexpected tears brimmed suddenly in Richard's eyes. He shook them angrily away and seized his uncle's outstretched hand. "You are too kind to me, sir!" he said gruffly. "I understand. And – God bless you too!" he added shyly. He turned quickly and walked firmly off. Captain Britten followed, watching the boy as he turned and went down the ladder. The strained look had gone from his eyes as he mounted the poop, and there was a slight curl to his fine mouth. Even naval captains are human.

Meanwhile, the studious Hugh had been writing a careful letter home.

"My honoured parents," he began, "and dear sisters, the time has come at last! We are all tired of waiting and glad that the enemy is now in sight. It is a beautiful morning, and their fleet is drawn up a few miles off the leeward. Our only worry is that with so slight a breeze behind us it may be some time before we can get at them!

They left harbour the day before yesterday, and as we followed them we had far less clement weather. Today, it is as if Heaven had sent the sun to smile upon our enterprise. Instead, we can only be surprised and thankful that yesterday's squalls did not send them scuttling back to harbour.

I have no time to write at length. We are even now clearing for action. I commend my soul to God and if He wills shall return triumphantly to embrace you all with thanksgiving. If not, may you have cause to remember with pride your devoted son and brother, Hugh."

He folded his letter neatly, addressed it, and laid it carefully in his chest on top of everything else, so that it might be seen the first thing when the lid was raised. Then he straightened himself, and trotted off quietly to his station as aide to Lieutenant Scott. Hugh was always most attentive to details.

He reached the quarterdeck, to find that Nonesuch was now sailing steadily eastwards towards the distant spread of sail which was the Combined Fleet. While Richard had been stuffing himself as far as possible, the French had begun a manoeuvre which made it look at first as if the cup would be dashed from English lips at the last moment. Straining through their glasses, the lookouts of the leading ships had seen the enemy turn simultaneously round and present their sterns to the English. They did not stop in this inviting position but went on swinging until their bows faced not southward but to the north. Now the last led the way and the first was last; the French admiral, thinking better of it at the last moment, was making a bid for home. Too late! Hugh had been right, and the bolthole was stopped. Still, this could be awkward. He saw that Lieutenant Scott's jaw had tightened, and ventured to ask why.

"I hope," the officer answered, "that the French will think better of their present northward course. It won't do to be forced so close to a lee shore with a gale brewing; particularly such a rocky coast as this. Far better to be blown through the Straits! Put your trust in God for tonight, my boy."

Hugh was surprised, for the sun was glinting on the calm sea, and the breeze was so slight that it scarcely fanned his cheek.

"A gale, sir?" he asked. "Are you sure?"

The lieutenant looked at him soberly. Then he smiled.

"Oh yes, I'm sure," he said, "and when you've been at sea a little longer you'll be a little more weatherwise, too. Have you never heard of the calm before the storm? Take no notice of the lack of wind, but heed the swell astern! It's too large and smooth by half, believe me! And the clouds are in tatters, too, when you can spare a moment to look at them. At this present moment I can't, and neither can you! Cut along to Lieutenant Yorke on the main deck and ask him if he has everything he needs!" Hugh sprinted off, glad of a definite order.

He pushed through the men milling about on the main deck, until he found the lieutenant. Lieutenant Yorke had paused beside the third gun on the starboard side to speak to Able Seaman Darby running an experienced eye over the gun, which was now ready to receive the first charge. Hugh waited until the lieutenant had finished what he was saying, then saluted smartly, and delivered his message.

"All's ready here!" came the reply. "All we want now is the order to start work – isn't that so, Darby?"

The gun captain grinned and nodded. He had stripped off his shirt, and tied a black cloth round his head, over his ears. So had most of the others busy about the guns, for these would help to deaden the crash of the firing and keep the sweat out of their eyes when they were too busy to wipe it away. "Ready when you are, sir!" he said, and Hugh was dismissed aloft. Up there, he found the sun still shining, the sea still sparkling, and the masts of the enemy fleet growing taller and nearer as Nonesuch sailed to meet them. The captain and the first lieutenant were deep in conversation, with Fellowes standing a little behind them. Fellowes turned and nodded as Hugh came up. He was never touchy with this quiet and studious boy. Now he smiled encouragingly at him.

"All right?" he asked, and Hugh smiled back and answered, "Right as can be; but the waiting is worse than anything!"

"To tell the truth – and I wouldn't say it to anyone else – I feel the same way! But I don't think we'll have to wait much longer."

As he spoke, Captain Britten lowered his telescope, through which he had been watching the advance of the ships ahead of them, and said quietly, "I think, Mr Scott, the men might take up their quarters now."

The lieutenant's eyebrow flickered, and he walked quietly off to where the bosun was supervising a group of men stringing nets to catch flying splinters. "Mr Bull!" he called, in the clear voice which he seldom needed to raise, "Send hands to quarters!" Then he turned and called to the waiting drummer, "Beat now to quarter! All hands to quarters!"

Immediately, the sticks began to beat a stirring rhythm on the tightly stretched parchment of the drum, and almost as quickly the high whistling of the pipes began. "Hands to quarters! Hands to quarters!"

Along the deck marched the drummer, pausing at the hatchways so that the call to arms should sound right down to the lowest decks.

"Hands to quarters! Hands to quarters!"

There was a stirring in Christopher's blood as the beat of his pulses echoed the thumping of the drum. For the first time this morning he felt a real battle-lust; just as he had the other evening, when Fellowes had goaded him once too often. He thought of those masts peeping over the skyline and thought of all they stood for; he looked aloft at the red, white and blue of the Union Jack fluttering from the fore and maintops, and his heart filled with pride and determination.

"Hands to quarters! Hands to quarters!"

The pipes were screeching down the hatches, for good measure.

"Hands to quarters! Hands to quarters!"

It was an exhilarating and awful moment. And if the ship had been busy before, it was now a scene of controlled frenzy as the men ceased their early preparations and ran to their battle stations.

"Hands to quarters! Hands to quarters! Look alive there! Hands to quarters!"

Long before it would have seemed possible for a man to fight his way through the crush to his own place, the gun crews were standing ready at their stations, and some of them had found time to collect the small arms with which they would take part in – or fight off – the boarding parties. The medical orderlies were standing by in the cockpit. The marines were swarming up aft. Those who were to help in passing supplies of ammunition were already at the magazines. And the guns were taking up their positions, too. There was an unaccustomed, dazzling light streaming across the main and lower decks as slowly the heavy port lids were raised on their ropes. Lieutenant Yorke and Lieutenant Welch, calling through speaking trumpets so that their voice carried the length of the decks above the squealing of tackles, the shuffling of feet and the creaking of the port hinges, shouted to the men to load the waiting guns. At the third gun on the starboard side on the main deck, Peters took the charge from the waiting boy who had brought it from the magazine stores and passed it quickly to Harris. Harris, standing by the cannon's mouth placed it inside the hungry muzzle, and Lewis rammed it well down. After that he pressed in the wadding, and then the shot itself was pushed in tightly. "Run out!" came the order, and before the words were fairly out of the lieutenant's mouth, there was a rumbling like an almighty thunderstorm as the crews hauled at the heavy ropes and the guns rolled forward through the open ports. Darby took his priming wire from his leather belt and probed it through the cover of the charge. The powder was poured in, and all was ready, waiting for the word. The crew sat philosophically down upon the planking, to wait.

"And that's that!" said Able Seaman Darby, easing himself into a more comfortable position. "Time to flex our muscles, boys, so let's make the most of it!"

Able Seaman Harris grunted. "This is the worst part," he muttered. "Here we are, all ready to go and got to hold back – shocking!"

"Not even in range yet," Peters pointed out. "And this ain't going to be a long-distance match. Close action; that's the way it's to be."

"Ah," agreed Lewis. "Look at it this way. The longer you wait to get into a fight, the keener you are when you get there!"

"That's so," agreed Harris, brightening up, "but it's a mortal long wait. Can't even have a bit of a game to pass the time!"

Darby was scandalized. "Cards!" he said, shocked. "Here we are with the eyes of the nation on us, and all you think of's playing cards!" He shook his head reprovingly.

"Eyes of the nation be damned," said Harris tartly. "They don't know where we are or what we're doing and they won't know either for days yet – weeks!"

"That's not their fault. They'll be pleased to know we've licked Johnny Frenchman for them – bound to be!"

"We've not licked them yet," said Lewis.

"Only a matter of time," Darby maintained. "Here we are and there they are and that'll be it, no help for it. My stars, these planks are hard. Won't be sorry to stand up for a bit."

"Why don't you stand up now then?" asked Peters reasonably.

"Because I'll be on my feet for hours belike and I'm going to rest 'em well beforehand!" came the unanswerable reply.

Lieutenant Scott, with Hugh trotting obediently at his heels, had been making a swift survey of the ship. Now he was mounting again to the quarterdeck, where Captain Britten stood tautly waiting for him. "All hands at quarters, sir." He reported. "The ship is fully prepared for action."

The captain's tall frame seemed to relax slightly. "That's well, Mr Scott," he said. "Nothing to do now but wait for it. What a beautiful day this is! It almost seems a shame to spoil it!"

Now that there was work for him to do, the empty feeling in the pit of Christopher's stomach had gone. He stood, tense but eager, with his pistol in his belt and the signal book in his hand, ready to read off the Admiral's instructions as they were relayed from the ships ahead of them in the line. "Prepare to anchor after the close of the day," he said firmly. Captain Britten nodded. The ominous groundswell was giving warning of a different enemy to engage before nightfall.

But first things first! Standing at his station on deck, Christopher thought that he never had, nor ever would see again, a sight at once so beautiful and so relentless. Ahead in a great crescent the enemy ships were waiting, a forest of canvas and timber. No fewer than six flagships were dispersed along the great curve of their battle-line. In the middle the French commander-in-chief, Villeneuve, was waiting in the Bucentaure. Immediately ahead of him was Rear-Admiral Cisneros in the tremendous Santissima Trinidad. Also near the centre and in Collingwood's way was the Spaniard Alava, in the huge Santa Ana of a hundred and twenty guns. To the rear of him was Rear-Admiral Magon in the Algéciras. To the south the rear was guarded by the Principe de Asturias under Admiral Gravina, while the same position among the northernmost ships was occupied by Dumanoir, heading his squadron in the Formidable. From the leading British ships it was now possible to see the Tricolour flying from the French mastheads, and the red and yellow Spanish flag from those of their allies. The Spanish ships also displayed large wooden crosses, asking a blessing on their cause. The Santa Ana carried as figurehead an immense carving of the Virgin, and the enormous Santissima Trinidad, which had no fewer than four decks, made the bravest show of all, brilliant with red and white paintwork and with her figurehead of the Holy Trinity sparkling in the sunshine.

"I wonder," mused Christopher, "what they're thinking, watching us. I wonder how they feel!"

"Much the same as we do," answered the lieutenant. "They're men like us, and they believe they're in the right of it. Some will be afraid, some will be confident, most of them determined to win because they know that this time it's death or glory. I suppose it's even possible they might win, but that's not very likely!"

"Why not?" asked Christopher, hopefully.

"Wrong place – wrong man!" was all the reply he got.

They could not know that at least one of the enemy captains fully agreed. From the quarterdeck of the southernmost ship, the San Juan Nepomuceno, Commodore Churucca declared, "We are lost. The French admiral does not understand his business." Nonetheless determined to fight to the last, he realised that with the entire fleet strung out singly on a broad front there would be no means of stopping that front being cut in two places by the advancing British columns. This would mean that while the central and southerly ships would be very heavily engaged, those to the north would have far less opportunity of entering the fight, and the full might of the Combined Fleet would not be brought into play. Moreover, with a dangerous coast behind them and the wind blowing in from the open sea, any damaged ship would be in a very nasty position if the threatened gale came. If only Admiral Dumanoir could be brought down behind the English, the English would be caught between two lines of ships and pulverised; but that signal to the van never came.

Still the sun shone, the waves rippled, and over to Nonesuch's starboard stretched a diagonal column of ships with Royal Sovereign in the lead, all sails set from royals thrusting into the sky to the studding-sails dripping over the yards to the water. The yellow and black paintwork on their sides gleamed bravely in the sunlight and the gay colours flying from the foretop and maintop stays belied the purpose of that graceful approach. Behind and to the right of Royal Sovereign came the Belleisle, bearing down joyfully into battle with her band playing, very confidently, "Rule, Britannia!" Close on her heels came the Mars, the Tonnant, and the Bellerophon. Three more sail followed, then after a gap, a final clump together. The end of the column came much closer to the tail of Nelson's own division, fanning out to the northward with Victory at their head. Very near together and close behind her were the Temeraire, the Neptune, the Conqueror and the Leviathan. Britannia, Ajax, Orion and Agamemnon were strung out more widely spaced, with Minotaur and Spartiate far to the rear. The three decker Prince, who really belonged with Collingwood's ships, had become part of the windward division instead. Nonesuch herself, when she reached the fighting would find herself involved with the leeward ships breaking the battle-line to the south. And the little Africa, separated altogether from the fleet, would approach and join from the north.

It was now a few minutes before noon, and suddenly a red streak danced along the side of the French ship in Collingwood's way. The reply from Royal Sovereign's forward guns hid her in her own smoke. As this dispersed, the watchers on Nonesuch's decks could still see her carrying on her stately way, bearing before her the figure of His Majesty King George III with Fame and Fortune on either hand to support him. Her own hundred guns biding their time, she sailed on regardless of the enemy shot falling around her. And at length she squeezed through a narrowing gap between a Frenchman and Spaniard to break the enemy line, and a cheer arose from the English crews who saw her do it. As she went, she fired a broadside full

The North

The Combined Fleet [France & Spain]

HMS Sirius (frigate)

HMS Euryalus (frigate)

HMS Africa

HMS Conqueror

HMS Neptune

HMS Mars?

HMS Britannia

HMS Ajax

HMS Orion

HMS Agamemnon

HMS Prince

HMS Minotaur

HMS Spartiate

HMS Victory [Nelson]

HMS Temeraire

The Battle of
Trafalgar
21st October
1805

HMS Royal Sovereign [Collingwood]

HMS Belleisle

HMS Mars

HMS Tonnant

HMS Bellerophon

HMS Colossus

HMS Orion

HMS Swiftsure

HMS Dreadnought

HMS Achilles

HMS Revenge

HMS Polyphemus

Neptuno
Scipion
Intrepide
Formidable
Duguay Trouin
Mont Blanc
Rayo
Heros
Santisima Trinidad
Bucentaure
Redoutable
San Francisco de Asis
San Augustin
San Justo
Neptuno
San Leandro
Indomptable
Santa Ana
Fougueux
Pluton
Monarca
Algeciras
Bahama
Aigle
Montanes
Swiftsure
Argonaute
Argonauta
Bahama
San Ildefonso
Principe de Asturias
San Ildefonso
Berwick
San Juan Nepomuceno

into the Santa Ana, and the Battle of Trafalgar had begun in earnest. It was just twelve o'clock.

10

Now the flags on the ship ahead of Nonesuch in the column were going up again. This was a long signal. There wasn't time to count them, but in fact thirty-two flags were flying from the stays. First the red and white "Popham" flag, then number 253 –
"England", read Christopher: 269 –
"Expects", read Christopher: then, one by one,
"That – Every – Man – Will – Do – His – Duty."
There was an audible breath from all those within hearing. Then Captain Britten said, "England shall not be disappointed! Lord Nelson need not doubt us! Mr Bull, call all hands on decks to hear the Admiral's message!"

The shrill of the pipes brought every man scrambling aloft at the double, and they fell in swiftly to hear what the captain had to say. "Men," he said directly, "there is a special message from Lord Nelson to every one of you. It is simply this – 'England expects that every man will do his duty'."

He was interrupted by a burst of cheering for Lord Nelson. One or two muttered that of course they would do their duty and he ought not to doubt it, but they cheered him just the same.

Captain Britten was speaking again. "The enemy," he said, "are now in sight; thirty-three sail of the line. Our country depends on us! Our ship may sink, but I know I can promise on your behalf that she shall not surrender. All I have left to say is – do not waste a single shot! Let each be expended to some purpose. Trust implicitly in the orders of your officers and act upon them immediately. And may everyone share in this day's glory. God Save the King!"

They gave another hearty cheer, then back they trooped to their battle quarters. Now, with ship and men ready stripped for action, the pipes sounded once more and every man fortified himself with a ration of cold salt beef, biscuit and grog, for the captain believed firmly that no one, not even an Englishman, could fight better than with his dinner inside him, and he intended everyone aboard his ship to give of his best. The "no-meat" rule was waived today, for this was no ordinary Monday. The men fell to where they were beside the guns, and afterwards had fresh enthusiasm for their task. Although the foremost ships were already engaged, their own position in the column gave them enough time for this relief.

Victory, breaking the enemy line at the head of the northern column just half-an-hour after Royal Sovereign had fired her first shot, had been almost immediately locked in mortal combat. She had suffered considerable damage and casualties even before her own guns had been brought to bear: still she held her fire until she could come to close grips. On the quarterdeck, calm amid the savage hail of shot that raked her, stood Nelson with Captain Hardy. His calculating mind was still hard at work. He knew that he must still surprise the enemy, though now he was not only in full view but well within their reach. That element of surprise was the kingpin of the whole enterprise. So Admiral Villeneuve must not be allowed to realise until the very last moment that Nelson intended to cut him off completely from the succour of his leading ships. If he could keep the Frenchman wondering until it was too late for him to dodge, the day would be half-won before it had begun. So while Collingwood was attacking the last fifteen ships in the line, Nelson steered northward as if to sail into the leading vessels in the orthodox style. Earlier in the morning, when Villeneuve had swung his fleet to the northerly course, Nelson had anticipated the move and allowed himself room to match it. This awkward development actually helped the English fleet, for it put the French in an almost impossible position from which to turn to the aid of their own rear. Like birds fascinated by a snake, the centre of the French line watched the English advance upon their van. Then, when he was so close that they could not go to assist the rear ships, already suffering from the fire of Collingwood's division, when it was too late for the van to turn and come to the rescue, Nelson sprang his surprise. The helmsman was ordered to turn hard to starboard. Now the ship came under the panic-stricken fire of four great sail of the line, and the fire from nearly two hundred guns had sliced her rigging, splintered her decks, ripped her canvas and cut down her crew. The sails were tattered and part of the mizenmast had gone before ever Victory fired a shot herself. But Nelson, unmoved, kept steadily on his way towards the slowly closing line of French ships. Dimly through the smoke it could be seen that the gaps were narrowing on either side of Villeneuve's flagship, and that the Victory would surely ram one of the opposing vessels. At last her moment had come and as she broke the line she poured into the French flagship, Bucentaure, shot from her broadside guns, muskets and carronades – those flat little guns with the big bore that could wreak so much havoc. Very quickly after that she grated against the Redoubtable on her other side, their rigging became interlocked, and Victory was attacking two of the enemy at once with both her broadsides pounding away.

Still beyond the scene of battle but making every inch of way possible, the men aboard Nonesuch knew nothing of this drama hidden in the smoke. All was hushed now. The bustle of preparation was over, and on the sanded decks time held its breath. Nonesuch was rolling heavily in the groundswell from the Atlantic. Righting herself on the crests of the wave, she sank again as they passed eastward from under her. Above the decks, the great spread of canvas stretched majestically to catch every breath of breeze. The poop and quarterdeck were lined by Marines, their muskets loaded and bayonets to hand. Below decks, the men at the guns stood tensely in the heat, sweat already trickling over their naked backs, eager to get at the enemy who had evaded them for so long. There was no fire now in the galley, and the firescreens hung heavily, drenched with water. The red port-lids were raised and the sunlight streamed through the openings which would soon provide an outlet for a brighter flash, a more blinding light. The great guns themselves were all primed and ready for the first order from the lieutenants: each held its cartridge and its shot, each had gunpowder in the pan, each had been rolled forward against the ship's side. Some received a final polish from their crews. It gave them something to do during the silent time before the enemy came within their range. And some men thought, superstitiously, that guns, like women, were in their best form when looking their best!

The cockpit had been turned into a hospital, and in the dim light of the hanging lanterns it had a brooding look. The surgeon and his assistants were already there making their grim preparations with the help of a handful of men detailed to act as "loblollies" – the medical orderlies. They would have to carry and hold down the writhing patients when splinters and bullets needed to be dug out of their tormented flesh: when cuts were bound: or when shattered limbs had to be amputated. Heroism of a different kind was needed here, but heroism just the same. The long tables had been dragged out to form crude operating tables, tubs of hot water held the sinister-looking implements (for Lord Nelson remembered to this day the sudden chill of the knife, and insisted on warm surgical instruments in his ships), and supplies of rum were at hand by way of a rough anaesthetic. This was the place, of all places, to disperse dreams of glory and fill the heart with pity for the wastage of war. Mr Campbell ordered his little hospital with cold rage at the man whose overweening ambition made such horrors necessary. If he could at that moment have had Napoleon Bonaparte at the mercy of his long surgical knife, he would without hesitation have buried it in the Corsican's heart.

Christopher had thought that to eat so much as a morsel would be quite beyond him, but he found that he was ravenously hungry after the busy morning, and the rough spirit filled him with a reckless eagerness he would never have suspected in himself. Now he could watch unmoved as one by one the foremost vessels joined the fray. He had lost sight of the flagship and her immediate companions; they were lost in a black cloud which crept ever closer to Nonesuch herself. The ship was steering slightly out of line now, and further to the south-east. Captain Britten could tell that he was so far to the rear that if he kept rigidly to his station he wouldn't get really close until the fiercest part of the fight was over. And hadn't the order been to get alongside an enemy vessel as soon as possible and stay there? Captain Britten intended to do just that. The enemy van were out of reach and one by one the ships ahead of him were engaging the centre. Collingwood's division were taking good care of the rear, but if that rear were to be destroyed as completely as Nelson wished every bit of help would be welcome. Since the windward column were sailing obliquely, Nonesuch wouldn't have very far to go to join the fight to leeward. Captain Britten turned and walked over to the Master. "Mr Dean," he said, "we will engage the enemy at that spot," and he pointed in front and to the right. Mr Dean's brows drew together a moment. Then as he saw what the captain intended he turned away to the man at the wheel and shouted a crisp order. The helm was put up, and Nonesuch headed straight for the immense cloud which hid Royal Sovereign and her followers from view. With almost painful regularity the black smoke turned to yellow speckled with points of orange fire, and the dull boom of the guns would perhaps be followed by the sharper crack of splintering timber. Beneath the rattle and roar of the conflict there could still be heard the flap-flap of the sails, the slap-slap of the sea; but the sound of voices died away, and the men were quite silent as their moment drew near. Suddenly, a new noise sounded over Christopher's head. There was a whirr and a smack, and a large jagged hole appeared in one of the topsails. The light of day was wholly obscured by smoke, and Christopher moved through it to Lieutenant Kent's side for orders.

Again he heard a whistling over his head and out of the corner of his eye he saw a seaman fall to the deck with a grunt, one leg dangling at a strange angle beside him. He had no time or wish to stop and stare. The ship on her new course was making for a gap in the enemy line. A vast shape loomed ahead on the starboard side, so close that it almost seemed that an outstretched hand could grasp the tricolour drooping at the rail. "Quickly now!" said Lieutenant Scott to Hugh. "Down to the main deck! Tell Lieutenant Yorke that the range is now forty yards, and to be ready to fire as we pass the enemy!"

Off sped Hugh, dodging through the ranks of the Marines, down to the decks below. There was a tense silence as he delivered his messages. The lieutenant nodded, raised the speaking trumpet to his lips for what seemed a long, long while, then – "FIRE!" he cried. The ship juddered, there was a crashing roar, and the force of the broadside was delivered full into the French seventy-four. Without pausing on her course, the ship sailed on, and the whole world became a medley of smoke and shot and shouting. The acrid smoke from Nonesuch's own guns billowed back across the deck, and Hugh made his way back aloft with choking throat and streaming eyes.

Through the swirl of the smoke he could see the crew and the Marines lying flat on the deck to avoid the musket shots aimed by men in the enemy rigging, though the officers still strode about the quarterdeck exhorting and commanding. The first broadside had been fired as the two ships came alongside, and it was plain that great damage had been inflicted on the enemy near the waterline. Again Nonesuch's guns boomed, and several shots which splintered the French mainmast sent it falling slowly across her own decks. It smashed the rail, draping split canvas and tangled ropes over the side, and some of her guns were for a time out of action, since the ports were smothered by the wreckage. Nonesuch's own foretopmast was gone, shot clean away, and the carpenter's mates were working frantically to plug the holes in her damaged hull. Christopher's eyes were watering, his nostrils stung with fumes, and the men about him were dim figures moving through the fog. But through the tumult and confusion purpose and discipline held firm, and the crash of the guns came regularly and devastatingly as they hammered away.

Like the quarterdeck, the poop was lost in a dense grey fog. Even the scarlet jackets of the Marines turned to a dingy rust colour as the dust and dirt of the battle showered upon them. Above the deeper roar of the guns cracked the sound of their muskets, shooting it out with the Frenchmen perched high above them in the rigging. On both sides the casualties were considerable, but whenever a man fell on the poop the ranks were closed and an unbroken line of fire kept going. Fellowes, crossing the deck, heard a sighing beside him, and turned to see a Marine slide to the deck, his musket clattering as it dropped.

Swiftly he bent and cautiously turned the man over. There was no mark on the white face, no rent in his uniform. He had fainted from sheer fright. Fellowes shook him as he knelt beside him, crying, "Get up, you hen-hearted creature! Get up and fight!" The man opened his eyes wide, gazing at him desperately; his jaw wobbled, and he was suddenly and violently sick. Fellowes lost his temper. Rising quickly to his feet he pushed the Marine as far from him as he could, snatched up the fallen musket and himself took his place in the line of red coats, firing from behind the protection of his hammocks in the netting.

Still the guns kept up the barrage. At the third gun on the starboard side on the main deck, the two messmates Harris and Lewis were hard at work. Harris was busy loading the shot for their share of the broadsides, sliding the cartridge and shot into the muzzle, and Lewis helped him to ram the charge down hard. Then, together, with the rest of the gun's crew, they hauled the gun right up so that it stuck out of the yawning port. The trigger was pulled, the gun rumbled back, driven by the force of its own explosion, and the whole business was to do again. Time after time after time. All the while the enemy fire was bursting through the ship's sides, and through the open ports, but Able Seaman Harris was almost too busy to wipe the sweat from his eyes, let alone take notice of one shot above another.

But he did glace round once, when an odd gurgling and thump sounded right behind him; and there was Peters, huddled under the gun, quite still. Grapeshot had hit him full in the face, and Peter's unlucky voyage was over.

"God have mercy on him!" muttered Harris, as someone dragged the limp form clear of the gun. "He wasn't a bad chap when the drink wasn't in him!" Then, ramming the shot home viciously as he spoke, "Well, here's one we'll send on your account, matey!"

The gun rolled forward yet again, the trigger was pulled by Darby, crouching well back clear of the recoil, and as the charge flamed out, "Hurrah!" cried Harris. "There's more where that came from!"

Once, twice more; and the French ship began to drift still

nearer. The yardarms were nearly touching already; now, almost completely hidden in the smoke, there came another hail of shot before, with an ear-splitting crash, the two great ships met, and a party of Marines and seamen armed with cutlasses and tomahawks went rushing to board. Caught up in the crush, Christopher found himself clambering over the bulwarks, cheering like a madman and brandishing his pistol.

Above the din he could hear the lieutenant of Marines yelling, "Come on, my lads! No quarter! Give 'em the cold steel!" Another and more familiar voice in his ear said "I'm blessed if it isn't blue eyes himself! Whatever are you doing among all these nasty rough men?"

"I don't know! I came along for the fun of it."

"Deserting your post, eh?"

"Why, I suppose so! But not deserting, anyway!"

Fellowes gave him a surprisingly friendly smile. "True enough! Come on, then!" and together they ran to join the scuffle on the French decks.

"There's more in you than meets the eye!" panted Fellowes as they trotted along. There was no time now for talking, and before Christopher could collect his thoughts in time to frame a suitable answer a sixth sense warned him of danger. Looking swiftly upwards he saw a heavy wooden billet, wielded by what looked a giant among Frenchmen about to descend on Fellowes' unguarded head. His reaction was automatic. Hardly knowing what he did or how he did it, he smashed his left fist against the Frenchman's chin. His victim staggered back and it was enough to deflect the blow. The club missed Fellows' skull, but hit his arm with a sickening crack. He reeled, and fell half-fainting on Christopher's shoulder. Christopher caught him in his arms and pushed him behind him against the ship's side while the fighting swept past them. He leant there for a moment, panting, with a bruise rapidly spreading across his torn knuckles.

"We must get you to Mr Campbell," he gasped. "Can you manage to get back, do you think?"

"I'll be all right – legs a bit wobbly, but if you don't mind me leaning on you a moment – I'll make it. I've still got one good arm but – oh lord, it hurts!"

"Hold on a moment and I'll pull you up," said Christopher urgently. "Don't faint now for the love of Heaven! Wait till you're back on board and faint then if you must!" He swung himself up into the chains and then to the rail, thanking his stars that the two ships were still grinding together. Taking firm hold with one hand he stretched the other down to Fellowes, bracing his legs to meet the sudden strain when it should come.

"Hold hard!" he commanded, "and when I give the word – come up! Now!" and he pulled with all his might. The impact of Fellowes' body against his own made him stagger, but fortunately help was near, and strong hands caught the wounded boy before he could collapse and fall on the slippery deck. As he wiped the sweat from his eyes, Christopher saw him being carried away to join the queue waiting for the surgeon's attention.

"At least he's safe now," he thought to himself, "and I would never have believed how glad I could be of that! Oh dear, I wonder how Richard's getting on!"

Richard's part in the battle had certainly been very different. He had been posted on the lower deck, keeping liaison between Lieutenant Welch and the powder magazine, guarded by Marine sentries who let no unauthorised person pass. From where he stood beside one of the guns, he could see the enemy fleet looming steadily larger.

"By George, but they're a fine sight!" he exclaimed.

A seaman who followed his glance grinned. "They'll look finer still in Plymouth Sound!" he commented, and Richard laughed.

One of the other men seemed inclined to argue.

"Frenchy ain't worth looking at anywhere," he declared. "Send him clean out of sight! That's what I say!"

"Well, do your best and keep a steady aim and we'll see what we shall see!" advised Richard. He saw Lieutenant Welch's raised finger, and hurried over. "The wind is dropping," the officer said. "Send up supplies of single shot in case we need to open fire at long range."

But Richard returned from his errand to find that the wind

had freshened again, and that Nonesuch would be joining the fray very soon now. The gun captains were already crouching back behind the guns, the trigger lines held firmly in their steady hands. The lieutenants stood well clear of the guns; the order to fire was given; and the word was still only half-pronounced when one after another along the line the trigger lines jerked, the first broadside boomed out and battle was fairly joined. Vision was dimmed in the belching smoke, and the repeated order to "Fire!" rang out more rapidly than a landsman would have thought possible. The men sweated and swore and manned the guns like so many machines, grimly holding on through the ruin around them – loading, ramming, wadding, then firing with the devastating effect Christopher was seeing from the quarterdeck. The greatest danger to the crews was the grapeshot which screamed through their own open ports, but despite the number who fell in this way the big guns were never so wholly unmanned as to be out of action. A tremendous cheer echoed down from the deck overhead, even though the crashing of the guns, and everyone looked up instinctively. Richard looked at Lieutenant Welch, who smiled and beckoned to him. "It sounds as if one of them has been forced to strike their colours!" he remarked. "Nip up aloft and find out!" Nothing loth, Richard scampered off, up to the main deck. There the smoke was every bit as dense as it had been below. The whole place reeked of sulphur, and he struggled on eagerly through the murk to the hatchway and so up to the deck above, where his grateful lungs caught a measure of clean air as the smoke billowed away between broadsides. He was crossing the quarterdeck when a rending noise above his head made him look up to see that one of the spars, sliced away from the mizzen, was about to come toppling down where he stood. He dodged quickly to one side, too quickly to see in the gloom where he was going. The falling timber caught him a glancing blow on the head; he staggered, tripped in one of the furrows carved by shot in the planking, and fell heavily, seeing stars and with blood spurting from a vicious cut across his foot. He was on his knees in a moment, shaking his head to clear it, when he felt himself being raised to his feet and then half-carried down below. Blackness whirled in his head and he lost consciousness.

When he came to, he found himself laid on the floor of the cockpit. There was a different smell here – not pungent and scorching as it was on the gundeck but sweet and sickly and disgusting, hardly to be breathed. He struggled to sit up, propping his back against the ship's side as he took in his situation. The deck above his head shook to the rumbling of the guns. He wished there were some way of knowing what was happening, but he was sufficiently master of himself to realise that as long as the guns were in action all was well for the ship. He turned his throbbing head cautiously and made out the figures of the surgeon and his assistants, busy in the dim light of the hanging lanterns. There were numbers of men ahead of him in the queue, although Nonesuch had been actively engaged for rather less than half-an-hour. He tried to shut his eyes and his ears to the sight and the sound of suffering around him, but this was not easy, and tried his fortitude far more than his own aches and pains did. He could only lie there and wait his turn and give silent thanks that his own hurts were so slight.

"My turn this time," he thought hazily. "Be too bad if poor old Hugh finds himself down here again today. I wonder how things are going with him?" As it happened, Hugh just then was ducking behind a boat on the forward deck to avoid the attentions of a man with a musket who, hidden somewhere on the rigging of the French ship's foremast, was shooting in his general direction and getting uncomfortably close with some of his shots. Actually, it wasn't such a bad place to choose, for the enemy fire was pouring in a constant stream over the bows, and to stand upright was foolhardy. He was on his way back to the quarterdeck after carrying a message forward, and he wasn't going to have it said that Mr Midshipman Stirling had failed in his duty; not after such a signal! Cautiously he peeped out; something zipped past his ear in a warm, stinging rush and he dropped back automatically into his shelter. "This won't do!" he said under his breath. "Curse the fellow! he shan't stop me!" and dropping down on the decks he set off on his front, wriggling along like a very dusty earthworm, feeling that a keen eyed early bird was watching and ready to pounce. "Most undignified behaviour for an officer and a gentleman!" he thought to himself. However, his assailant had either been picked off himself or had lost sight of him in the smoke, for out of the corner of his eye he saw that he had crawled level with the mainmast and should now be out of range of the Frenchman's musket. He stretched his cramped legs and scurried off to find Lieutenant Scott. "Good thing Richard didn't see that!" he grinned to himself. "I'd never hear the end of it!"

But Richard just then was more concerned with the hammer in his head than with anything else. He shifted against the timbers, trying to find a softer spot and so relieve the ache, and found that he was sitting beside a wounded sailor. It was Able Seaman Darby, his face grey under its covering of soot, carefully resting the remains of his shattered left hand on his lap.

"I know you," said Richard. "Wait a minute! Darby – that's your name, isn't it?"

"That's right, sir! So that knock you took on the head hasn't quite addled your wits! Out cold, you were, when you came down here."

As full consciousness returned to him Richard noticed the blood-soaked rag wrapping the man's hand.

"I'm sorry to see you here," he said sincerely. "I'm afraid you're badly hart."

"Can't be helped, sir! And I've still got a good right hand to strike a blow when I need it!"

Darby's voice was growing fainter, but he managed the ghost of a grin.

"I do wish," said Richard fretfully, "that one could know how things are going!"

"Why, sir, pretty fairly to be sure! While that old rumbling's going on you know we're still in the fight!"

As he spoke, the timbers above their heads echoed to the crash of a broadside and Richard said, "That's right enough! Why didn't I remember that? Oh, there I go again, never thinking of anything. But I did think – and I forgot!"

Darby looked anxiously at him, thinking his wits were wandering again. Richard put a hand gingerly to his temple; when he drew it away the fingers were scarlet. He looked stupidly at them for a moment; then he shrugged and leaned back against the ship's framework. He said no more, and Darby too was silent from pain and respect. Richard closed his eyes, acutely aware of the grinding of the timbers behind him as Nonesuch grated against the enemy and, clinging together, they rose to the increasing swell. It didn't really help much to lean his head back, because every time the guns thundered out the whole ship jarred, and nearly as often an ear-splitting jolt told that the enemy fire too was finding a target. He came out of a reverie to see that Darby was being led away, and raised a friendly hand in farewell. Better not think of what was going to happen to Darby! He shut his eyes again, and tried hard to think of pleasant things.

He had lost all sense of time when at last he felt a hand on his brow and heard a hearty voice saying "Now then, my lad, let's have a look at you! What have you been doing to yourself, eh?"

"It's not what I've been doing; it's what somebody else has!" returned Richard, with an echo of his usual good humour. "I've got a shocking headache and something's happened to my foot, but if you'll just bandage me up I'll be off back to my post on the instant!"

"Indeed! and perhaps I'll have something to say to that!" – but the surgeon's assistant was working swiftly and soon straightened himself with a reassuring pat on Richard's shoulder. "You'll do, my boy – and give thanks for your good fortune!" he said. "Lucky for you that that cut is only a fleshwound! The blood had clotted beautifully before I reached you and you've not lost as much as I feared!"

"Then will you be so good as to help me up?" asked Richard. "I can't lie about here all day! I've got work to do!"

"There you are my boy – and mind you look after it! I don't expect to see you here again. I'm busy too!" and the surgeon had already turned to attend to his next patient before Richard was fairly on his way out of the sick bay. He was limping eagerly away from that heart-breaking place when he heard his name, and turning, saw Fellowes half-sitting, half-lying, propped against a frame. He trod over to him and sat beside him.

186

"Hello!" he said. "We meet again, and what a place to choose! Arm?" he asked sympathetically, noticing the dangling sleeve.

"Yes – 'fraid so, but at least it's better than leg! How are you? All right?"

"Oh Lord, yes! I'm a fraud and just been told so. I hope they get round to you soon, old fellow. This isn't too jolly a spot to be in, is it?"

"No – but it's not very pretty up aloft, either."

"We're all right, aren't we? How's it going? We can't see a thing down below on the gundeck."

"It seems to be going our way – I know several of the enemy have struck, and we were boarding when I got this."

"Come, that's good news at all events. Tell me, have you seen the young 'un?"

"He was there too, and doing well –" and Fellowes would have gone on to say just how well Christopher had been doing, when a spasm of pain made him close his eyes. Richard looked at him for a moment; then he gently pressed his uninjured hand and went thoughtfully away, determining to find out later how his fellow midshipman was likely to go on if he should get the chance. At least Christopher had been unhurt until a short time ago. That was one good thing!

Down in the darkness of the cockpit, with only the rumble of the guns to tell them that the battle was still going on, and with no indication of the passing of time, neither boy could know that Nonesuch was now engaged in a more desperate struggle, nor that Christopher was at that moment as near to joining them as he could be. The boarding party had been recalled, for when the hand-to-hand fighting had been at its height another of the Combined Fleet had steered alongside out of the smoke. So many casualties had been suffered that Captain Britten was reluctant to press home his threat in the face of this new danger, and his victim had drifted thankfully away, leaving the field to the newcomer. This brought None-such's other broadside into action, and as they blazed out thundering her late adversary, passing in front of her, sent a farewell over her bows that virtually silenced the forward guns. Luckily, she vanished then into the gloom. The enemy ship that now loomed alongside was a vague shape in the greyness, sparked with rippling lines of red and yellow light as the shots were exchanged. Both ships took advantage of the extremely close range to inflict severe punishment upon the other. None-such's fo'c'sle was terribly torn about, but what was worse, and presented a ghastly danger, was the loss of the mizenmast: for by an unlucky chance a piece of blazing matter set the topsail on fire, and in no time the rigging was also alight. This in its turn spread swiftly to the mast itself. Already weakened by the many hits it had suffered, it crashed down across the poop. The crew fell upon the flaming mass, some slashing away with axes, cutlasses and pikes to free the wreckage and pitch it over the side, while others doused the deck with water to stop the fire spreading.

It began to seem as if the nightmare would never end. What should have been a bright sunny afternoon had been turned to midnight, the murk was so dense. Christopher's ears had grown so used to the groans of the wounded, the shouting, the cheering, the booming of the guns and the pop-pop of the musket-fire, that a thunderbolt landing beside him would scarcely have made him turn his head. Suddenly, a terrific thump between his shoulders sent him flying. He landed flat on his face on the deck, all the wind knocked out of him. He lay there whooping for breath; from far away he heard Lieutenant Scott's urgent voice. As his breath came slowly back he realised that the officer was down on one knee, supporting him against his shoulder. He managed a feeble grin, and struggled to get up.

"You're hit, my boy," said the lieutenant anxiously. "We must get you below at once."

"No, sir – I'm not hurt, I'm sure of it – only winded!"

"Let me see" – and gently the lieutenant removed his jacket and felt underneath his shirt. Christopher winced.

"No," said the officer thankfully. "There's no wound there, but I'm afraid it'll be very uncomfortable for a time. A blow like that will give you a bad bruise. Lucky for you it was only the flat side of the splinter – it would have killed you otherwise! You have a charmed life, it seems!"

"Indeed I think so, sir!" agreed Christopher, as he struggled back into his jacket.

And now, even when the battle was hottest, help was at hand. A second English ship had sailed across the enemy's stern and, comfortably out of range herself, was briskly pumping away with every available gun. This murderous fire afforded the crippled Nonesuch a much-welcome respite, and she fell away to starboard, clear of the drifting smoke.

11

Coming out into the afternoon light, it appeared that more signals had been sent from the Victory, ordering the British ships to come into the wind, away from their captures. While he gave the orders that would swing Nonesuch round to the north, Captain Britten, peering through his telescope, realised that the reason for this manoeuvre was the approach to larboard of a previously unengaged number of enemy ships. Ten more sail – the isolated French van – were about to enter the lists against them; but even as he watched, three pulled back and headed for the safety of Cadiz, two sailed on into the thick of the battle, and five only were left to be tackled. But for Nonesuch, the battle was over. Far to the rear of the newly-forming column, hampered by the damage she had suffered and hindered by the lightness of the breeze, she could only observe the new development from a distance. The range was too great for her, and all that her crew could do was to watch and send up a thundering cheer as one by one the newcomers met with a warm reception. Seven British ships had formed into a fresh column of sorts and plunged northwards; the Minotaur and Spartiate, who had now caught up with the rest and sailed across the enemy leader's bows, were almost at once involved in a very close action. Although the enemy obviously intended to stop these two joining the column coming up from the south, they managed to sail safely past. As she went by, the Minotaur had sent her fire thundering into these French reserves, and she was ably backed by the Spartiate, coming close behind. The Spartiate passed on towards the rear of the English column, and placed herself where she could fire conveniently at the Spanish ship Neptuno, last of the five. The Neptuno's ropes and canvas were already badly torn, and her companions drew away, leaving her to her fate. Since the Spartiate had approached from an awkward angle, the Master gave orders to swing the ship round, so that her guns could be brought to bear from the best possible position. It worked; first one mast fell, then the other two. The Neptuno was surrounded, and could do no more.

This opposition was too much for the French, led by no less a person than Admiral Dumanoir himself, in the Formidable. With his rigging in tatters, he led his squadron on southward out of danger: five sail of the line chased off by two British seventy-fours.

"Will you just look at that now?" cried a gleeful voice on Nonesuch's main deck, where the gun crews were peering through the ports now for all the world as if they were sitting in a box at the opera. "Didn't the Admiral himself say one Englishman was the equal of three Johnny Frenchmen?"

"That's a fair and pretty compliment coming from you, Paddy!"

"Well, and 'tis a fair and pretty sight!" the Irishman retorted with unabated good humour.

With the heat of battle cooling down, it was possible for those on the quarterdeck to gain some idea of how things had gone with the rest of the fleet. Although many had obviously taken a terrible pounding, no British vessel appeared to have struck her colours, and this in itself was cause for rejoicing. The one who seemed to have come off worst, as far as they could see, was the Belleisle, which had followed Vice-Admiral Collingwood's flagship into battle. Completely dismasted, she floated on the water an oddly blunted shape, like a child's toy boat; but though crippled, she still kept her colours flying from the stump of the mizenmast, and the men on board were waving from her decks and gunports. She had been in the thick of it from the start and had suffered heavy casualties before firing a shot. In fact she had taken worse punishment during the approach than Royal Sovereign herself. But her chunky, spunky little captain, never a man to waste time talking, had declared that his ship was to pass under the sides of the Spanish Santa Ana. This particular target carried a hundred and twelve guns, but this didn't matter to Captain Hargood. He insisted that no one was to pull a trigger-line until the Belleisle was near enough to do spectacular damage; then he calmly placed himself on the slide of one of the quarterdeck guns and said no more, apart from instructing the Master as to the course they should take. Although the enemy fire was raging in across his decks, although his mizentopmast was already gone and he himself bruised on the chest by a flying splinter, he kept his own fire in check until he judged that the critical moment had come. About ten minutes after Royal Sovereign had broken through, Belleisle fired broadsides almost at the same time at the Santa Ana on the one hand and the Fougueux on the other. Sailing on through the gap between these two, with her own rigging in a terrible muddle, she had headed for the Indomptable, lying to leeward. As she swung round to starboard across her enemy's stern, the Fougueux had appeared again out of the smoke and crashed against her. The Indomptable, with a farewell broadside, made good her escape, while the other two battered away at each other at point-blank range, but by sound and instinct rather than by sight, for everything was hidden in the thick black smoke, and the guns were brought to bear simply by the crews' blind faith in the orders passed to them from above, where vision was not so completely blotted out. Later, the French ship Pluton had joined in, coming upon the British ship in a sadly shattered condition; but now, at the end of the battle, the Belleisle was still proudly defiant, though her crew had suffered horribly and the upper deck was an incredible tangle of wreckage.

Two of the other ships which had followed Collingwood in the rear division had had the bad luck to lose their captains. One was Captain George Duff of the Mars, third in line, which suffered an attack from both sides as she came up with the enemy. With every stitch of canvas set that the yards could hold she had flown across the water in a race to break first through the line. But the swiftly-sailing Royal Sovereign, freshly arrived from England after refitting, was too fleet for her, and she had to be content with third place, and was open to heavy fire as she entered the gap made by the flagship and the Belleisle. The Fougueux, locked to the Belleisle, had left the line, but the Pluton had swiftly filled the gap. Sideways on, the two ships sailed north together, and when the Mars had to stop to avoid colliding with the vast Santa Ana ahead of her, her flanks were wide open to raking fire from the Pluton and her bows from the Spanish flagship; and a broadside from the Fougueux killed Captain Duff as he stood on the quarterdeck. The Bellerophon too was now commanded by her First Lieutenant. She had been attacked at the very beginning by four enemy ships at once, when an unlucky "mid" had stumbled over a trigger-line on one of the gundecks. The four enemy ships had immediately opened fire and their shots started smashing into her before she was ready. It was a quarter of an hour before she could retaliate, although she had fired her forward guns to make a smoke-screen until she could find her own close range. Getting into a gap between two ships, she had opened fire on both; then another loomed so close that although the crew worked quickly to reduce speed and change course to avoid a collision, the yards met and clung together. A fourth enemy ship came up, and Bellerophon was now the centre of a concerted attack. Captain Cooke, who was shooting with his pistol at the men on the French ship Aigle's deck, was hit by musket balls in the chest, and died almost at once. But both ships had survived to tell the tale. Bellerophon's embittered struggle with the Aigle was at such close quarters that their gun crews fought each other through the open ports with what weapons they could find; and the Frenchmen, throwing grenades, did tremendous damage. One even set fire to the stores, hideously close to the magazine, but the same blast which flung open the door of the one had slammed shut the door of the other, and prompt action quickly put out the blaze. Other shots cut down the colours but a seaman grabbed the flag and started up the mast to replace it, and the French marksmen, paying tribute to his motive, forbore to shoot. With only one mast left, and in a terribly shattered condition, it seemed hardly possible that the Bellerophon could outlive the day: but when the three-decker Dreadnought came to her aid she was not only able to cease fire but to send a party aboard a nearby Spanish wreck and take possession of her in the King's name. The Mars too took full revenge for the loss of her captain, for when the Bucentaure herself hauled down her colours to the Conqueror it was actually to the first Lieutenant of the Mars, commanding in place of Captain Duff, that Admiral Villeneuve surrendered his sword.

Among the other ships in Collingwood's division, the Tonnant had gone into battle with her band playing "Britons, Strike Home!" (Belleisle's band had played "Rule, Britannia!"). Tonnant had been captured from the French at the Battle of the Nile; now, taking part on the British side, she forced her way through the line between a Spaniard and a Frenchman, with barely room between them for her to pass. At that range there could be no doubt at all of the result. Her first broadside sent down a French mast, her second damaged the Spanish yards, the third sent the Spaniard limping out of the fight. She would have gone then to help the Mars, but another French ship turned to cross her. Captain Tyler swung his ship round again, and the two clashed together, with the French bowsprit stuck in the British rigging. Tonnant, broadside on, and firmly fixed in that position, had her enemy at her mercy. The broadside guns boomed away while her "upstairs" artillery removed the French rigging. The two great ships scraped each other's sides, for the Algésiras had managed to swing round until they were alongside. At one time both were set on fire together, and prompt action had to be taken to prevent a holocaust. It was a strange sight to see British seamen playing the water from their fire-engine on their enemy as well as on themselves! Both ships suffered acutely, and the Frenchman lost all three of her masts. Finally, having repelled an attempt to board her, Tonnant sent over a boarding party of her own, and that, for the Algésiras, was the end of it. Then the battered San Juan came within range, and surrendered to Tonnant after losing her foremast.

The Colossus had been sixth in the stately line which Christopher had admired so much. She had scarcely reached the French line when the Argonaute came suddenly out of the smoke. The crunch as they met jerked the men aboard sharply from their stations, but they recovered themselves quickly and set about a furious fire – below decks from the big guns, up above from the muskets. The fight was short and sharp, and when at last they parted company Colossus was engaged by the Spanish ship Bahama. Unluckily for the Spanish, their French ally the Swiftsure came barging in between. This meant that while the Colossus was screened from the Bahama's guns she could rake the Swiftsure with deadly accuracy, and when the French ship drew away astern the Bahama was left bare to a cruel and relentless onslaught. The constant barrage from the Colossus' guns crippled the ship and killed her captain, and soon after that, she surrendered. Captain James Morris, though wounded, gave crisp orders, and his ship swung about as fast as she could, with her seamen pulling for dear life at the sheets; and after the next broadside, the Swiftsure was left with only her foremast and part of her mainmast still standing.

The Orion now appeared out of the smoke. Three surprisingly swift broadsides saw off the remnant of the French mainmast, and did a lot of other damage besides. Very soon the foremast went the way of the others, and when the French captain saw that he was cut off from the rest of his fleet, and his ship was taking in water fast, he admitted defeat. He had hardly done so when Colossus herself lost her mizenmast. Riddled with shotholes, it could no longer stand upright and fell with a crash over the side of the ship, narrowly missing Captain Morris as it came down. All the same, Colossus had two captures to her credit.

Achilles, following behind, had spent an hour or so fighting the Spanish ship Montanes, which reeled with the impact of the British ship's larboard broadside as she broke through the line. The Montanes could not match the speed of the Achilles, and Captain King was able to bring his ship right up alongside. Wrapped in a blanket of reeking smoke, the two thumped away at each other; and when the smoke cleared and the Montanes fell back, Achilles found she had another Spanish ship, the Argonauta, on her starboard side. Later on, she was attacked by two French vessels at once, but the British crew's fighting blood was up, and when one of them, her namesake Achille, pulled away, they could give all their time to the other. This was the Berwick, and half-an-hour after the two had engaged, the Achilles was able to take possession.

About half-an-hour after her leader and at the same time as Nelson in the Victory was smashing through to the north, the Revenge had taken on two of the Combined Fleet together. Her captain was a particularly brilliant gunner, and his splendidly trained teams went gleefully into action. They had been given strict orders not to fire until Captain Moorsom himself gave the signal by firing one of the carronades on the quarterdeck. No sooner had they heard that long-awaited "crump!" than both broadsides boomed out, and the French Achille's mizenmast went crashing into the water. The Revenge broke the line so close in front of the French ship that its long jibboom tore away one of her topsails, and for a moment it looked as if a crowd of Frenchmen would leap onto her decks. They were driven back by the vicious fire poured at them by the Marines, and the Revenge turned tightly into the wind so as to attack the Achille from her other side, while her starboard guns tore into the naked stern of the Spanish San Ildefonso. These two were soon joined by a third, the Principe de Asturias with her armoury of hundred and twelve guns, and for a lonely while the Revenge had to endure a three-sided fire until the rest of the column caught up with her. Then, with the pressure off him, Captain Moorsom was able to concentrate on the luckless Achille, which sagged out of the fight with only her foremast left standing. Revenge herself was badly damaged; none of her masts was intact, she was leaking badly and had suffered a great many casualties.

The arrival of the rest of the column was the final proof of the Spanish captain Churucca's prophecy. The northernmost ships of the Combined Fleet, separated from the rest, still had to enter the fight, and now all that Collingwood's tailenders needed to do was to job at the southern end. Of these, the Defiance had fallen foul of the Berwick, which had hurried to close the gap and crunched against her as she tried to storm through; but Captain Durham tore himself away and chased after the Principe de Asturias where she was taking part in the fight against the Revenge. It was galling to him when the damage to his rigging made him give up the chase, but then he came upon the Aigle. After two previous encounters, the French ship was in poor way, but she fought most bravely, even after a boarding party forced its way onto her decks. The boarders were driven back, with the Frenchmen hurling grenades at them. The broadsides were called upon once more, and it was not until the Aigle had been rendered an almost helpless wreck, and her captain killed, and a fire started on board, that she could be induced to strike her colours at last. Meanwhile, the Swiftsure, the Thunderer and the Polyphemus had come up, together with the vast but slow-moving three-decker Dreadnought who made up for lost time by reaching Commodore Churucca's San Juan Nepomuceno just in time to save the struggling Bellerophon from her. In ten minutes, it was all over. The brave Spanish captain was dead, his ship's guns were out of action, and she was too badly damaged to follow the Principe de Asturias out of the fight. The Combined Fleet's rear had been overwhelmed, just as Nelson had intended.

And what of Royal Sovereign herself, at the head of the column, who had fired the first British shot of the day? No one in the entire line could have gone into action more calmly than Collingwood, despite his heavy responsibility. Fully sensible of the honour, he remarked to his captain as the first French shots splashed round him, "What would Nelson give to be here!" And Nelson himself, watching from Victory's quarterdeck the relentless advance of his old friend's flagship, cried to his Captain Hardy, "See how that noble fellow Collingwood carries his ship into action!" Carry it he did, into the action and through it from that first shattering broadside to the end of the battle. As he approached the curve of the enemy line, well ahead of his column, first one and then another belched smoke and flame in his direction. Collingwood remained unmoved, even when his ship was near enough to suffer a hit or two. Seeing that he was not to be put off, the seventy-four Fougueux set more canvas, and the huge Santa Ana ahead of her backed hers in order to close the space between them and bar the way. But Collingwood refused to be thwarted. "Steer for the Frenchman," he ordered, "and carry away her bowsprit." Just in time the Fougueux's captain slowed up to save his ship from collision, and Royal Sovereign was through, blazing away at the Spaniard as she went. Immediately after breaking the line the helm was put hard over to swing the flagship round and bring her alongside. In doing so she formed a target for the Fougueux and the Indomptable. Staggering under the impact from the close fire of the hundred and twelve gun Santa Ana, Royal Sovereign came under fire from two more Spanish ships ahead in the line, which turned together with a third Frenchman to meet her. Attacked by six enemy ships at once, Collingwood walked about the deck advising and encouraging, and as the rest of the line followed him into the fight the immediate pressure on his flagship was relieved. She had her reward; although crippled, with only one mast remaining, and eventually taken in by the frigate Euryalus, she received the surrender of the Santa Ana. And Collingwood, who had gone through most of the day with a bandage covering a wounded leg, echoed the Victory's signal and sent his division off to windward to meet the short-lived threat from Dumanoir's van squadron, abandoning the chase of Admiral Gravina in the Principe de Asturias, who was making for home with the survivors of the rear.

All these stories would be pieced together later. For the present, all that the surviving officers and men aboard None-such could tell was that the remaining enemy vessels were leaving the scene, and that the whole of Collingwood's division had completed their task. What of that other column, which had followed Nelson into the battle upwind? How had they fared? Victory herself, determined to fight a close action, wait-ed until the very last moment before returning fire. She was closely followed by the Temeraire, who broke the line on the other side of her chief antagonist, the Redoutable. Victory, realising that she was there, directed her own shot downwards, for fear of going clean through the Redoutable and smashing into her ally on the other side! She came under heavy, crippling fire from the French ship Neptune, next in line; but with rigging and masts terribly torn about almost before the battle had begun, Temeraire still managed to wreak havoc aboard the Redoutable, sandwiched between the two English three-deckers. Still locked together with the Victory, the Redoutable had collided with the Temeraire on her other side. Immediately, Captain Elias Harvey ordered the French bowsprit to be secured, and from this position he could launch a savage onslaught in safety, so relieving the pressure on Nelson's flagship. Attacked at such close quarters on two sides, the Redoutable put up a tremendous resistance, and though reduced to a wreck it was some time before she finally hauled down her colours. Temeraire, damaged as she was, had not done yet: for on her starboard side the Fougueux, deserting the combined attack on Royal Sovereign, was drifting slowly nearer through the dense banks of smoke. Nearer she came and nearer, until she was little more than a few yards away. Captain Harvey's gunners held themselves in check until she was almost upon them; a shattering broadside was released; and the now helpless Frenchman drifted on to collide with the Temeraire. The carnage aboard had been frightful among officers and men alike, and since she could not hope to repel the inevitable boarding party the Fougueux too gave up the struggle. With Victory now loose and sailing away to windward, and with two captives to his own credit, Captain Harvey looked about for more.

The French Neptune had savaged the Temeraire as she broke the battleline in Victory's wake, but the British fleet also boasted a Neptune, eager to take advantage of every opportunity. The first came in the shape of the spreading gap which the two leading ships had forced in the French line, and Captain Thomas Fremantle took Neptune straight through, coming between the Victory and the Bucentaure and taking Villeneuve's flagship for his own target. Sailing straight across her stern, and out of range himself, he reduced her to a stricken condition; then, following his leader's example, he waited until the guns could be trusted to do the maximum amount of damage before opening fire. One shattering broadside was poured in by the larboard crews. Then, as Captain Fremantle passed on his way, his guns crashed again into the Bucentaure. Once more: then, leaving her to fall to the share of those behind, he found another victim in the towering Santissima Trinidad, and was lucky enough to attack her from a similar position and to pummel away at close quarters without suffering too much himself. The Bucentaure, having taken a broadside from the British Leviathan as she in turn passed through the gap now fell to the Conqueror. On board his battered flagship, Admiral Villeneuve had signalled to his van to wear round and come to the relief of the fleet from the north. He had hardly done so when the Conqueror overtook him. Once again the unlucky Bucentaure was exposed to heavy fire from a British ship passing along her stern; the most valuable part of any ship, because unarmed. Two tremendous broadsides thundered into the already shattered Bucentaure, doing her the most shocking damage, and a third dismasted her. Villeneuve's command was at an end, and Conqueror sailed on to join the Neptune in her fight with the Santissima Trinidad.

Now the pride of the Spanish fleet had the Neptune on one side, the Conqueror on the other, pounding away and sending two of her masts, one of which proudly carried the gay red and yellow colours, crashing down into the water in a confused mass. Splintered wood, rope and canvas lay sprawled over her sides in a hideous tangle, and the cheers of the British seamen mingled with the shrieks of the Spaniards who went overboard with the rigging. The beautiful big ship was being reduced to a ruin; badly holed below the waterline, she had lost all her remaining masts, and so much of her own wreckage littered the decks that her remaining guns were too smothered to answer back.

Meanwhile the Leviathan, having passed the Bucentaure immediately ahead of the Conqueror, and having watched the French Neptune, for whom she was heading, take to her sails and depart from the danger zone, was somewhat at a loss. She had managed to turn and get in a shot of her own at the Santissima Trinidad when Captain Bayntun thought he saw the French van heading for the battle. This seemed to give him the chance he was seeking. So it was some time before Leviathan could take a really active part, but with the arrival of Dunamoir's ships from the north the picture changed. From their vantage point, Christopher and his companions could see Leviathan leading the line into the attack. Only two of the French reinforcements came down into the thick of the fight, and of these two the San Augustin had a noisy welcome. Leviathan made straight for her, banged away with her broadside guns, and at the third attempt got a boarding party onto her decks.

The San Augustin's companion, the Intrépide, fully justified her name. Sailing down to the relief of the hard-pressed French centre, she suffered a fantastic punishment, but fought bravely on against the odds. Fired on by several British ships as they passed in pursuit of the three now making all sail for Cadiz, she found herself fully occupied by the little Africa. This duel lasted some time, until Orion, followed by the Britannia, joined in. Still the courageous captain fought his ship, and did not surrender till the very end of the entire battle, when completely dismasted, without sails, and with incredible damage done both to the Intrépide and to her crew.

The Britannia, next through the gap after the Leviathan, had in passing fired at the stricken Bucentaure and at the already heavily engaged Santissima Trinidad, before following northward and joining the fight against the gallant Intrépide. The other British ship involved, the Orion, had previously mingled with Collingwood's division, and lent considerable help to the Colossus, fighting it out with the French Swiftsure. Ajax, meanwhile, under the command of her first lieutenant because her captain had returned to England with Robert Calder, was pursuing the retreating ships heading for Cadiz.

The Prince, several miles to the rear of the Victory, had joined the column as an "extra". She was a huge first-rate of ninety-eight guns and had been meant to lead Collingwood's lee division; but she was naturally slow, and after being forced to adjust one of her sails she was so far behind that she found herself instead to the rear of the windward line. So she was a latecomer into the battle, but lost no time when she did reach it. First she fought the rear Spanish flagship, the Principe de Asturias; then she came to close quarters with the already badly damaged and captainless French Achille. Her first broadside was really all that was needed, for not only did it carry away the mainmast, but it set the only remaining mast on fire. In its fall it set light to the deck, and the ship's fire-engine was destroyed. There was nothing to be done but to scuttle the ship, and let those who could escape do so in whatever way they could. Many who swam for it were rescued by boats sent off by the Prince and whoever else saw their plight; and among them were two women who had followed their menfolk to sea and had helped during the fight by passing ammunition for the guns. The Achille was now completely ablaze, and in the end she exploded.

In fact, the Prince was luckier than several of Nelson's rear ships in being able to engage so closely although she was so late. Unlike Collingwood's division, which had broken through diagonally between individual ships and so separated the enemy ships from each other, Nelson's own division had followed through the gap he had made and found the enemy there already occupied. Only the Temeraire, following too closely behind the Victory to take advantage of the space she had created, had been forced to break though entirely on her own. Those rear vessels had seen the approach of the French van almost as the answer to a prayer; even so, some were thwarted, for Dumanoir's squadron had not, for the most part, cared to face their thundering fire, for these were not battered hulks but ships in full fighting array, barely touched, although the battle had been going on for some time. One such was the Agamemnon, which although toward the end of the column, caught up in time to fire at Villeneuve's flagship before she surrendered. After that, she went on to meet the French van. The last two ships, Minotaur and Spartiate, were the ones who had so delighted the Irish seaman on Nonesuch's main deck. One other ship should have sailed into action behind Nelson, the little sixty-four gun Africa. She had somehow lost the rest of the fleet during the dark night, and in the morning sailed to meet them from the north. This meant that she had to pass along the waiting line of the Combined Fleet's van, but, nothing daunted, she had fired back at them and then, full of spunk, like a very small terrier worrying a mastiff, she set to work on the tremendous Santissima Trinidad. The beautiful Spanish ship, although the largest in the world, could not hope to succeed against the odds facing her. Alone against three British ships, she fought bravely to the end, before being forced to admit defeat. But when Dumanoir's squadron was seen sailing southward as if to the rescue, and the two big British ships joined in pursuit, the Santissima Trinidad changed her mind. The Africa left her to lick her wounds, and instead joined the fight against that other superlatively brave enemy vessel, the Intrépide.

Late in the afternoon Collingwood sent some of his division up to what was expected to be a fight. Their departure gave the Spanish Admiral Gravina the chance to make the best of his way home. Firing had become spasmodic, and the terrific cheers of the men who saw the Principe de Asturias retreating told those below decks that at last the day was theirs. Some of the enemy ships continued their fire until the bitter end in the face of almost certain defeat; "Almost," said Lieutenant Yorke with feeling, "as if they were our own!" Praise could go no higher. But their case was hopeless, and the sun finally set on a day which, more than all his former triumphs, set the seal of greatness on Lord Nelson's achievements.

12

The battle was over: the battle was won: and now the clearing-up began. It was a very different scene from the one that had excited Christopher that morning! No majestic column of fighting ships now, with all sails spread like so many gigantic birds skimming the water; only a surly sea on which floated the ruins of two fleets, many of them shattered hulks. It was a desolate and awful sight; and in the midst of it rode Nonesuch, battered and broken but still afloat and still seaworthy. Her mizenmast was gone and her foremast was little more than a stump. Half the remaining sails were in shreds. The poop was a nightmare heap of charred and splintered timber where the blazing rigging of the fallen mizen had been hacked away with axes before being cast overboard, the quarterdeck was a sham-bles, and the fo'c'sle a blackened wreck. It was difficult to know where to begin, but those who could were set to work to restore the ship, as far as was possible, to fair seagoing order. The question uppermost in every man's mind was "How are my friends?" and grief and joy were felt in equal degrees as one by one the fate of shipmates became known to the survivors. Christopher and Richard came upon each other on the main deck, two dishevelled figures. Both their faces were blackened by smoke, their clothes torn and covered in dust, but each greeted the other with undisguised delight. Christopher had come through the thick of the action with nothing worse than bleeding knuckles and an aching bruise between his shoulder blades, but alas! For Richard! A large plaster disfigured his brow, and a grimy bandage swathed one foot.

"By George, young 'un, I'm glad to see you!" he exclaimed. "All in one piece too! How splendid."

"I'm pretty glad to see you too," said Christopher, with a twinkle, "especially as you're not quite ruined after all!" and he glanced mischievously at the bandage. "How did you manage to do that? I thought you were going to be so careful!"

"It's really the most disgusting bad luck!" came the mournful answer. "I got knocked on the head by a bit of falling timber and staggered straight into a hole in the deck – there's a dashed great gash in my foot at this moment – and the battle had hardly started when it happened, by Jove! Never mind, here I am and here you are, and worse things happen at sea – I mean – I mean – oh lord, I am a fool!" And the pair of them burst into a fit of laughter that released their over-strung young nerves and was better, as Christopher remarked when he could stop whooping, than crying, as they might have done all too easily.

Together they crossed the mangled deck, looking ahead of them to avoid the sight of those silent figures who were even now being laid gently beside each other before being sent to rest, together, irrespective of rank, at the bottom of the sea. Richard's face was grave, and he murmured, "I'm not so sure that these poor fellows aren't better off than some, young 'un. You wouldn't recognize our merry cockpit now. It's like hell on earth down there; I don't think I could begin to describe it."

Christopher glanced quickly at him, unused to his friend in

this sober mood that had followed so quickly on his laughter.

"I was forgetting," he said. "You've been hurt! Is it painful?"

"Oh lord, no! – aches a bit, but that's nothing. They patched me up in no time when my turn came and scolded me into the bargain for being careless! But if you had seen what some of them are enduring down there – and hear, too…" He broke off with a shudder and clung for a moment to a stanchion for support. "It's as dark as Hades there," he went on tonelessly, "and you can hardly breathe for the fug and the stench, and I think I'll hear some of those shrieks and groans until my dying day." His voice had sunk to a whisper, and Christopher looked at him in growing horror.

"Fellowes was down there," Richard went on. "I saw him on my way back."

"Yes," said Christopher. "I knew he'd been hurt. How was he?"

"Broken arm, but it's going to be all right. One of Mr Campbell's men told me afterwards that the bone hadn't splintered and there's no question of his losing it. In fact, he'll soon be back on duty."

"I'm glad," said Christopher simply. "I should have hated anything to happen to him." He looked sharply at is friend. "What do you mean – afterwards?"

"I had to go back with a message and I asked about him. I'll tell you now that that was the worst errand I ever had – going back down there among the horrors. Lieutenant Mann's gone, you know."

"Gone? Do you mean killed?"

Richard nodded. "Yes. One of their beastly sharpshooters got him with a musketball. Lieutenant Kent got burned when the mizzen went, on the hands. And Lieutenant Ross has lost a leg. It's wonder to me that any of us are left alive, let alone whole, after this dreadful day."

Christopher looked again, uneasily, at his friend's pallid face and at the beads of sweat gathering on his forehead.

"Look here," he said, "you'd better go and sit quietly somewhere for a bit! You're not fit for any more. Let me go up on my own! I haven't had a bang on the head, and you don't look at all the thing! I'll explain to Lieutenant Scott."

With something of an effort, Richard pulled himself together. "No," he said more firmly. "I shall be all right. Mustn't
disgrace myself at this stage! Duty is duty, young 'un, and I'll
report to Lieutenant Scott myself. Only – I can't help thinking
of our jolly mess this morning and what a charnel-house it is
at this moment – and thinking of breakfast, I'm fearfully hungry."

"I feel empty too," admitted Christopher. "In fact, I've had no
inside all day! I could drink the Thames dry if I had the chance,
I'm so parched with smoke and shouting! Still – as you say –
duty first!" and up the hatchway and into the air they went. The
confusion was unbelievable. The quarterdeck was littered with
torn canvas, tumbled rigging and piles of splintered timber;
and the crew were busy clearing away the wreckage so that
fresh ropes and sails could be brought from the stores which
had so fortunately escaped damage, and so that makeshift masts
could be put up to replace those shot away.

Lieutenant Scott was in the thick of all this activity, directing
the work of salvage, but he took in Richard's limp and the
paleness of his face beneath the plaster. "You're wounded, are
you? You should be laid down and resting that foot, my lad! Mr
Campbell has enough work without extra worry. There will be
food for us all in the captain's cabin in half an hour's time. Until
then, you have my permission to retire!"

So Richard went down the steps and out of sight, while
Christopher found himself if anything busier than before, and
more than grateful when at last Lieutenant Scott tapped him on
the shoulder and sent him below for rest and refreshment.
Never had food been so welcome as the fresh fruit that awaited
them, together with more solid fare, and their spirits began to
rise again, although a deadly tiredness began to creep over
bodies exhausted by the fantastic strain of the last few hours.

Captain Britten greeted them with relief. There was a grimy
bloodstained bandage round his head, and his face was streaked
black with smoke. "Well done, gentlemen!" was all he said. "I'm
glad to see you safe!" but some of the strain left his eyes when
his nephew came limping in. There would be sad gaps in the
wardroom that evening; Lieutenant Mann was gone, and two

others, crippled and badly injured, lay in the sick bay, mercifully drugged out of their pain for a short time with raw rum. Then Fellowes appeared, his arm in a sling, and with him came a lieutenant from another ship, who had come across in a small boat and asked in a shaken voice to be taken to the captain. The news he brought was shattering. Lord Nelson had been shot in the chest and through the spine by a musketball early in the action, and had died later in the afternoon, having lingered only long enough to be assured that the day was his, the Combined Fleet destroyed, and the "Nelson Touch", as he himself had termed it, fully vindicated.

It was a crushing, unbelievable blow. No one could imagine a Navy without Nelson; to them, Nelson was the Navy. But everyone there, who had had the privilege of serving under him in this, his greatest battle, knew that the best memorial he could ask would be for them to continue to do their duty and follow his example. So the work of clearance and repair went on, while the wind rose and the clouds gathered. The news of the Admiral's death had spread through the ship, and many a weather-beaten cheek was furrowed by tears shed freely and unashamedly. For Nelson had not been simply an Admiral; he had been a sailor. There had been a magic in his leadership that had fired the very humblest to follow blindly where he led, and a warmth in his generous nature that had rubbed off even on men who had perhaps never known a kindly word or an affectionate gesture in all their lives before. He had shared the seamen's hardships and knew their problems, and they had loved him – rough, tough sailormen that they were.

Able Seaman Harris sat down where he was and blubbered like a baby, the tears he would have scorned to shed for his dead and wounded messmates streaking greyly down his smoke-blackened cheeks. "So we beat Frenchy," he growled, "and what's it worth now? Frenchy got the last laugh when he killed the Admiral, that's what! Seems there's no point in anything anymore!" For once Able Seaman Lewis, gulping beside him, could not argue, and together they mourned their Admiral even more than their comrades; more than for Darby, who, whatever the future might hold for him, could never again climb, one-handed, to the top yards.

That evening, while Nonesuch rolled and the waves increased beneath her, three boys sat on the deck discussing this day of days. They were Richard, pale and subdued, his aching foot propped on a rolled-up jacket; Fellowes, just as pale and strangely altered, his arrogance gone and real feeling showing in his voice and expression; and Christopher, unharmed (more or less), awed, and full of tremendous relief. Hugh, who this time had come through unscathed, was busy above; but then, as Richard pointed out, he had already taken his whack at Copenhagen.

"You mean his fingers?" asked Christopher.

Richard looked at him in surprise. "Hugh's blind in one eye," he said. "Got a little bit of timber in it – only a little bit, but enough. Do you mean you never noticed?"

"Good lord! I did think he had a bit of a squint but naturally I wouldn't mention that. It never occurred to me that there was anything really wrong. No wonder he said once that Lord Nelson's wounds were horrible, however he came by them."

At the mention of Nelson's name, all three fell silent. They were too young not to feel jubilant at their safety and at the outcome of the day, but not too young to feel the shadow of the Admiral's loss.

"Do you know!" Richard exclaimed suddenly, "I've just thought – the war's over! Do you realise that? It must be! Boney can't invade us now! He hasn't got a Navy anymore!"

"He can't invade us, certainly," agreed Fellowes, "but I think you're wrong about the war being over. He can still do plenty on land, and he will do it, too. You wait and see!"

"Pooh, you're nothing but a pessimist! We've got his ships and we've got the Mediterranean – and that means Sicily – and he can't get past there with us in the way. And England's safe with the French Navy out of action, and that's all that really matters."

"But is it? There's more at stake than that, you know!"

"What d'you mean? There's nothing more important!"

"Lord, Richard, when will you learn to see farther than the end of your own nose? We can't sit back on our laurels. We must press home the advantage."

"How d'you mean?"

"For one thing, now that we've freed the trade routes we've got to keep them that way. An island's very vulnerable to starvation, you know. So we've got to go after the remains of the French fleet and we've got to stop them building another Navy and starting all over again."

"Don't see how they can do that!"

"I do! If I know anything of the old fox he'll start pressing for a peace with us to give himself breathing space. But he's tried that one before, so let's hope to goodness 'they' won't be taken in again."

"Did you ever think of going in for politics instead of the navy?" broke in Christopher curiously.

"Me? Good gracious, no! 'Twouldn't suit me at all. Why?"

"Because you've got it all worked out. These things wouldn't have occurred to me any more than they have to Richard. We were asked to stop the invasion – and we've done that – and there's an end to it."

Fellowes shook his head. "That's only a part of the job," he said patiently. Look, let me explain! Napoleon wants us in his empire, like so much of the continent. But Europe isn't enough for him – he wants the world! Particularly the East. So he desperately wanted to control the Mediterranean – Richard's admitted that! – because then he would have two routes open to him. One – Egypt. Two – Turkey. And then through India. But with our Navy in the Med and our army in India he'll have to go the long way round, through Russia – and it's a very long way round! It would take him a devil of a time and at least the attempt would relieve the pressure on us. Even better would be his not making the attempt at all. Because you cannot have one man dictating to the rest of the world! That's unthinkable. You have to stand up to a bully – Christopher knows that!" He grinned at them, and went on. "Today may very well turn the tide, but it will be a long time going right out. It'll show that Boney isn't, after all, unbeatable, and that's a big step forward. If you think he is, you're beaten yourself before you've begun, and that's been the trouble with most people. And it might – it just might – shake his own faith in himself a little bit, and that'll be very good for him, too, even if it does make him mad as fire. I hope it does! A furious man makes mistakes. So you see, we can't afford to let up. And I'll tell you what – if we can pull it off – and there's no earthly reason why we can't – we'll be able to make an England stronger and grander than she's ever been before!"

Fellowes sank back, and the other two were quiet for a moment, taking in all he had been saying. Then Richard broke the silence, saying, "But one thing's certain, all the same. He'll blame it all on his unfortunate admiral! He won't have had anything to do with it!"

"That's very true. All the more reason to watch that massive army of his! He may not be much of a naval strategist, but you have to admit he's a splendid general!"

"Then I see what you mean about making him lose his temper! The more mistakes he makes, the better!"

Fellowes nodded. "As long as we don't make any ourselves," he warned. "That's why I rather hope there won't be any peace talk. That would be the biggest mistake of all."

"Because of today?" asked Christopher.

"Yes – because of today. This will make us supreme at sea, I'm sure. You see, no matter what Napoleon may do on land, we're still an island, and a good job too! He has to reach us by sea, and he can't do that without ships. Ten to one he'll try to grab another breathing space to get his shipyards busy, and we mustn't let him have it!"

"I see what you're getting at," said Richard. "Also, to starve us out he's got to stop the merchant ships, and that's out too, now."

"True. We won't have to worry about the trade routes – but you've forgotten the other ships, haven't you?"

"What others?"

"The ones behind the blockades, of course! Once the siege is lifted they'll come scuttling out like rabbits, and then what happens?"

"What happens? We'd have to send 'em to the bottom, I suppose. What else could we do?"

Fellowes looked at him incredulously. Haven't you had enough fighting to last you a while?" he asked. "I'm sure I have!"

"It was horrible, wasn't it?" asked Christopher.

Fellowes nodded again, "Quite horrible," he said. "Lieutenant Welch told me it was the worst fight he'd ever been in, and he's seen plenty of action, goodness only knows!"

"Yes," said Richard. "I'll admit I didn't enjoy it as much as I thought I would, but if only everyone else could have been as lucky as us I wouldn't mind doing it all again, just to send the French to the rightabout!"

Christopher was amazed. "But you said," he began hesitantly, "you said – you'd never forget the – the ugliness – as long as you lived!"

"I know I did, and I mean it. The point is, if the job isn't properly finished we'll have betrayed those men more than if we'd struck our colours at the start. They won't have died for nothing if we can stop Boney for good and all. I don't want to see such things again, but I can't run away from them. He didn't after all."

They sat for a while in subdued silence. Then Christopher said slowly, "I suppose he thought it was worth it, but why did he expose himself so? I mean, he was out there in the open, and they would know him so easily. Even if he hadn't been wearing his orders, it's not so easy to hide an empty sleeve. If only he'd kept out of sight, he might have been here now."

"That wouldn't have done for him," said Richard proudly. "He wouldn't hide himself away when his men were going through it. He didn't lack courage. He was the Admiral! Perhaps that was the way he would have wanted it. He'd done what he had to do – and I'm so glad he knew we'd won before he went!"

There was another silence; then Fellowes' voice, surprisingly said softly,

"Nothing is here for tears, nothing to wail
Or knock the breast; no weakness, no contempt,
Dispraise or blame; nothing but well and fair,
And what may quiet us in a death so noble."

"I say!" exclaimed Richard, "that's exactly it! Where did you find that?"

"Milton," said Christopher.

Richard looked at them with great respect. "I never knew Milton could turn out that kind of thing," he said. "I always thought him as dry as could be, but then I never was bookish. I wish I had been; that's absolutely splendid. Do you know, I think the Admiral would have liked to hear you say that about him? It's – it's everything in a nutshell. Fancy you both knowing that!" He shook his head in wonder.

"It's amazing how surprising other people can be," returned Fellowes. "You can live on top of each other for days and weeks on end, as we have, and then something like today happens and you see them in quite a different light. You know, I always thought you were simply cruising along on your uncle's interest. I just couldn't believe he was treating you the same as everyone else. And I couldn't stand your everlasting cheerfulness! Until you came to see me in the cockpit, and I saw that you did have feelings after all. I'd always thought you were completely callous about the whole business."

"Yes, I can quite see that the captain being my uncle would be galling," agreed Richard, "though honestly it doesn't make the slightest bit of difference. He's not that kind of man. But what's wrong with being cheerful? I admit that today has been horrible and there are things I'd sooner forget than remember, but I couldn't be anything but a sailor. I just couldn't! I love it, so I'm happy. Be honest, now! Can you think of anything you'd rather do than be at sea?"

"No, I can't think," Fellowes answered straight away. "I truly can't."

"Then there's the young 'un here. He was a regular Johnny Raw but he did all right when he had to."

"By George, yes! And now I come to think of it, I've never said thank-you, though if it hadn't been for you I probably shouldn't be sitting here now. Will you shake hands; and let bygones be bygones?

He held out his sound arm, and they shook hands very heartily.

"What did he do?" asked Richard, curiously.

Christopher flushed with embarrassment, Fellowes explained the incident with the Frenchman, and Richard exclaimed delightedly he was a regular bruiser, no doubt about it!

"You said you knew he'd been hurt," he said reproachfully, "but you never said you'd been a hero!"

"What I can't understand," said Christopher shyly, "is why you always had such a down on me. Why were you so unfriendly? I never could make out what I'd done to offend you so."

"Jealousy again," said Fellowes with a shrug. "There you were, sprung from nowhere, bosom friends with the captain's nephew and getting all the attention. And I had to fight somebody – to prove to myself that I wasn't a coward. Because I was. This morning I was most horribly afraid; but do you know, once we were fairly started, I wasn't frightened anymore!"

"There you are," said Richard, "what did I tell you? When it comes to the point there isn't really any time to be frightened – any more than there was when you fished that poor man out of the sea!" He went quickly on, to cover Fellowes' confusion, "And when the time comes you'll go through it all over again as a matter of course. And as you seem to think the war's going on for ever it's just as well!"

"I didn't say for ever, but I can't see any end to it yet. I really can't. Even if Boney does lie quiet for a bit he'll come bobbing up again somewhere! I'm sure of it!"

"I wish you wouldn't keep harping on it!" exclaimed Richard. "In any case, you've got to be wrong because now – there's no Nelson."

"I'm not the gloomy one. I'm as unhappy as you are about Nelson, but I can see that there are other people to carry on as he would want. Collingwood, for a start!"

"Collingwood!" said Richard scornfully. "Careful Cuthbert!"

"Yes, Collingwood. He may not have Nelson's glamour but he's a splendid officer and a first-class man in a fight."

"Pooh! He can't hold a candle to Nelson!"

"Why not? He knows what to do and does it and he doesn't make a fuss about it, either. I don't think you're being fair."

"Nor do I," chimed in Christopher. "You couldn't see it down below as well as I could, but I've never seen anything so splendid as the way he got in amongst 'em today. It was great!"

"And the rest backed him up splendidly," went on Fellowes. "It was Nelson's plan, but he couldn't have carried it through without Collingwood! I think he knew that, too, and he trusted him, didn't he? He always did, and that ought to be enough for you!"

"Were they all that close?" Richard sounded doubtful.

"You see! You're so blinded by Nelson – not that I blame you! – that you don't even know who his best friends were! They've been as close as can be for nearly thirty years, and I don't want to guess what Collingwood must be thinking to-night."

"You do surprise me," said Richard, and he meant it. "They're so different – I mean – what could they have in common?"

"Do people have to be alike to be friends? Perhaps it was just because they were so different! They balanced each other, do you see?"

"You mean like me and the young 'un?"

Fellowes smiled faintly. "If you like. What I mean is, that Collingwood might calm Nelson down if he got too excited…"

Christopher chuckled. "Which of them is me?" he asked innocently, and Fellowes looked prim.

"I'll leave you to decide!" he said.

Richard was unconvinced. "You must admit," he said, "that chalk and cheese aren't in it!"

Fellowes looked exasperated. "But that's the whole point! Collinwood might not act so much on the spur of the moment, but he'd always back Nelson up – and keep a cool head into the bargain!" He grinned. "Did you never hear the story of what he said at Cape St Vincent?"

"Can't say I have."

"Well, I got it from a man who was on the Excellent with him. Nelson was banging away at half-a-dozen enemy ships at once, and Collingwood came up to help him – and in the middle of it all he got quite hot and bothered because he realised they'd gone into battle with new sails and he didn't want to get them spoiled!"

Christopher gave a crack of laughter, but Richard looked disgusted. "Fancy thinking about sails in the middle of a battle!" he said. "What an old woman!"

"Not at all – it showed how confident he was. It didn't occur to him, you see, that his ship might go under, and he wanted the sail to use another day."

Even Richard had to admit the sense of that, and Fellowes pressed home his advantage. "What's more," he went on, "he's a splendid man with a gun-crew. Do you know what his timing is for each broadside? Half-a-minute! Thirty seconds, my boy! How about that?"

"I'm not surprised," said Christopher. "They were going at it like billyo, the last I saw of them."

"Exactly! That just proves how efficient he is – and his crews think the world of him."

"Well then, I'm prepared to admit I've misjudged the man," said Richard magnanimously. "But that surprised me too, be-cause he looks too rigid to be an object of hero-worship."

"You can't always go by appearances! He looks unmoved, and he's a great one for discipline, but maybe that's why. You can't think much of a man who can't command respect. I'll tell you something else, too. He hardly ever uses the 'cat' on a bad lot – he turns him into a sailor instead!"

"What with? A magic wand?"

"Don't be silly! Punishment isn't the only way to make a man toe the line and Collingwood's shrewd enough to see it. Some-times it's the only thing to do with a really hard case, but more often than not you can make 'em see sweet reason without it. For instance, he'll take away a privilege but he'll leave a man his self-respect. He'd rather deprive them of their privileges than their belief in themselves. So they know he looks on them as human beings and they respect him in his turn. It's as simple as that. And it works! What's more, Nelson admitted it."

Faint but pursuing, Richard said, "Anyone would think he was greater than Nelson, to hear you talk! But you can't deny that Nelson had the vision, can you?"

"Good lord, I don't want to! He was a master of strategy, and I know it as well as you do! You said he wouldn't turn his back on danger, and I'm simply trying to point out that he's set such an example – a tradition, if you like – that the people who knew him best will be bound to take up the torch and carry on. They'll have to!"

"I tell you, you're nothing but a pessimist!" Richard cried again. "Maybe I'm not as farsighted as you are, but I can't see any reason why we shouldn't make for home and a quiet life or a little while at any rate."

Fellowes shook his head. "We're not home yet," he pointed out, "and I still say that Napoleon won't give in just because he's had a setback. It will make him very angry, but that's all! Really, he's his own worst enemy, all on account of his temper. He's too impatient by half! You'll never find him playing a waiting game!"

Richard looked rueful. "As we have!" he said feelingly. "All those months of hanging about! These last weeks, too! They seemed more like years to me."

Fellowes nodded. "We know," he said, "and I think, though it's only my own very humble opinion, that Napoleon could never have done it himself. He'd have sailed straight in and forced a battle in the harbour, come what might. But Nelson had enough strength of mind to wait until the time and the place were as nearly of his own choosing as they could possibly be. And it paid, in the end."

"You mean the French did!" chuckled Christopher.

"Yes, they did. I think this is probably the beginning of the end, and Napoleon will never be so strong at sea again. Well, he can't be! He's got to rebuild his fleet first! But there's a long hard road to go before he'll admit defeat. When the army does as much as the Navy has, his time will be up. Not before."

Richard looked pitying at the mention of the army, but Christopher, who had been following all that Fellowes said with close attention, nodded earnestly.

"I see what you mean," he said. "This victory isn't in itself enough, but without it we couldn't do anything. Now there's a good chance if only we don't let up."

"That's right! And the great thing is that we've got him contained within Europe. What we must do now is to see that he stays there."

"Then at least you admit that when Napoleon does come a cropper at last it will be owing to Nelson?" demanded Richard.

"To a very great extent, yes. That's why I think he must have died satisfied. He must have known he'd saved England."

"I wish he'd lived, all the same," said Richard softly. "Things just won't be the same without him."

"We shall have to carry on," retorted Fellowes. "If we don't, his example will be wasted. Did you hear what they said his last words were? 'I thank God I have done my duty'."

Eight bells sounded. Life was returning to normal. Christopher groaned.

"My watch," he said. "What were you saying about duty? Look after yourselves, won't you? You'll probably be asleep before I come back." With a mock yawn, he picked himself off the deck and made his way back up the ladder.

By now the wind had risen almost to gale force and Nonesuch was really pitching. Her sails were reefed and her hatches battened down, and a fine spray blew into his face as he leaned for an instant on the rail peering through the darkness over the scene of battle. Of the thirty-three sail which had faced the English fleet that noonday, a handful had managed to escape towards Cadiz. One, the Achille, had exploded and disappeared. The rest lay mangled and helpless about their captors. There had been no British losses, though it had been a near thing for some of them, and their crews were now busy making their vessels seaworthy, while the swell grew beneath them and the wind gathered strength. The seamen were busy knotting new ropes, fresh sails were brought up from the store-rooms and the carpenters worked frantically to repair the broken masts. In some ships the pumps had been set going, while the holes were plugged in the riddled hulls. It had been a busy day, but there would be little or no sleep for anyone that night. Apart from getting the ships put to rights, watches had still to be kept, and there were prisoners to be guarded, some illustrious, some humble. There was so much still to do, and there were fewer men to do it. Bits of wreckage floated all around the shattered hulks, but the saddest sight of all was the dark shadow of the Victory, where the lights of the Commander-in-Chief no longer shone. They were to be seen glinting from the frigate Euryalus, now being used by Vice-Admiral Collingwood since his

216

own flagship had been so roughly handled. Loneliness and desolation reigned. Only defeat, thought Christopher, could have left him feeling flatter than this great victory. Or was it simply the relief of success and safety after those crowded hours? It was hard to believe that it was all over, after those keyed-up weeks of waiting.

The moon was hidden now behind the fast-gathering storm clouds and above his head he could hear the wind whistling in the spars. He closed his eyes for a moment. He wouldn't have believed he could feel so tired. When he lifted his head, the sun was low in the sky, and the empty sea was streaked with pink and gold. It would be a beautiful day tomorrow.

Christopher shivered in his thin T-shirt; the grass felt damp through his jeans. Gosh, he was hungry! He wriggled out from the thinking-place, wincing from the pain in his back, and ran off along the cliff-path. Just before he turned the corner, he stopped, and looked back. Nobody was following him. He squared his shoulders and set off home, whistling.

"Rule, Britannia…"

Select Bibliography

The Dictionary of National Biography

BRYANT, Arthur   The Years of Endurance, 1793-1802
                         The Years of Victory, 1802-1812

FENWICK, Kenneth   H.M.S. Victory

LEGG, Stuart   Trafalgar: An Eye-Witness Account
                         of a Great Battle

LEWIS, Prof Michael   A Social History of the Navy, 1793-
                         1815

MAY, Cmdr W.E., R.N.   The Dress of Naval Officers

POPE, Dudley   England Expects

SOUTHEY, Robert   Life of Nelson

WARNER, Oliver   A Portrait of Lord Nelson

www.ingramcontent.com/pod-product-compliance
Lightning Source LLC
Chambersburg PA
CBHW050357030726
47503CB00006B/1896